The Telephone
A Spy Story

Max Barrington

Max Barrington

For the love of my life,

my darling wife and my inspiration,

Lynette

First published in Australia in 2025 by Etteleah Books - Cairns Australia

Max Barrington

Contents

The Telephone Call

The sound of an old Australian 1950s telephone ringing was distinct and commanding. It had a loud, mechanical **BRRRRINNNGG! BRRRRINNNGG!,**

BRRRRINNNGG! BRRRRINNNGG!

A sharp, metallic trill produced by two brass bells being struck by a small hammer inside the phone.

The ring wasn't a soft chime or a modern digital tone but a strong, insistent clatter designed to be heard throughout the house, even over the noise of a busy kitchen, or a crackling fireplace. It had a slightly harsh, almost electrified edge to it, with each two rings, lasting about a second each, followed by a brief pause before repeating.

If you were nearby, you could hear the faint vibration of the metal bells continuing to tremble for a fraction of a second after each strike. If you were far away, the sound seemed to echo through the house, bouncing off wooden floors and walls, making sure no one could ignore it.

The old Bakelite telephone, now silent, stands as a witness to the joys and sorrows exchanged over the years. It was more than just a device; it was a keeper of stories, each call connecting moments in time and weaving the fabric of their lives in this beloved home on a farm in outback Queensland.

Its black surface, dulled by years of dust and handling, still bore the smudges of fingers that had once dialled its heavy rotary wheel with urgency, excitement, or trepidation. The thick, coiled cord, stretched and twisted from decades of anxious tugging, lay limply beside it, as if exhausted from the weight of the conversations it had carried.

Located in the centre of the long hallway, the old Bakelite telephone rested on a small wooden desk, purpose-built for its presence. The hallway, with its polished timber floors and high, ten-foot ceiling, carried every sound with remarkable clarity. When the phone rang, its sharp, unmistakable brrring, brrring... brrring, brrring sound, ricocheted off the walls, filling the house with urgency.

No matter where you were, the kitchen, the sitting room, or out on the veranda, you could hear its insistent call, demanding attention. It was a sound that once sparked excitement, sometimes dread, but always a moment of connection.

This telephone had been the bearer of all manner of news, the joyous, the mundane, and the heartbreaking. It had carried the sound of laughter as new babies were announced, as wedding dates were set, and as old friends reconnected after years apart. It had been the messenger of community news, passing along word of town meetings, upcoming socials, and the occasional bit of gossip that travelled faster than any telegram ever could.

But it had also delivered the kind of news that made hands tremble as they gripped the receiver. The quiet, measured tones of a neighbour calling to say a bushfire was closing in. The solemn voice of a doctor on the other end of the line, delivering news that would change a family forever. The hushed, tearful words of a relative calling from far away, sharing the loss of a loved one.

For decades, it had been more than just a device; it had been a witness to life's greatest joys and deepest sorrows, an ever-present link between the home and the world beyond its walls.

The woman was jolted awake by the distant, urgent calls.

"Mum... Mum!... Telephone, Mum!"

The voice was familiar, insistent, but thick with something unplaceable, urgency, perhaps, or a desperation that sent a shiver

Max Barrington

down her spine. Still half-dreaming, she didn't pause to question it. She didn't consider, even for a moment, that she was alone in the house.

Her movements were automatic, almost rehearsed, as she threw back the covers and swung her feet onto the cool wooden floor. With groggy determination, she fumbled for her dressing gown, clumsily pulling it over her shoulders before stepping into the hallway. The house was bathed in a soft, eerie glow, the moonlight spilling in through the glass panels of the front door, casting long shadows across the floorboards.

She moved forward, her slippered feet making no sound against the worn timber. The air felt different, charged, expectant. As she reached the small table where the telephone sat, a strange unease prickled at the back of her neck. The receiver was already off the hook, resting on the table beside the telephone, as if someone had answered it before she arrived.

For a long moment, she simply stared at it. The silence pressed in around her, heavy and unnatural.

Then, with a deep breath, she reached out and picked up the receiver.

As the woman lifted the heavy Bakelite telephone and pressed it to her ear, she was met with an unnatural silence, no reassuring hum of a dial tone, just the hollow stillness of a disconnected line. Yet, against all reason, a voice emerged from the void, crisp and clear as if the line were still alive.

"This is the Dalby Police Station."

Her breath caught in her throat. The words, spoken with quiet authority, sent a chill down her spine. She gripped the receiver tighter, her pulse quickening. How was this possible? The phone had been out of service for months, perhaps even years, its connection to the outside world long severed. And yet, here it was, carrying a voice from miles away, as though time itself had folded inward.

Swallowing hard, she hesitated, then whispered, "Hello?"

The silence stretched for a moment too long. Then, the voice spoke again, calm, deliberate, and unmistakably real.

"Mrs. Collins… we need to speak with you about your………"

The voice on the other end was steady, professional, yet tinged with a gravity that made her grip the receiver tighter. A chill crept up her spine. She knew exactly what the voice was about to say, she had heard these very words before.

Forty eight years ago.

Her breath hitched as memories surged forward, unbidden and sharp. The humid summer air of that fateful evening, the distant rumble of a storm rolling in from the west, the way her hands had trembled as she clutched this very receiver, listening as the officer delivered the devastating news. The words had carved themselves into her soul, each syllable weighted with finality.

And yet, here she was, almost half a century later, hearing it all again.

A part of her clung to the impossible hope that this time, just this once, the story would change. That the officer would say something different, something that would rewrite the past and undo the loss that had shadowed her for a lifetime.

She swallowed hard, steeling herself.

"I'm listening," she said, her voice barely above a whisper.

But there was no answer.

The telephone was silent, the empty stillness stretching unnervingly. She frowned, tightening her grip on the receiver. "Hello?" she repeated, her voice slightly louder this time. Her eyes flickered around the dimly lit hallway, scanning the shadows pooling along the walls, then toward the front door, where the moonlight cast a pale glow across the floorboards.

"Hello?" she tried once more, her voice edged with uncertainty.

Nothing.

Slowly, she pulled the heavy handset away from her ear, staring at it as if it might somehow explain itself. And then, like a sudden gust of cold wind, the realisation struck her.

This telephone hadn't been connected in years.

Telstra had disconnected the old copper lines long ago, cutting off its tether to the outside world. She hadn't used it since. Her sister had given her a mobile phone, urging her to move on with the times. And yet, this phone, someone had called her, it was Lindsay, her son, Lindsay had called her. She had heard a voice, was it Lindsay's voice that had called her. The telephone receiver was laying beside the telephone, someone had answered it and called her? She had heard the voice through the telephone.

Hadn't she?

A wave of disorientation swept over her. Perhaps she had been dreaming. That had to be it, a vivid, lingering dream, tangled with memories that refused to fade.

Taking a steadying breath, she replaced the handset onto the cradle with the old familiar single light ring of a bell and soft click. For a long moment, she stood there, listening to the silence that followed, as if expecting the phone to ring again, to prove that she hadn't imagined it. But the house remained still.

With a quiet sigh, she turned and made her way back down the hallway, her slippers brushing softly against the wooden floor. Slipping into bed, she pulled the blankets around her, though she knew sleep would not come easily now. Her mind was too full of ghosts, of voices from the past.

Lying in bed, Matilda, though everyone called her Maddy, felt a growing sense of certainty that the entire episode had been nothing more than a vivid dream. A strange, unsettling dream, perhaps, but a dream nonetheless. The idea that she had been walking in her sleep troubled her. She had never sleepwalked before, not that she could remember. It seemed dangerous at her age, and she made a mental note to mention it to her doctor at her next visit.

As she settled deeper under the covers, her thoughts began to drift, carried backward through the years like leaves on a slow-moving stream.

Seventy one years ago.

She had been twenty one then, very young, full of life, though already weathered by its trials. This house, now filled with memories and echoes of the past, had been her home since 1954, the year she married Bernard Collins and moved in as his wife. She had been just twenty-one, a bright-eyed girl stepping into a future she could not yet fully grasp.

Seventy-one years.

So much time had passed, yet in the quiet hours of the night, it felt as though it had all happened only yesterday.

She had been living on the Gold Coast when she first met Bernard, Bernie, as he had introduced himself with a warm smile, at the restaurant where she worked. He was on holiday, taking a break from his life on a sprawling property between Chinchilla and Dalby, a remote town approximately 170 miles west of Brisbane. There was something about his easygoing nature and quiet confidence that immediately caught her attention, and as the weeks passed, their connection deepened.

During Bernard's three-week stay, they spent much of their free time together, exploring the coastline, strolling along the sun-drenched beaches, and sharing meals at some of the Gold Coast's finest dining spots. What had begun as casual companionship quickly evolved into something more meaningful, a bond neither of them had quite expected but both were eager to explore.

As Bernard's departure loomed, he hesitated before making a suggestion, one that had clearly been on his mind. He invited Matilda to visit him in Dalby, offering her a glimpse into his world, far removed from the bustling energy of the Gold Coast. "A proper country holiday," he called it, describing the vast, open landscapes, the quiet rhythms of rural life, and the clear, star-filled skies.

Matilda had smiled, pretending to give it some thought before agreeing that it sounded like a wonderful idea. In truth, there had been no hesitation in her heart. She already knew she wanted to see Bernard again, to spend more time with him, to find out if what had sparked between them in the coastal city could truly catch fire in the wide, open spaces of the outback.

They kept in touch through letters, each one carrying a piece of their growing affection. The anticipation of receiving Bernard's replies became the highlight of Matilda's days, and with each exchange, the bond between them deepened.

In one of her letters, Matilda shared her plans, she had arranged time off work and was eager to visit. She would book a ticket on the twice-weekly train service that departed from Brisbane, a journey that would take approximately seven hours to reach Dalby. The thought of finally seeing Bernard again filled her with excitement and a touch of nervousness.

Bernard's reply came swiftly, his handwriting neat and deliberate. He assured her that he would meet her at the Dalby railway station bond drive her the rest of the way to Girraween, his parent's property. "It's about an hour's drive from Dalby," he wrote, "but I reckon it'll pass in no time with good company."

Matilda traced the inked words with her fingers, smiling to herself. The idea of travelling deep into the countryside, away from the coastal life she had always known, felt like the beginning of something significant, perhaps even life-changing.

Matilda was born in 1933 in Queanbeyan, a small but bustling town in southern New South Wales and on the border of The Australian Capital Territory, to Mabel and Ralph Simmons. She was the younger of two daughters, her sister Kathleen being just a year older.

Queanbeyan, though situated just beyond Canberra's borders, was more than a satellite town, it was a highly prized rural centre with a rich agricultural heritage. Known as the home of wheat pioneer William Farrer, it had long been recognised for producing some of the finest wool in the region, its pastoral lands yielding fleece of exceptional quality.

Despite its economic contributions, Queanbeyan bore a less flattering nickname among Canberra residents, 'Struggle Town'. The moniker, though affectionate, reflected the town's working-class roots and the stark contrast between its modest, no-nonsense character and the meticulously planned grandeur of the nation's capital. Yet, for those who called it home, Queanbeyan was more than just a place to endure; it was a place of resilience, community, and quiet prosperity.

Matilda's father, a skilled saddler, operated a modest yet well-respected shop on Rutledge Street, where he meticulously handcrafted and sold saddles, bridles, and other fine leather goods. His craftsmanship was widely recognised, and his products were sought after by both local stockmen and passing travellers.

Their mother, Mabel, played an equally vital role in the family's livelihood. From the same shop, she offered mending and ironing services, skilfully repairing garments and household linens with care and precision. Her work not only supplemented the family's income but also strengthened their reputation within the community as hardworking and dependable.

Together, they built a business that provided for their family while fostering strong ties with the townspeople who relied on their services.

Life had been simple but happy until tragedy struck one bitterly cold winter's night. Their home on Donald Road caught fire, and despite desperate efforts, both Mabel and Ralph perished in the flames. Like many of the home fires at the time, wood burning heating fireplace was blamed. The sisters, just 11 and 12 at the time, were left orphaned, their once-stable world suddenly consumed by grief and uncertainty.

With no immediate family nearby, their father's only sister, Aunt Josie, took them in, bringing them to live with her in Southport, Queensland. The transition from the crisp winters of Queanbeyan to the warm, salt-tinged air of the coastal town was a stark change, but under Josie's care, the girls slowly rebuilt their lives.

Both girls had completed their high schooling at St. Hilda's Girls Boarding School, in Southport, though their paths diverged significantly from there.

Matilda, restless and unable to find a passion for academics, left school at the end of Year 10. She drifted between various unskilled jobs, trying her hand at different roles but never feeling truly satisfied. Eventually, she found a sense of stability in the hospitality industry, despite the demanding hours and meagre pay. Her choice of career was a point of contention with her aunt, who had hoped for a more prestigious or secure path for her niece. But Matilda, ever independent, was determined to carve out her own way in the world, even if it meant hard work and little recognition.

Kathleen, on the other hand, was a natural student, excelling in nearly every subject she studied. Her discipline, intelligence, and keen sense of justice led her to pursue a career in law enforcement. Upon finishing high school, she joined the Australian Federal Police, embarking on a path that would demand resilience, strength, and a deep commitment to serving her country. Where Matilda had sought a life of independence and exploration, Kathleen had found her purpose in structure, duty, and the pursuit of justice.

The sisters' beloved Aunt Josie passed away in 1952, leaving behind her modest yet charming two-bedroom unit in Southport. In her will, she bequeathed the property in equal shares to her two nieces, a final act of love and generosity that would provide them with a place of their own.

The unit, located on Norman Street, was unassuming yet perfectly positioned, offering stunning views of the Coral Sea. The salty breeze, the gentle rhythm of the waves, and the golden glow of sunrise over the water made it a serene retreat. At the time of Josie's passing, Kathleen was living in Canberra, where her career with the Australian Federal Police had firmly taken root. However, she made the journey back to Southport for the funeral, standing by Matilda's side as they said their final goodbyes to the aunt who had been a steady presence in their lives.

In the days that followed, the sisters worked together to reorganise the unit, ensuring it could now accommodate them both with a bedroom each whenever Kathleen was in town, rather than sharing a room as before when the three of them lived there.

They cleared out old belongings, sorted through their aunt's possessions with bittersweet nostalgia, and rearranged the modest space. Though their lives had taken different paths, the unit in Norman Street became a shared haven, a place where they could always return, reconnect, and remember the woman who had once held them together.

In 1993, the Gold Coast was in the midst of a property boom, with developers aggressively buying up old buildings, outdated home units, and aging motels to make way for luxury resorts, high-rise holiday apartments, and modern beachfront accommodations. The city was rapidly evolving, shedding its older, low-rise charm in favour of sleek, high-end tourism infrastructure.

Surfers Paradise, Broadbeach, and Main Beach were at the heart of this transformation, where entire blocks of older-style units and small family-owned motels were being demolished to make way for towering resorts with ocean views, swimming pools, and state-of-the-art amenities. The skyline was becoming increasingly dominated by high-rises, reflecting the growing demand for upscale holiday experiences.

Developers were capitalising on the booming tourism industry, as domestic and international visitors flocked to the Gold Coast for its golden beaches, vibrant nightlife, and theme parks. The expansion of resorts also catered to a growing number of investors looking to profit from the short-term holiday rental market.

However, this rapid development was not without controversy. Long-term residents of older units found themselves being pushed out as their buildings were bought and demolished, and concerns were raised about the impact of high-rise expansion on the character of some coastal suburbs. Despite this, the Gold Coast continued to reinvent itself throughout the 1990s, solidifying its reputation as Australia's premier holiday destination.

It had been only a year since their Aunt Josie's passing when a property developer arrived on the scene in Norman Street, setting his sights on the sisters' small unit complex. The once-quiet block of twelve modest units, perched with views of the Coral Sea, had become prime real estate in the midst of the Gold Coast's rapid transformation.

The developer wasted no time in arranging a meeting with all twelve owners, presenting an offer that was simply too good to refuse. The sum was far beyond what any of them had ever expected to receive for their aging units, and one by one, the owners agreed to sell. The decision was unanimous, and the sale was finalised swiftly.

For Matilda, the reality of the situation hit hard. While the payout was generous, it came with an urgent deadline, she had just ninety days to find a new place for both herself and Kathleen. With her sister's career keeping her stationed in Canberra, the weight of the move fell entirely on Matilda's shoulders. The thought of packing up their shared home, a place filled with memories of their late aunt, left her feeling both overwhelmed and untethered.

Still, there was no time for hesitation. The Gold Coast property market was shifting rapidly, and securing a new home in a city undergoing such relentless redevelopment would not be easy. With a mix of anxiety and determination, Matilda set out to find a place where she and Kathleen could once again put down roots.

As fate would have it, a timely opportunity presented itself. The mother of one of Kathleen's colleagues from the academy had recently passed away, leaving behind a well-maintained three-bedroom unit in Thornton Street, Surfers Paradise. The property was soon to be listed for sale, but thanks to Kathleen's connection, the sisters received an early heads-up before it officially hit the market.

With this valuable insider information, Matilda wasted no time in making inquiries. The unit's location was ideal, close to the beach, within walking distance of cafes and shops, and offering the kind of coastal lifestyle they had grown to love. It was larger than their previous home, with ample space for both of them, and the thought of having an extra room for guests or storage was an unexpected bonus.

The timing could not have been more perfect. Unlike the rushed uncertainty that had initially accompanied the sale of their Norman Street unit, this opportunity allowed them to plan their move with ease and confidence. Matilda handled the logistics, ensuring that their transition would be as smooth as possible.

By the time Matilda met Bernard, she had been living at The Gold Coast for ten years, the coastal lifestyle deeply ingrained in her. The ocean had become her solace, its vastness both a comfort and a reminder of how far she had come. But when Bernard entered her life, with his stories of the sprawling countryside and quiet, open landscapes of Dalby, she felt the stirrings of something new, a pull toward a different kind of life, one she never imagined she would consider. Now as the train neared Dalby in the late afternoon she was excited but also apprehensive about seeing Bernard.

Dalby - 1954

In 1954, Dalby, a rural town in the Western Downs region of Queensland, was a thriving agricultural hub known for its rich black soil plains and strong wool, cattle, and grain industries. The town served as a key service centre for surrounding farms, supporting a community largely dependent on wheat, sorghum, and sheep grazing.

The population of Dalby in 1954 was approximately 5,000 to 6,000 people, reflecting steady post-war growth as farming technologies improved and demand for agricultural products increased. The town featured classic Queenslander-style homes, a modest commercial district, and essential services such as schools, churches, banks, and railway connections that linked it to Brisbane and other regional centres.

Dalby was also notable for its railway station, which played a crucial role in transporting produce to markets, and its community spirit, with locals gathering for events at the show grounds, racecourse, and town hall. While life in Dalby was relatively quiet, the town's importance in Queensland's agricultural economy continued to grow throughout the 1950s.

In 1954, Girraween was a vast and sprawling 7,000-acre property located approximately 45 miles north of Dalby, Queensland. Passed down through generations of the Collins family, the land bore the legacy of hard work and resilience, shaped by both its natural beauty and the ever-changing demands of the agricultural industry.

Originally established as a wool and lamb station, Girraween had long been renowned for the quality of its fine Merino wool, a reputation built over decades of careful breeding and pasture management. The gently undulating landscape was dotted with hardy eucalypts, sprawling paddocks, and stretches of native grassland, ideal for grazing livestock. A network of creeks, some seasonal and others fed by natural springs, meandered through the property, ensuring a reliable water source for both stock and homestead.

By 1954, under the ownership of Edwin and Phyllis Collins, Girraween was on the cusp of change. The demand for wool remained strong, but diversification had become a necessity. Experimentation with different crops had begun, with small parcels of land set aside for trial plantings of wheat and sorghum. There was also talk of expanding into cattle, with Edwin having recently acquired a small herd of Herefords to test the viability of beef production alongside the traditional sheep operations.

The homestead itself was an imposing, yet welcoming structure, a grand timber house with deep verandahs that provided shade from the relentless Queensland sun. Wide-planked floors bore the scuffs of generations, and high ceilings kept the interiors cool during the sweltering summers. The gardens surrounding the homestead were well tended by Phyllis, featuring vibrant flower beds, neatly trimmed hedges, and an orchard with fruit trees that had stood for decades.

The property was also home to an array of working buildings, large shearing sheds, storerooms stacked with bales of wool, and sturdy stockyards constructed from timber hewn from the land itself. Windmills and water tanks stood tall against the horizon, their rhythmic creaking a constant background to the daily workings of the station.

Edwin and Phyllis's two sons, Bernard and Bruce, had grown up with Girraween as their playground, learning from an early age the skills and responsibilities that came with life on the land.While Bernard was deeply invested in the future of Girraween, he was also drawn to a different calling. His keen interest in medicine had sparked a desire to become a doctor, a path that would take him far from the rhythms of station life. Though he loved the land and respected the legacy his family had built, he felt a pull toward higher education and the opportunity to help others in a different way.

Bruce, on the other hand, had little interest in the responsibilities of running Girraween. He had always been restless, his mind filled with thoughts of distant places and the untamed landscapes of Queensland's far north. Tales of vast rainforests, remote cattle stations, and frontier towns fascinated him, and he longed to break free from the expectations that came with being a Collins. While his parents hoped he might take on a role within the family business, Bruce's heart was set on travel and adventure.

This difference in aspirations created an unspoken tension within the family. With one son eager to pursue a medical career and the other yearning for exploration, the question of Girraween's future loomed large. Edwin and Phyllis, deeply rooted in tradition, quietly worried about what would become of the land that had been passed down for generations.

Despite these uncertainties, Girraween in 1954 remained a proud and productive station, a testament to the hard work and perseverance of the Collins family. It stood as both a legacy and a question, one that would be answered in time.

It was a beautiful September afternoon when the train slowly pulled into Dalby railway station, the rhythmic clatter of the wheels against the tracks fading as it came to a stop. As Matilda peered out the window, her heart gave a little flutter of anticipation. Stepping down onto the platform, she immediately spotted Bernie, his tall, broad-shouldered frame unmistakable among the small gathering of people waiting to greet arriving passengers. At 6 feet 4 inches, he stood out with ease, his weathered hat pushed back slightly, revealing a warm, eager smile that instantly put her at ease.

Bernie was nine years older than Matilda, having just turned thirty, and he carried himself with the quiet confidence of a man who had spent his life working the land. He lived with his parents on Girraween, a sprawling sheep station that had once been one of the most productive properties in the region. Though the years had brought challenges, droughts, shifting markets, and the hard realities of life on the land, Bernie remained deeply connected to Girraween, determined to keep the property going despite its struggles.

As they drove through the golden Queensland countryside in Bernard's gleaming new FJ Holden Special, Matilda listened intently, her fingers resting lightly on the smooth upholstery. The warm September air carried the scent of sunbaked earth and eucalyptus, and the hum of the engine filled the comfortable silence between bursts of conversation.

Bernard, clearly eager to share, spoke animatedly as he navigated the open road. "Mum and Dad are really looking forward to meeting you," he said with a grin, glancing over at her. "Mum's already made up a room for you, fresh sheets and all. She doesn't do things by halves."

Matilda smiled, touched by the thoughtfulness. It was a small gesture, but it reassured her that she was welcome.

Then, almost as an afterthought, Bernard casually revealed something that took her by surprise. "I'm a doctor, you know. General practitioner. I work at a practice in Dalby on Tuesdays and Wednesdays."

Matilda turned to him, eyes widening slightly. She hadn't expected this. A sheep farmer and a doctor? The combination was unexpected, but somehow, it only added to the growing admiration she felt for him.

Noticing her surprise, Bernard chuckled, shifting the column gear stick smoothly into second. "I was fed up with living out in the bush," he admitted. "As soon as I turned eighteen, I applied to The University of Queensland Medical School and got in. Graduated four years later."

She could hear the pride in his voice, but there was something else, too, an unspoken weight behind his words.

"I wanted a different life," he continued, his tone more reflective. "But when I finished, Mum and Dad were doing it tough, and I couldn't just leave them to manage on their own. So, I came back to Girraween. I still work the property, but I take on patients in town two days a week. It's a good balance, I suppose."

Matilda absorbed it all, her admiration deepening. Not only was he dedicated to his family, but he had also carved out a meaningful role for himself beyond the farm. She suddenly felt a little out of place, her life had been simple by comparison. But as she glanced over at Bernard, his strong hands steady on the wheel, his expression relaxed and open, she couldn't help but feel a flicker of excitement.

She had come here hoping for a holiday, a chance to see a new world and spend more time with a man who intrigued her. But now, as they sped along the dusty road toward Girraween, she couldn't shake the feeling that this trip might change her life in ways she had never imagined.

As the FJ Holden crested the final rise in the road, Matilda caught her first glimpse of Girraween. The vast landscape stretched before her, rolling paddocks bathed in the golden light of late afternoon, dotted with grazing sheep that moved like scattered clouds over the dry grass. Sturdy eucalyptus trees lined the winding dirt road, their leaves shimmering silver-green in the breeze, while a distant windmill turned lazily against the endless blue sky.

Bernard slowed the car as they approached the main homestead. It was a sprawling, classic Queenslander, raised on stilts to catch the breeze. Wide verandas wrapped around its weathered timber exterior on three sides, providing shade from the relentless summer sun. The tin roof gleamed under the sky, and Matilda could already picture warm evenings spent sipping tea, or cool drinks, and watching the sunset from the veranda's edge.

Beyond the homestead, a collection of outbuildings stood, shearing sheds, machinery sheds, and stockyards, all testaments to a once-thriving sheep station. The scent of dry earth, lanolin, and sun-warmed timber filled the air, mingling with the occasional bleat of sheep from the paddocks.

"This is Girraween," Bernard said, his voice tinged with both pride and something else, perhaps the weight of responsibility that came with running a property of this size.

Matilda took it all in, feeling a mix of awe and uncertainty. She had grown up surrounded by the salty sea breeze of Southport, but this, this was something entirely different. The land was vast and untamed, stretching endlessly in all directions. It was both beautiful and intimidating.

As the car rolled to a stop near the homestead, a pair of blue heelers bounded towards them, barking excitedly. Bernard laughed. "Looks like you've got a welcoming committee."

The front door swung open, and a woman stepped onto the veranda. Bernard's mother, no doubt, from inside, the low murmur of voices suggested his father wasn't far behind.

Matilda took a deep breath, smoothing her skirt as she stepped out of the car. This was her first look at Girraween, and though she had only just arrived, she already sensed that this land, and this family, would soon become a part of her story.

"I do hope you are Matilda…?" The woman's voice was firm, edged with seriousness as she studied Matilda with sharp, assessing eyes. "He swaps and changes so much that we can't keep track," she added, arms crossed over her apron.

Matilda hesitated, unsure how to respond. She felt her stomach tighten, but before she could find the right words, the woman's expression softened into a mischievous smile. "I'm sorry, I couldn't help myself," she admitted with a chuckle, reaching out to touch Matilda's arm reassuringly. Then, turning to Bernard, she playfully scolded, "You didn't tell me she was so beautiful!"

Bernard grinned but said nothing, only glancing at Matilda with quiet amusement.

"Come on in, my dear," the woman continued warmly. "I'm Phyllis."

Matilda exhaled, relieved by the sudden shift in tone. "Matilda, or call me Maddy if you wish," she replied, offering a smile of her own. As she stepped forward, she leaned in to give Phyllis an airy kiss on the cheek, an instinctive gesture of politeness.

Phyllis, seeming both pleased and slightly amused, stepped aside to let her in. Matilda took her first steps into the entrance vestibule, her eyes adjusting to the dim interior after the brightness of the late afternoon sun. The scent of freshly baked roast lamb and eucalyptus polish filled the air, and from deeper inside the house, she could hear the faint clatter of dishes and the murmur of voices. She was ushered further into the house,

     Max Barrington

the warmth of the homestead wrapping around her as she followed Phyllis down the hallway. As they neared the lounge room, the hum of conversation grew louder, voices rising with excitement.

"Oh… they're here!" a woman's voice rang out, brimming with enthusiasm.

Before Matilda could fully step into the room, two figures emerged from the dining area almost in unison.

"Hello! You must be Maddy, the one we've heard so much about!" the pair exclaimed, their voices overlapping with cheerful energy.

Matilda blinked in surprise, taking in the beaming faces of a man and woman who were clearly close in age to herself. Bernard chuckled, stepping forward.

"Maddy, this is my younger brother, Bruce, and his wife, Dawn."

Bruce extended his hand in a firm but friendly handshake while Dawn, full of warmth, pulled Matilda into a brief but affectionate hug.

"We've been dying to meet you," Dawn said with a grin. "Bernie never stops writing about you in his letters."

Matilda, feeling a little overwhelmed by the sudden attention, managed a genuine smile. "It's lovely to meet you both," she replied, her voice steady despite the flutter in her chest.

Before she could say more, another presence entered the room, an older man with a measured step and a dignified air. His silvered hair and weathered features hinted at years of hard work under the Queensland sun.

"And this," Bernard said with a touch of reverence, "is my father, Edwin."

Edwin studied her for a moment before offering a nod of approval. "Welcome to Girraween, Matilda," he said, his voice deep and steady. "We're pleased to have you here."

Matilda felt herself relax just a little. The house, though unfamiliar, pulsed with warmth and energy, as she took in the smiling faces around her.

The dinner that night was a true country feast, the kind that had been a tradition in homes like Girraween for generations. The large wooden dining table, polished to a soft sheen, was set with simple yet elegant white china and sturdy cutlery. A golden glow from the overhead light cast a warm ambience, flickering against the crystal water glasses and the delicate floral centrepiece that Phyllis had arranged earlier that afternoon.

At the centre of the table, a large serving platter held the star of the meal, a beautifully roasted leg of lamb, its surface crisp and golden, glistening with juices. The aroma of rosemary and garlic filled the room, mingling with the comforting scents of freshly baked bread and rich gravy.

Beside the lamb sat a heaping dish of crispy roast potatoes, their golden-brown exteriors promising a satisfying crunch, along with generous portions of honey-glazed carrots and buttery green beans. A steaming dish of cauliflower cheese, its creamy sauce bubbling under a golden crust, added to the hearty spread. A large gravy boat, filled to the brim with rich, homemade gravy, was passed around the table, ensuring everyone could drizzle as much as they pleased over their plates.

Phyllis moved with ease, dishing up servings while Bernard poured glasses of red wine, its deep, ruby hue catching the light. Laughter and conversation flowed as Bruce and Dawn, who were visiting down from Cairns in the states far north, recounted humorous stories from their own travels, and Edwin shared snippets of the station's history, speaking of the challenges and triumphs that had shaped Girraween over the years.

Matilda, though slightly nervous at first, found herself settling into the warmth of the gathering. The meal was simple yet abundant, a reflection of country hospitality, food made with care, shared with love, and enjoyed with good company. As the last bites were taken and plates emptied, Phyllis rose to retrieve dessert, her famous apple pie, served with fresh cream from a nearby dairy.

It had been a truly wonderful week, one that Matilda would remember for the rest of her life. Her time at Girraween had been filled with warmth, laughter, and a growing sense of belonging. The sprawling landscape, the endless blue skies, and the hospitality of Bernard's family had made her feel at home in a way she hadn't expected. She had spent her days exploring the vast property, riding horses alongside Bernard, learning about station life, and sharing quiet moments with Phyllis in the kitchen as they prepared meals together. Evenings were spent on the wide verandah, watching the sun dip below the horizon, painting the sky in hues of pink and gold, while Bernard's father, Edwin, shared stories of the land and its history.

But all too soon, her visit had come to an end. Now, she stood on the platform of the railway station, the hum of the waiting train filling the air as the final call for passengers echoed across the platform. Matilda turned to Bernard, feeling a bittersweet tug at her heart. Just as she was about to say goodbye, he took both of her hands in his, his expression suddenly serious yet filled with a quiet determination.

"Matilda," he began, his voice steady despite the slight nervousness in his eyes. "I don't want to say goodbye, not like this, not knowing when I'll see you again."

Before she could respond, he reached into his trouser pocket and pulled out a small, velvet box. Time seemed to stand still as he opened it, revealing a stunning diamond engagement ring that sparkled even in the soft afternoon light.

"Will you marry me?" he asked, his gaze locked onto hers.

Matilda's breath caught in her throat. Hadn't she once imagined this moment, finding someone who made her feel safe, cherished, and truly seen? She had only known Bernard for three months, but in her heart, she knew. She knew.

A slow smile spread across her lips as she whispered, "Yes."

Bernard's face broke into a broad grin as he slipped the ring onto her finger, sealing the promise between them.

As the train whistle blew, signalling its imminent departure, Matilda felt the weight of the moment settle over her. She was leaving today, but she would return, not as a visitor, but as Bernard's fiancée, and soon, his wife. The thought filled her with a sense of joy and certainty.

Who cared that they had only known each other for a short time? Some things in life just felt right, and this was one of them.

About a month had passed since Matilda had returned to Surfers Paradise, and although she and Bernard had been exchanging letters almost daily, she longed to be back at Girraween.

Lambing season at Girraween, near Dalby, Queensland, was a crucial time for sheep graziers, typically occurring in late winter to early spring (July to September). During lambing season, ewes required careful monitoring to ensure safe births, as cold snaps or wet weather could threaten newborn lambs. Farmers and station hands would often conduct regular paddock checks, assisting any struggling ewes and ensuring lambs were feeding properly.

Whilst on an early morning lamb patrol, Edwin, had suggested to Bernard, that they pay a visit to their neighbours, Anton and Kalina Petryczek. The middle aged Polish couple had lived in the district since 1944, settling on a modest farm not far from Girraween. Though quiet and reserved, they were known for their kindness and resilience, qualities that had earned them the respect of everyone in the community.

Their story, however, was one of unimaginable hardship.

Anton and Kalina had fled Poland in fear for their lives after the German forces, under the new chancellor, Adolf Hitler, invaded their country. Before their escape, they had been active members of the Armia Krajowa, the Polish Home Army, working as spies in Warsaw. Their resistance efforts had been dangerous but necessary, as they passed information to the underground movement, aiding in the fight against the brutal Nazi occupation.

Their work had not gone unnoticed. The same year they had married, Poland was invaded, and they were captured by the Wehrmacht, then handed over to the SS for interrogation.

The punishment was swift and merciless. In a cruel attempt to extract information, the SS executed both of their parents before their eyes. Anton and Kalina were subjected to relentless beatings, so severe that Kalina would later learn she could never have children. The pain of that loss would stay with them for the rest of their lives.

Yet, even in the face of such horror, fate had offered them an escape. A friend within the resistance managed to help them flee the city. Through a network of safe houses and secret passageways, they made their way to the Croatian seaport of Rijeka. From there, they secured passage on a ship bound for Colombo, Sri Lanka. It was in Colombo that they found an opportunity to travel to Australia, a land they knew little about, but one that offered the hope of safety and a new beginning.

By the time Anton and Kalina arrived in Queensland, they were utterly exhausted, psychically battered by their past but mentally resilient. Their journey to Australia had been long and harrowing, yet it had given them the chance to start anew, far from the horrors of war. They settled in the district near Dalby, choosing a reasonably sized farm of 1700 acres of good grazing land and a large house that boarded the property Girraween, where they could live in peace, away from the chaos that had defined much of their early lives.

Despite their traumatic past, they became an integral part of the close-knit rural community. Over the years, they built a modest but comfortable income by working the land with the same diligence and determination that had carried them through their darkest days. They rarely spoke of their past, yet there was an unspoken reverence for them among the locals, a deep respect for the strength they embodied.

As Edwin navigated his Land Rover along the rough backtrack leading to the Petryczek's farmhouse, he voiced his concern.

"I usually see them around when I'm moving through Girraween," he said, his voice carrying a note of worry. "But I haven't seen or heard from them in a while. Your mother even tried to reach them through the exchange, but there's been no answer, I don't think that they have gone away as they normally advise us, you know, being the neighbour."

Bernard, sitting in the passenger seat, furrowed his brow. Anton and Kalina were private people, but they were also reliable, never ones to disappear without word.

When they reached the Petryczek's property, Edwin slowed the vehicle to a stop near the gate. The place was eerily still, with no sign of movement. Bernard climbed out first, unfastening the latch and swinging the gate open, allowing his father to drive through.

The farmhouse stood ahead, its white weatherboard walls glowing warmly under the morning sun. The pitched roof, edged with rusting tin, bore the marks of time, while the wraparound verandah, shaded by a few creaking posts, hinted at years of quiet country living. A gentle breeze stirred the dry grass around the house, carrying with it the faint scent of eucalyptus from the distant tree line.

Beyond the house, a scattering of small outbuildings and fenced paddocks stretched toward the horizon, their neat yet weathered appearance reflecting a property once well cared for. The land, though parched from the relentless Queensland sun, showed signs of careful management, paddocks recently rotated, fences mended, and water troughs filled.

Just across from the back door of the house, in perfect alignment with the path leading from the verandah, stood the open shed where the Petryczek's kept their vehicles. Inside, the dust-covered Land Rover and the Ford Pilot sat side by side, their exteriors layered with a fine coat of red earth.

The silence of the property was unsettling, an unnatural stillness that clung to the air. No distant sounds of livestock, no barking dogs, no faint hum of a radio from inside the house, just the occasional rustling of leaves and the sigh of the wind through the dry grass.

Bernard exchanged a glance with his father. Something wasn't right.

As the Land Rover rolled to a stop, Edwin cut the engine, and an unsettling silence settled over them. The usual sounds of a working property, dogs barking, birds calling from the trees, the distant hum of insects, were absent. Instead, there was only an eerie stillness, thick and oppressive. Bernard hesitated for a brief moment, glancing toward his father, before stepping out onto the gravel path. The crunch of his boots against the stones was the only sound as he approached the house, his pulse quickening with an unspoken sense of unease.

Something felt off. The silence was too complete, too unnatural. The curtains were drawn tight across every window, and not a single wisp of smoke rose from the chimney. Bernard rapped his knuckles firmly against the front door, the sound echoing hollowly through the house. He waited. Nothing. He knocked again, harder this time. Still no response.

Frowning, he moved to the side of the house, where a second entry door led from the verandah into the kitchen. He knocked again, listening intently for any sign of movement inside. Silence.

Edwin joined him as they tried the third and final entry point at the back of the house. Every door was locked, every window sealed shut. Not a single curtain had been drawn back, leaving the house feeling even more lifeless.

Bernard exhaled sharply, frustration creeping into his voice. "We should force our way in and check," he suggested, his hand resting on the doorframe.

Edwin shook his head firmly. "No," he said, his voice measured. "We won't break in. But I do think we should contact the police. Something isn't right here."

Bernard studied his father's face, reading the concern in his furrowed brow. He gave a reluctant nod. "Agreed."

With a final glance at the eerily still house, they turned back toward the Land Rover, both of them feeling a growing certainty that something was very, very wrong.

Back at Girraween, Bernard wasted no time in heading straight for the telephone in the farmhouse. The familiar surroundings of home did little to ease the uneasy feeling that had settled in his chest. He picked up the receiver and dialled 013 and asked for the police station number, the operator had offered to put him through and asked him to hold the line, his fingers drumming impatiently against the worn wooden bench as he waited for the operator to connect him to the local police station.

When the constable answered, Bernard spoke clearly and deliberately. "Good afternoon, Constable. My name is Bernard Collins. My father and I just returned from checking in on our neighbours, the Petryczek's, and we're quite concerned. We haven't seen them around for a while, so we decided to stop by their place on Chinchilla-Miles Road."

He took a steadying breath before continuing. "When we got there, we found the house completely locked up, doors secured, windows shut, curtains drawn. Nothing looked disturbed, but both of their vehicles, the Land Rover and the Ford Pilot, are still there, covered in dust. It doesn't seem like they've been moved in some time. We knocked on every door, but there was no response. It's just… off. We're worried something might have happened to them."

There was a brief silence on the other end before the constable responded, his tone shifting to one of concern. "I understand, Mr. Collins. Given the circumstances, we'll send someone out to take a look. Will you be at home if we need to follow up?"

Bernard glanced at his father, who was standing nearby, arms folded, his face lined with worry. "Yes, we'll be here at Girraween. Please keep us updated."

As he hung up the phone, Bernard turned to Edwin. "They're sending someone out."

His father nodded, his expression unreadable. "Good. Something's not right over there."

                    Max Barrington

Neither of them said anything more, but the weight of unspoken fears hung between them. Now, all they could do was wait.

The police officers Constable's Jim Carter and Ray Mitchell stood on the front porch, the heavy stillness of the property pressing in around them. After repeatedly knocking on the doors and rapping on the windows, calling out the names of Anton and Kalina Petryczek, they exchanged uneasy glances. The eerie silence, the motionless vehicles in the shed, and the drawn curtains all contributed to a growing sense of foreboding. Something wasn't right.

Determined to cover every possibility, they stepped off the veranda and began a slow, methodical walk around the house yard. The sun was relentless, casting long shadows over the dry, compacted earth. As they rounded the back of the shed, one of the officers suddenly stopped, his breath catching in his throat.

"Over here, Jim," he called grimly to his partner.

Lying on the hard ground, their bodies unnervingly still, were the Petryczek's' two border collies. Both dogs remained tethered to their chains, their water bowls bone-dry, their food bowls long emptied. The sight of them, silent, lifeless, sent a cold wave of unease through the officers. Whatever had happened here, it had been days, perhaps longer, since anyone had tended to them.

One of the officers crouched down, removing his hat as he examined the dogs. "No one would leave dogs like this."

His partner exhaled sharply and straightened. "That settles it. We've exhausted every attempt to make contact. No movement inside, no response, and now this…" He trailed off, glancing back toward the locked house, the unanswered questions looming over them like storm clouds.

The senior officer made the call. "We're going back to Dalby. We'll get a warrant for forced entry."

Neither spoke as they made their way back to the patrol car. There was nothing more they could do at that moment, but the unease clung to them like the heat of the afternoon sun.

As the police officers returned to the property, warrant in hand, a sense of foreboding settled over them. The weight of unanswered questions bore down as they stepped onto the wide veranda, the wooden boards groaning beneath their boots. Dust motes swirled in the afternoon light filtering through the lace curtains, undisturbed for far too long.

One of the officers adjusted his grip on the crowbar, meeting his partner's gaze with a silent nod before wedging it between the door and its frame. With a firm push, the lock gave way, the door swinging open with a reluctant creak, as if in quiet protest against their intrusion.

Inside, the air was thick, unnaturally still, heavy with something indescribable yet unmistakable. The scent of aged wood, dust, and something faintly metallic settled in their throats. The living room, visible from the doorway, appeared undisturbed; a crocheted throw lay draped over the arm of a floral-patterned couch, and a tea set sat neatly on a side table, as if awaiting an afternoon visitor who never arrived.

But beneath the quiet domesticity lurked a deeper unease. The officers exchanged a glance before stepping inside, their boots leaving faint imprints in the thin layer of dust that had settled on the floorboards. Somewhere in the house, a clock ticked, steady, unhurried, but it did little to mask the suffocating hush that wrapped around them like a shroud.

Then, in the dim interior, they saw them.

Two figures sat in the lounge, perfectly still, their posture almost unnatural in its stillness. Anton and Kalina Petryczek had not simply vanished. They had been here the entire time.

Anton and Kalina sat in the lounge, side by side, their bodies unnaturally composed, as if they had merely drifted into a quiet afternoon slumber. Their hands rested gently in their laps, fingers slightly curled, their expressions serene, too serene. It was a stillness that felt deliberate, a scene frozen in time.

The dim light filtering through the heavy curtains cast soft, shifting shadows across their faces, lending them an illusion of warmth, of breath, of life, if only for a fleeting moment. The air inside the house was stale, unmoving, carrying the faint trace of something acrid beneath the lingering scents of old wood and fabric.

A delicate china teacup sat on the table beside Kalina, its contents long evaporated, a thin line of residue marking where liquid had once touched porcelain. A book lay open on Anton's lap, its yellowed pages frozen mid-sentence, as if waiting for him to pick up where he left off.

Yet, the longer the officers stood in the doorway, the more the illusion unravelled. There was something profoundly wrong with the scene, an unnatural hush that pressed against the walls, a hollowness to the quiet.

Then, one officer stepped closer, eyes narrowing as he took in the minute details, the slight discolouration around their lips, the telltale glassy sheen in their half-lidded eyes. A slow exhale escaped him, his throat tightening as understanding settled in.

They hadn't dozed off.

Anton and Kalina Petryczek had died sitting right where they were.

Constable Jim Carter swallowed hard, his eyes fixed on the still forms of Anton and Kalina. They looked almost peaceful, as if they had simply drifted off to sleep. But the unnatural silence of the house, the lingering scent of something metallic in the air, and the two lifeless border collies outside told him otherwise.

Behind him, his partner, Constable Ray Mitchell, let out a slow breath. "We need to get back to Dalby and report this," he said, voice low.

Jim nodded, then turned toward the narrow hallway where an old Bakelite telephone sat on a small wooden desk. He lifted the receiver, pressed it to his ear. Nothing. Dead.

"Damn thing's out," he muttered.

Ray stepped back from the doorway, his boot scraping against the floorboards. "Radio won't reach from here either. We're too far out."

That left them with only one option.

"I'll stay here," Jim said. "Keep the place secure."

Ray hesitated for a moment, glancing toward the bodies. Then he gave a sharp nod. "I'll head over to Girraween and use their phone. Won't take me long."

With that, Ray strode out of the house, his footsteps crunching against the dry earth as he made his way to their patrol car. The engine rumbled to life, and within moments, he was gone, leaving Jim alone with the silence.

Jim stepped outside onto the veranda, sucking in a lungful of warm country air, trying to rid himself of the uneasy tightness in his chest. He had seen death before, farm accidents, old timers passing in their sleep, but this was different. The locked house. The dead dogs. The way Anton and Kalina had been sitting, side by side, as if waiting for something.

He leaned against the railing, his fingers tapping absently against the wood as he kept his eyes on the tree line. Until the others arrived, there was nothing to do but wait.

Meanwhile, at Girraween, Ray pulled the patrol car to a stop in a swirl of dust. He barely had to knock before Bernard Collins opened the door, concern etched across his face.

"We found them," Ray said, wasting no time. "They're gone."

Bernard's expression darkened. "Inside the house?"

Ray gave a short nod. "Sitting in the lounge. Everything locked up tight. Phone's dead, too. I need to use yours."

Bernard stepped aside without another word, leading Ray into the homestead. The constable wasted no time dialling the Dalby station, gripping the receiver tightly as he waited for the line to connect.

When the dispatcher answered, Ray spoke quickly, detailing everything: the locked house, the lifeless bodies, the untouched vehicles, the dogs.

"We need backup out here," he finished. "Senior officers, a forensic team, and the coroner. And tell them to bring extra men, we don't know what we're dealing with yet."

"Understood," came the reply. "I'll get a team out there immediately. Stay put until they arrive."

Ray hung up and exhaled.

"How long?" Bernard asked.

"Hour, maybe more."

By the time the convoy of police vehicles arrived at Szansa, Jim had paced the length of the veranda more times than he could count.

Senior Detective Frank Morrison stepped out first, surveying the farmhouse with a practiced eye. "Show me."

Jim led them inside. The officers moved with quiet efficiency, their sharp gazes sweeping over every detail, the locked doors, the drawn curtains, the still figures in the lounge room.

The forensic team followed, unpacking their cameras and equipment.

The coroner knelt beside the bodies, checking for any immediate signs of injury. He pressed two fingers gently to Anton's neck, then Kalina's, though he already knew what he'd find.

"Cold," he murmured. "They've been dead for days."

One of the forensics officers, a woman with dark hair tied back in a braid, scanned the room. "No signs of a struggle. No forced entry. But something's off."

Detective Morrison nodded grimly. "Let's get them photographed and then move them for autopsy. We need to know what killed them."

Jim stepped back, watching as the team went to work.

The unease in his gut hadn't faded. If anything, it had only deepened. Something about this didn't feel right.

And he had a feeling they were only just beginning to understand why.

As they climbed back into their patrol vehicle, the late afternoon sun cast long shadows across the dry, compacted earth of the driveway. The dust from their tires rose lazily into the warm air as they turned back toward Dalby, the weight of unspoken concerns hanging heavily between them.

The autopsy confirmed what the investigators had begun to suspect, Anton and Kalina had both died from cyanide poisoning. The telltale markers were unmistakable: the faint but distinct scent of bitter almonds, the bright red discolouration of oxygen-starved blood, and the rapid cellular asphyxiation that accompanied ingestion of the deadly compound. It was a swift and merciless end.

But the examination did not stop there. As the forensic pathologists continued their work, a more unsettling discovery came to light. Small, jagged shards of glass were found embedded in the soft tissues of their mouths, microscopic slivers caught between their teeth and lining the inner walls of their throats. The presence of the glass immediately altered the investigation's course. It was no accidental poisoning, no careless exposure to a toxic substance. The coroner concluded that Anton and Kalina had each ingested a lethal dose of cyanide encased within a fragile glass capsule, an intentional and calculated act.

Had they taken it willingly, a final, desperate act of their own choosing? Or had someone else placed the poison in their hands, convincing them, by force or persuasion, to end their lives?

As these questions swirled among investigators, one thing was certain: the answers would not be easily found, and the mystery surrounding Szansa was only deepening.

These capsules, commonly known as L-pills, carried a dark and storied past. Widely used during World War II, they were a secret weapon of desperation, tiny glass vials filled with lethal cyanide, designed to grant a swift and irreversible escape from capture. Spies, resistance fighters, and high-ranking military officials often carried them as their last line of defence, a grim safeguard against the horrors of torture and forced confessions.

A single, sharp bite was all it took. The fragile glass shattered instantly, releasing the deadly poison directly into the bloodstream. Death came in moments, agonising, yet mercifully swift. It was a method employed by those who knew too much, those who refused to fall into enemy hands.

But what were such capsules doing here, in this quiet farmhouse on the Chinchilla-Miles Road, a decade after the war had ended? Had Anton and Kalina carried these deadly pills with them all these years, a lingering remnant of a past they never spoke of? Or had someone else introduced them to their fate, ensuring their silence with a method as chilling as its history?

Determining the exact time of death proved challenging due to environmental factors, including temperature fluctuations and the natural process of decomposition. However, based on forensic analysis, the coroner estimated that Anton and Kalina had been dead for approximately three to seven days before their bodies were discovered.

An additional clue came from the two Border Collies found chained outside. Deprived of food and water, they had succumbed to dehydration, a process that typically takes around three days for a healthy dog. This suggested that whatever had transpired within the walls of Szansa had occurred no more than a week prior, with the couple likely perishing before their animals.

Had Anton and Kalina chosen this fate, invoking an unspoken past they had long kept buried? Or had someone else made the choice for them, silencing them forever?

The circumstances surrounding their deaths carried a chilling historical weight, one that reached back a decade into the shadows of war. Anton and Kalina had escaped the horrors of Nazi-occupied Poland, surviving the unimaginable brutality inflicted by the SS. They had endured, rebuilt their lives in a foreign land, and found solace in the quiet expanse of the Queensland countryside. Yet, in the end, they met their deaths by the very method once intended as their final safeguard, a bitter, cruel irony that only deepened the mystery.

Had they foreseen a threat from which there was no other escape? Or had ghosts from their past finally caught up with them, leaving them with no choice but to surrender to the fate they had once carried in secret?

After a meticulous investigation, authorities ultimately ruled out foul play. There were no signs of forced entry, no indications of a struggle, and no evidence to suggest the involvement of a third party. Every detail, locked doors, drawn curtains, untouched belongings, pointed to a deliberate and carefully planned act. The presence of the cyanide capsules, relics from a time of war and desperation, suggested a pact, one made in solitude and secrecy, bound by a history few could ever truly comprehend.

With no suspicious circumstances to pursue, the case was officially closed. Yet, despite the finality of the ruling, an air of mystery lingered. Why now? Why after a decade of building a new life had Anton and Kalina made this decision? Had they feared something, or had they simply grown weary of carrying the weight of the past?

Their deaths left a quiet sorrow in their wake, among neighbours who had respected their hard work and resilience, among friends who had known them only in fragments, never the full story. Szansa, the home they had built for themselves in a land far from the one they had fled, now stood empty, its silence echoing with unanswered questions.

With no known relatives to claim responsibility, the task of handling Anton and Kalina's final affairs fell to the Queensland Public Trustee, the government agency charged with managing the estates of those who pass away without identified next of kin. It was a cold, bureaucratic process, efficient yet impersonal, ensuring that even in death, the couple's affairs were settled according to legal protocol.

The Public Trustee oversaw the respectful burial of the deceased, arranging for a modest yet dignified service. Few attended, mostly distant acquaintances and curious locals, drawn less by personal connection than by the lingering mystery surrounding the couple's deaths. There were no grieving family members, no tearful goodbyes, only the quiet rustle of wind through the cemetery trees and the dull thud of earth as it covered their final resting place.

Beyond their burial, the Public Trustee assumed full control of the couple's estate. A formal search was conducted for any distant heirs or rightful claimants, but none were found. Their property, financial assets, and personal effects were cataloged, assessed, and eventually liquidated. What could not be sold was either archived or discarded. The proceeds from the estate were placed in government trust, held indefinitely in case a rightful heir should ever emerge.

And so, the lives of Anton and Kalina Petryczek, survivors of war, of exile, of hardships known only to them, ended not in the embrace of loved ones but in the quiet annals of legal administration. Their story, once one of resilience and reinvention, was now reduced to numbers in a ledger, a case file collecting dust. In the end, the questions that surrounded their deaths remained unanswered, swallowed by time and the vast, indifferent machinery of the state.

It had been three months since Matilda had returned to Southport, yet her thoughts often drifted back to Girraween, to Bernard, to the open skies and quiet strength of the land, and more recently, to the unsettling story of the neighbouring property.

Bernard's letters arrived with comforting regularity, filled with warmth, affection, and a longing that mirrored her own. He spoke of the changing seasons, of the work that never ceased, of quiet evenings spent thinking of her. But one letter, in particular, had captured her attention more than the others. It was different, not just in tone, but in the weight it carried. Within its pages, Bernard had recounted, in stark and careful detail, the tragic and deeply unsettling suicide of Anton and Kalina Petryczek, the elderly Polish couple who had lived on the neighbouring property, Szansa.

Matilda had read the letter twice that night, then once more the following morning, unable to shake the unease it stirred within her. The Petryczek's had been quiet, private people, their past veiled in mystery. That they had chosen to end their lives together, in such a deliberate and methodical way, sent a chill through her. She could almost picture the stillness of the farmhouse, the locked doors, the drawn curtains, an entire world sealed off in silence.

As she sat by the window of her Surfers Paradise apartment, listening absently to the rolling waves beyond, Matilda couldn't help but wonder: What secrets had Anton and Kalina carried with them to their graves? And why, after decades of survival, had they chosen to leave this world in such a final and calculated manner?

According to Bernard's letter, the fate of Szansa had been left in the hands of the Queensland Public Trust. With no known relatives to claim the estate, the property and all it contained had fallen under government control. Any personal belongings of value, documents, jewellery, money, had been carefully catalogued and placed in a secure container, where they would be held for a regulated period in the unlikely event that a rightful heir came forward.

Yet, given the couple's history, their escape from war-torn Poland, their quiet and isolated existence in the Australian countryside, it seemed doubtful that any surviving family would emerge. The tragic weight of their past now extended beyond their lives, lingering in the form of an unclaimed estate, a home left to gather dust under bureaucratic oversight.

Bernard's words carried a tone of inevitability, a resignation to the idea that Szansa, a place the Petryczek's had built as their refuge, would eventually be sold off, its story fading into history. And yet, Matilda couldn't help but wonder, had they truly left behind no one? No hidden ties to the past waiting to be uncovered? Or had they chosen, deliberately, to erase those connections long ago?

Due to its remote location, the Public Trustee's decision was made to sell the property 'as is', a full estate auction, lock, stock, and barrel. The sale was widely advertised in both state and national newspapers, drawing interest from buyers looking for rural land. But what struck Matilda as strange was the alteration of the property's name. Szansa, meaning "Chance" in Polish, had somehow been misrepresented, or deliberately changed, in the auction listings to Stanlee.

Whether this was an innocent mistake, an administrative error, or something more intentional, Bernard hadn't been able to determine. But the change nagged at him, and by extension, at Matilda. It felt as though something important had been erased or rewritten, whether by accident or design, she couldn't be sure.

What truly caught Matilda's eye as she neared the end of Bernard's letter was a passage that made her heart race:

"The auction is on Saturday week. I really think we should attend and, if possible, buy it! … I think we could make it a perfect home for us. I know we don't have that much money at the moment, but Dad said, 'Not to worry about money, just buy the bugger.' I'll pick you up at the station on Friday arvo."

"Love, Bernie."

She read the words over again, letting them sink in. Our home. The idea of it sent a shiver through her, part excitement, part uncertainty. It was all happening so fast. Just months ago, she had been working at the restaurant in Southport, leading an ordinary life, and now she was engaged to a man she adored, with the prospect of moving to a remote property with a dark and mysterious history.

Could she really see herself living there? In a house that had belonged to a couple who had, for reasons still unknown, chosen to take their own lives? A home once called Szansa, now inexplicably renamed Stanlee?

But then she thought of Bernard, his unwavering confidence, the way he made everything seem possible. If he believed they could turn the place into something beautiful, maybe she could believe it too.

She folded the letter carefully, holding it to her chest for a moment before placing it on her nightstand.

There was no doubt in her mind, she would be on that train to Dalby next Friday.

Inspections inside the house were permitted only on the morning of the auction, a decision made due to the sheer volume of belongings left behind. The property had remained untouched, other than the Public Trustee's search, since the passing of its former owners, and curiosity about its contents had only added to the intrigue surrounding the sale.

On the day of the auction, the air buzzed with anticipation. Bernard's mother, Phyllis, had taken it upon herself to ensure that the event was well catered, enlisting the help of her local branch of the Country Women's Association. Under a large canvas tent near the auctioneer's stand, the women bustled about, setting up trestle tables laden with plates of sandwiches, freshly baked scones with jam and cream, and large urns of hot tea and coffee.

While the refreshments were a welcome distraction, it was the gossip that truly fuelled the gathering. Phyllis, never one to miss an opportunity for socialising, seemed to know almost everyone in attendance. She floated effortlessly between groups, exchanging pleasantries before rejoining her circle of close friends, who were engrossed in whispered, yet distinctly audible, conversations about the macabre history of the property.

"Well, they say the police found them sitting right there at the dining table, as if they were just about to have supper," one woman murmured, tilting her head towards the house.

"With cyanide, no less!" another chimed in, lowering her voice just enough to sound scandalous. "Glass capsules, just like the war spies used. Imagine living in a house where something like that happened!"

"Oh, and what about that name change?" someone else interjected. "It was Szansa, wasn't it? But now they're calling it Stanlee? Why would they change it? What if that means something?"

A few heads turned towards the house with a mix of intrigue and unease, but none of the speculation seemed to deter the bidders. If anything, it heightened the sense of drama, drawing in more onlookers and potential buyers.

Bernard stood beside Matilda, watching the scene unfold. He leaned in and whispered, "They're turning this into a proper town event."

Matilda smirked. "Your mother certainly knows how to create an atmosphere."

He chuckled, slipping his hand into hers. "Let's just hope that the atmosphere doesn't drive the price up."

The hum of conversation died down as the auctioneer, a seasoned man with a booming voice and an air of authority, stepped up onto the wooden platform. Adjusting his hat, he surveyed the crowd, allowing a brief pause before he spoke.

"Ladies and gentlemen, welcome, and thank you for attending today's auction of the property known as Stanlee," he began, his voice carrying over the gathering. "Now, as you know, this sale includes the homestead, all furnishings, and outbuildings on approximately one thousand and seven hundred acres of land. There is also some stock on the property and as of right now the successful bigger will own all and any stock that is on the property. A rare opportunity indeed!"

A murmur rippled through the crowd as people shifted into position, some stepping closer to the platform, others tightening their grips on auction paddles or nodding to their representatives. Bernard and Matilda stood side by side, his hand resting lightly on her back.

"Alright then, let's get straight into it," the auctioneer continued. "We'll start the bidding at twenty-five thousand pounds. Do I have twenty-five to open?"

A tall man in a dark suit raised his hand. "Twenty-five."

"Thank you, sir. I have twenty-five. Do I hear twenty-six?"

Another bid came swiftly from a local grazier. "Twenty-six."

"Twenty-six, thank you. Twenty-seven?"

The numbers climbed steadily, with eager competition pushing the price higher. Bernard remained silent, standing motionless as he gauged the other bidders. At thirty-eight thousand pounds, several potential buyers had already dropped out, and the pace of bidding slowed.

A man in a grey hat lifted a finger. "Forty-two thousand."

A hush fell over the crowd as the stakes grew higher. Bernard finally made his move. With a calm, decisive nod, he raised his hand.

"Forty-three."

The auctioneer's eyes locked onto him. "Forty-three thousand pounds. A fine bid! Do I have forty-four?"

The man in the grey hat hesitated. A long pause stretched out before he gave a small nod of his head.

"Alright, ladies and gentlemen, we are at forty-four thousand. Do I hear forty-four?"

Another bidder, a middle-aged woman with a shrewd look about her, raised her hand. "Forty-five."

Bernard didn't waver. "Forty-six."

The woman bit her lip, considering. She lifted her hand again. "Forty-seven."

The man in the grey hat once again raised his hand and gave a slight nod.

The auctioneer called "We now have forty-eight thousand pounds, ladies and gentlemen!"

Bernard inhaled deeply, glanced briefly at Matilda, then lifted his hand one final time. "Forty-nine."

A whisper spread through the crowd. The auctioneer nodded approvingly.

"I have forty-nine thousand pounds. Going once… going twice…" He scanned the gathering for any final movement and just before he called for the third. The man in the grey hat called out in a German accent, "Fifty thousand pounds!"

Bernard, without hesitation called "Fifty five!"

A loud murmur passed from the crowd.

The auctioneer, not rattled, but with an appearance of job satisfaction embedded on his face, called strongly "I have fifty five thousand pounds. Going once… going twice…" Again he scanned the gathering, particularly the man with the grey hat, for any final movement. The man in the grey hat moved his head in the negative.

"Sold! To the gentleman at fifty-five thousand pounds!" The gavel came down with a sharp crack, sealing the deal.

A round of polite applause rippled through the onlookers, and Phyllis let out a delighted sigh, nudging her husband Edwin. Bernard turned to Matilda, his eyes shining with excitement.

"It's ours," he whispered.

Matilda smiled, slipping her arm through his. "Our home."

After Bernard handed over the deposit of five thousand five hundred pounds and signed the contract, he was officially locked into the purchase of Stanlee. The agreement stipulated that full payment was to be made within thirty days, at which point ownership would be legally transferred to him as recorded in the council land titles. With the paperwork completed and the auctioneer's firm handshake sealing the deal, Bernard turned away from the solicitor's table and made his way back toward Matilda.

She stood with his parents, Edwin and Phyllis, along with several of their friends, all of whom had gathered to celebrate the momentous occasion. The air was filled with murmurs of approval and quiet excitement as Bernard approached.

"All done," he announced, exhaling with a mixture of relief and satisfaction.

His father, Edwin, reached out, gripping Bernard's hand in a firm shake, nodding with pride. Phyllis, her eyes brimming with emotion, simply gazed at her son before shifting her attention to Matilda.

"That," she said softly, her voice thick with sentiment, "is your wedding present from us."

Matilda's eyes widened in disbelief, her hand instinctively reaching for Bernard's arm as if to steady herself. Bernard himself blinked, momentarily taken aback.

Phyllis stepped forward, embracing them both in a warm, motherly hug before pressing a kiss to each of their cheeks. "And you know?" she added, dabbing at the corner of her eye with a lace-trimmed handkerchief, "I don't think I could wish for better neighbours."

The words settled over them like a blessing, and Matilda, overwhelmed with gratitude, could only smile as she squeezed Bernard's hand. The dream of their future together had just taken a giant step forward, and with it came a home, a history, and a new beginning.

All the people standing within earshot of Phyllis's news put their hands together in applause and congratulated the couple.

As soon as the last of the auction attendees had departed, Phyllis asked Edwin if he had known the man in the grey hat "The man that was bidding?" She looked inquisitively at Edwin, "he bid up to £50,000"

"I saw him, but I have never seen him before, not that I know everyone around here." Replied Edwin, somewhat nonplussed.

"Well I saw him give Bernard such a filthy look once he had placed the winning bid" Phyllis insisted.

After little consideration Edwin had replied that the fellow was probably a bit sour that he had not secured it, "might have run out of money, fifty-five thousand pounds is probably about ten thousand pounds too much for that particular property, anyway,…but!..who knows and ..who cares, really?"

"I just didn't like the horrible look that he gave Bernard, that's all" and then she had out it from her mind, just like that.

Bernard and Matilda were eager to step inside their newly acquired home and begin exploring. Edwin, always one to come prepared, had already purchased new locks for the three external doors, as well as a sturdy padlock for the entry gate to the house yard. Without hesitation, he busied himself changing the locks, ensuring that they alone had access to the property from that moment forward.

The moment they stepped inside, they were all struck by the remarkable cleanliness of the home. Given its history and the tragic circumstances surrounding its previous owners, they had expected at least a layer of dust or a sense of abandonment. Instead, it felt as though the house had been meticulously maintained, as if someone had prepared it for their arrival.

What also surprised them was the sheer size of the home. From the outside, Stanlee had appeared to be a modest country dwelling, but once inside, they realised it was far more spacious and grand than expected. The most striking feature was the long, elegant hallway that stretched through the heart of the house, lined with polished timber floors that gleamed in the soft afternoon light. The hallway seemed to whisper of history, its walls adorned with faded floral wallpaper, heavy wooden doors leading off into rooms yet to be explored.

Matilda ran her fingers along the smooth wooden banister that framed a recessed alcove near the entrance. She could almost picture the life that had once filled these rooms, quiet conversations over tea, footsteps echoing down the hall, laughter, and perhaps even secrets.

"This house has good bones," Edwin remarked as he tested the sturdiness of the doorframes. "Built to last, and well looked after. You won't find many places like this anymore."

Phyllis, standing in the doorway with a keen eye for detail, nodded approvingly. "It's got character," she said with a smile. "And now, it's yours to make a home."

Bernard and Matilda exchanged a glance, excitement flickering between them. There was so much to discover, so many possibilities ahead.

As they moved through the house, a strange, lingering odour filled the air, a sharp, acrid scent that clung to the walls and furnishings. It was the unmistakable aftermath of the fumigation process, carried out to eliminate the remnants of decay left behind by the tragic passing of the Petryczek's. Though the house had been thoroughly cleaned and treated, the unsettling reminder of its history still lingered in the air.

In the kitchen, they noticed that every cupboard and drawer bore a small label or sticker, each marked with a tick and an initial. It became immediately clear that the public trustee had conducted an exhaustive search, leaving no corner unchecked. Presumably, this was done to ensure that any valuables, money, or important documents had been accounted for before the property was handed over. It was a sobering sight, an official, methodical process that left no room for sentimentality.

As they continued exploring, they saw that all the bedding had been stripped from the beds, leaving only bare mattresses propped against the walls. Lounge cushions had been removed from their usual places and stacked neatly beside their chairs, as though everything had been carefully inspected and then abandoned in a hurry. The house, despite its grandeur and cleanliness, felt strangely hollow, as if it were waiting to be brought back to life.

Realising that the heavy, chemical-laden air needed to be cleared, they threw open every window, allowing the crisp country breeze to circulate through the rooms. The evening air carried the familiar scents of dry grass and distant eucalyptus, slowly pushing out the artificial sterility left behind by the fumigation.

Satisfied that they had done all they could for the moment, they decided to leave the house for the night, locking up securely behind them. Tomorrow would be a new day, one filled with cleaning, sorting, and the first steps toward making this place truly their own.

By the time Bernard and Matilda's much-anticipated wedding day arrived, the homestead at Stanlee had been completely transformed. What had once been a house filled with lingering remnants of the past had now been cleaned, refreshed, and reimagined into a warm and inviting home.

The process had been no small feat. Every inch of the house had been scrubbed, repainted, and thoughtfully redecorated, restoring its charm and making it truly their own. The once faded walls now gleamed with fresh coats of paint, the wooden floors polished to a warm shine. Every item they had chosen to keep from the estate, furniture, heirlooms, and trinkets of the past, had been meticulously cleaned, restored, and placed with care, blending the home's history with their own new beginnings.

By the time they stood back to admire their work, the transformation was nothing short of remarkable. Gone was the stale, lifeless air of the past, replaced by the fresh scent of clean linens, beeswax polish, and country florals wafting through the open windows. Every room now radiated warmth, comfort, and a renewed sense of purpose, no longer just a house but a home brimming with possibility.

The Post Master General's department, (PMG) had re-connected the telephone in the hallway, a luxury that would make communication with Girraween, Dalby, and beyond far more accessible. The small, polished oak desk, provided the perfect place for the telephone, and Matilda had already imagined cozy evening conversations with friends and family by its side.

With everything finally in place, they could now turn their attention to their wedding day.

Bernard's mother had invited both Bernard and Matilda to sit with her in the warmth of the farmhouse kitchen, a pot of freshly brewed tea between them, to discuss their wishes for the upcoming wedding. She listened intently, her eyes alight with curiosity and excitement, as they shared their vision for the day they would become husband and wife.

When Bernard and Matilda revealed their desire to have a beautiful lawn wedding on the expansive grounds of Girraween, she clasped her hands together in delight. The thought of hosting such a special occasion on the land that had been in their family for generations filled her with deep honour and joy.

"The homestead will make the perfect backdrop," she mused, already picturing the scene, the rolling green paddocks, the towering gum trees swaying gently in the breeze, and the golden light of late afternoon casting a glow over the gathering of friends and family.

She leaned forward, eager to help bring their vision to life. "We'll set up a marquee under the old fig tree. And imagine the tables, draped in white linen, with fresh wildflowers in the centre…" Her enthusiasm was contagious, and soon, they were swept up in the excitement of planning every detail, from the ceremony to the celebration that would follow.

The couple envisioned an elegant yet relaxed outdoor ceremony, surrounded by the natural beauty of the property, with towering gum trees and rolling pastures providing the perfect backdrop. Following the exchange of vows, the celebration would continue with a reception held under grand marquees, set up on the estate's lush lawns. The atmosphere would be one of charm and sophistication, blending country elegance with warm hospitality.

For the catering, they had chosen the highly regarded Dalby Imperial Hotel, known for its exceptional off-site catering services. The hotel's expertise in providing gourmet cuisine at external venues meant that guests would be treated to a sumptuous feast, featuring locally sourced produce and fine wines. It was to be an occasion that blended tradition with personal touches, an event that not only celebrated their love but also honoured the deep connection they both felt to Girraween.

The wedding itself had surpassed even their most hopeful expectations. The weather had been perfect, the ceremony heartfelt, and the atmosphere filled with warmth and joy. Guests mingled beneath the soft glow of festoon lights, the gentle evening breeze carrying laughter and music across the sprawling grounds of Girraween.

With so many guests choosing to 'camp out' on the property, the celebration took on a festival-like feel, stretching well into the night. It quickly became apparent that the reception was not going to end anytime soon, as the sound of clinking glasses, lively conversation, and bursts of laughter continued to echo through the trees. The caterer, initially confident in his provisions, soon found himself caught off guard by the guests' unstoppable merriment. Twice, he was forced to return to the Dalby Imperial Hotel for additional kegs of beer, much to the delight of the guests.

As the evening wore on and the final embers of the bonfire flickered in the distance, it was clear that this was not just a wedding, it was a celebration for the ages, a night that would be fondly remembered by all who had been lucky enough to attend. Matilda's sister, Kathleen, who had arrived a few days before the wedding, had vowed to return to Dalby in her retirement as it was the nicest and friendliest towns she had ever been to.

On a sombre note, Bernard's brother, Bruce, and his wife, Dawn, did not attend the wedding. Their absence was not due to distance or unavoidable circumstances but rather a resentment that had festered into outright bitterness.

When Bruce and Dawn learned that Edwin and Phyllis had gifted Bernard and Matilda the property Stanlee as a wedding present, they were deeply offended and consumed by jealousy. Their own wedding gift, a brand-new car, suddenly seemed insufficient in their eyes. Instead of sharing in the joy of the occasion, they allowed their sense of entitlement to drive a wedge between themselves and the family.

This grievance eventually led to a complete breakdown in their relationship with Edwin and Phyllis. Years passed, and the silence between them remained unbroken. The final consequence came when Bruce and Dawn discovered, too late, that their estrangement had led to their removal from Edwin and Phyllis's will.

"Families," Matilda had sighed when she and Bernard reflected on it later. "It's amazing how something so petty can tear them apart."

The excitement of their new life together was matched only by the anticipation of their honeymoon on the sun-drenched shores of Hayman Island, a well-earned escape before returning to celebrate their first Christmas as husband and wife in their beautifully restored home.

Bernard had been busy discussing the future of Stanlee's vast seventeen hundred acres with his father. Given that the property bordered Girraween, it presented a seamless opportunity for expansion. Together, they had devised a practical plan, with strategic fence removals and additional gates, they could increase livestock capacity while also sowing crops for stockfeed and cultivating lucerne for baling.

As the reality of managing the combined properties set in, Bernard began to consider a significant shift in his career. Balancing his medical practice in Dalby twice a week with the demands of a working farm would soon become unsustainable.

It was beginning to look as though he might have to step away from medicine temporarily, committing to the farm full-time, at least for a year or so, until they were in a position to hire additional staff to oversee the daily operations.

It was a big decision, but one that felt right. With their new home, their growing responsibilities, and their bright future ahead, everything was falling into place exactly as it was meant to be.

Going through each cupboard had been an adventure in itself, a blend of discovery and nostalgia as they carefully sorted through decades' worth of belongings. Some items held sentimental charm, others were genuine treasures, while many were simply junk, long past their usefulness. Every drawer, every shelf, every trunk told a story, whispering hints about the lives of the home's former owners.

The sheds had been no different, a maze of tools, machinery, and forgotten odds and ends. Stacks of equipment lined the walls, some in pristine condition, others rusted beyond recognition. And then of course was the Series One Land Rover, a 1950 model, its rugged frame solid and well-maintained. Though dusty from sitting idle, it was evident that it had been well cared for and still like new for it's four years of service, its simple yet sturdy design a testament to the reliability of British engineering.

Even more astonishing was the British Ford Pilot, a 1951 model in near-showroom condition. The sleek black sedan gleamed beneath its protective cover, a true British masterpiece of post-war luxury. With its V8 3622cc engine, it was a far cry from Bernard's 1954 Holden Special, a workhorse of a car but hardly one to turn heads. Bernard ran his hands along the smooth, curved bodywork of the Ford, admiring its classic design and stately presence.

"Now this," he said with a grin, turning to Matilda, "is far more befitting for a doctor."

She laughed, shaking her head. "And where exactly is your chauffeur, Dr. Collins?"

Bernard chuckled, trying to open the driver's side door to inspect the interior, but all the door were firmly locked. While the Land Rover keys had been found tucked beneath the driver's seat, resting on the petrol tank, the keys to the Ford Pilot remained elusive. They both knew they had countless more boxes, drawers, and hidden compartments to search through, but the thrill of the hunt only made it more exciting.

This house, with all its mysteries and history, had already begun to feel like home.

The search for the elusive Ford Pilot keys had turned into something far more unsettling. A discovery neither of them had anticipated.

It was Matilda who had stumbled upon it first. As she stood on the small step ladder, reaching deep into the high-set laundry cupboard, her fingers brushed against something unexpectedly solid beneath a folded cloth. Expecting perhaps an old tin or a forgotten box of keepsakes, she instead found herself recoiling slightly at the sensation of cold, unyielding metal. Her pulse quickened.

"Bernard, can you please come here!" she called, an unmistakable urgency in her voice.

Bernard was at her side in seconds. As she climbed down from the step ladder, she gestured toward the shadowed recess of the cupboard.

"It's at the back, half-wrapped in a tea towel, or something," she said, her voice tinged with unease.

Bernard reached in, his fingers closing around the heavy object, and withdrew it carefully. The weight of it was unmistakable. As he climbed down, he carefully placed it on the laundry bench, unfolding the cloth that had concealed it for who knew how long.

Matilda's breath caught as the object came into full view. A handgun.

"What... is that...? Is that a... gun?" she asked, her voice barely above a whisper, her concern palpable.

Bernard didn't answer immediately. Instead, he methodically unwrapped the weapon, revealing its dark, well-maintained frame. It wasn't rusted. It wasn't neglected. It looked as though it had been cleaned, stored with care, hidden with intention.

His hands, steady but cautious, worked with practiced precision. He ran his thumb over the grip, his fingers feeling for the magazine release clip. With a soft click, the magazine slid free, revealing live rounds. Then, ever so carefully, he pulled back on the cocking slide, exposing another chambered bullet.

Matilda could only watch, her amazement mingling with apprehension. This wasn't just an old relic or a forgotten heirloom.

"Bernard... why would they have a loaded gun?" she finally asked, her voice laced with unease.

Bernard exhaled slowly, turning the weapon over in his hands. It had been years since he'd last handled a handgun, not since his time in the Dalby High School Pistol Club. Even then, he had only ever fired standard competition pistols, nothing quite like this.

He studied the engraving along the slide, running his thumb across the cold steel as he read aloud:

"F.B. RADOM VIS Mod. 35 Pat. No. 15567."

The name meant nothing to him. Radom? He had never heard of that manufacturer before. It certainly wasn't something commonly seen in Australia.

Glancing at the round of ammunition he had just ejected, he examined the small lettering stamped onto the casing:

"9 x 19 P."

Bernard frowned. A 9mm round. That, at least, was familiar. It was the same caliber used in many military and police sidearms. But this gun, this particular make and model, was a complete mystery to him.

He turned it over once more, weighing it carefully in his palm. Despite the layer of dust from its hiding place, it was well-maintained, oiled, and in working condition.

"I have no idea," he finally admitted, a curious fascination creeping into his voice. "But it's a neat-looking gun."

Matilda, who had been watching him intently, narrowed her eyes.

"You're not going to keep it… are you?" she asked, her voice a mixture of disbelief and concern.

Bernard chuckled, but there was an unease behind it. This wasn't a harmless old pistol left forgotten in a drawer. This had been hidden, intentionally concealed, and still loaded. Someone had kept it ready for use.

He sighed, setting the gun down on the bench. "I don't know yet," he admitted. "But probably," he said as he studied the coat of arms that was stamped into the side of the weapons slide receiver. It resembled a bird wearing a crown with its wings and legs outstretched.

While Bernard was still engrossed in examining the pistol, Matilda turned her attention to another cupboard mounted on the opposite side of the laundry copper, it was a strange location above the entrance door to the laundry room. Using the small steps, she reached up, feeling around the dark interior, but the depth of the space made it difficult to see what lay at the back.

Frowning, she stepped down from the small ladder and made her way to the kitchen, retrieving the bicycle torch she always kept handy. Returning to the laundry, she flicked it on and directed the beam into the shadowed recesses of the cupboard.

The light caught something, a smooth, polished surface that gleamed faintly in the glow. She reached in and carefully grasped the object, pulling it free. It was a wooden box, about an inch thick, four inches wide, and roughly ten inches long. The craftsmanship was evident, the wood dark and well-maintained, with brass hinges and an ornate, yet subtle, clasp.

Matilda's pulse quickened as she turned it over in her hands.

"Look at this!" she called out, her excitement growing.

She carefully stepped down from the ladder and carried the box over to the laundry bench, setting it down next to the pistol. Bernard, momentarily distracted from his inspection of the firearm, looked up.

"What is it?" he asked, his curiosity now aroused.

Matilda ran her fingers over the smooth wood, hesitating for a brief moment before glancing at him.

"I don't know," she said, "but I think we're about to find out."

"Be careful opening it," Bernard warned as Matilda flicked open the two small brass clasps and slowly lifted the lid.

Inside, nestled in dark, aged velvet, lay a dagger in a scabbard, its polished metal fittings gleaming under the overhead light. But what caught their immediate attention was the emblem adorning the scabbard: the unmistakable German eagle clutching a swastika.

"Wow… look at this!" Matilda breathed, tilting the open box toward Bernard so he could see.

Bernard reached in carefully, his fingers closing around the hilt as he lifted the dagger free. The weight of it was solid, the craftsmanship undeniable. As he withdrew the blade from its scabbard, the highly polished carbon steel flashed under the light, revealing an inscription running down the centre of the long, spear-pointed blade:

"Meine Ehre heißt Treue."

Bernard frowned. His German was rusty, but he recognised enough to know it translated to "My honour is loyalty." This wasn't just any dagger, it was a military weapon, almost certainly from the Third Reich.

He carefully slid the dagger back into its scabbard and turned his attention back to the box. But Matilda was already focused on something else. Beneath where the dagger had rested, she had discovered a folded envelope.

She carefully lifted it out, her fingers brushing against the brittle paper. As she opened the unstuck flap, something caught her eye, small, black celluloid squares, each barely a sixteenth of an inch, taped to the envelope flap. The tape, once clear, had yellowed with age, but the tiny squares were still visible through the discoloured adhesive.

Matilda sucked in a sharp breath, her voice barely above a whisper.

"What… on… earth…?"

Bernard leaned in, his gaze shifting between the dagger, the envelope, and the mysterious black squares.

"What the hell did we just find?"

That evening, after dinner, Bernard reached into the liquor cabinet and pulled out a bottle of Dimple Haig Scotch Whisky, a Christmas gift from a grateful patient, along with a bottle of dry ginger ale. Holding them up toward Matilda with a raised brow and a knowing smirk, he silently posed the question.

Matilda glanced at the bottles, then at Bernard, and exhaled with a small, weary smile. "Yes!... I think so. I think we could both use a drink."

They settled into the wooden rocking chairs on the front verandah, the warm night air wrapping around them as they listened to the distant sounds of the bush. Bernard poured the whisky into two glasses, topping them with a splash of ginger ale. He handed one to Matilda, then took a slow sip from his own, letting the smoky warmth settle in his chest.

"What a day," Matilda murmured, stretching her legs out.

Bernard nodded, swirling the amber liquid in his glass. "And what a find."

Their thoughts drifted back to the strange discoveries in the house, the hidden pistol, the German dagger, the envelope with the mysterious black squares. They had spent the rest of the afternoon speculating about the former owners, trying to piece together what kind of lives they had led and why their belongings hinted at secrets long buried.

Then, of course, there was the Ford Pilot.

After hours of searching, they had finally given up on finding the keys to the Ford Pilot. It was only by a complete fluke, a few days later, that Matilda had noticed them sitting on top of the right hand side, back wheel. She had briefly thought it was a strange place to leave the keys to a car.

Excited, they had rushed to open the vehicle, eager to see if it would start. But the moment they pulled back the thick woollen blankets covering the seats, their enthusiasm turned to disappointment, and confusion.

The upholstery had been ruthlessly slashed, deep gashes ran across both the front and back seats, as though someone had taken a knife and torn through the leather in a frenzy. The roof lining hung in tatters, and the carpet had been ripped apart, exposing the floor panels beneath.

Matilda had run her fingers over the ruined seats, shaking her head. "What the hell were they looking for?"

Bernard could only shrug, baffled. "More importantly… did they find it?"

Now, as they sat in the dim glow of the verandah light, their drinks in hand, the question still lingered in the air, unanswered.

Bernard took a slow sip of his whisky, letting the warmth spread through him before exhaling deeply. He stared out into the darkness beyond the verandah, where the faint outline of the paddocks stretched toward the horizon. Then, almost as if voicing a thought he had been wrestling with all evening, he said slowly, "Did they really commit suicide?"

Matilda, who had just taken a sip from her own glass, snorted mid-drink, coughing as a few drops splashed over the rim. She quickly wiped her mouth with the back of her hand, eyes widening as she turned to Bernard. "I was just about to ask the same thing," she admitted, her voice tinged with surprise.

She set her glass down on the small wooden table between them and shook her head. "It's strange, isn't it? The way people talk about what happened here… it's almost as if no one really believes it."

Bernard tapped his fingers against the side of his glass, his brow furrowed in thought. "It doesn't add up," he murmured. "The house, the way it was left… and now this mess with the car? Someone was looking for something."

Matilda leaned forward, resting her elbows on her knees. "And they didn't find it."

Bernard met her gaze, his expression unreadable. "Maybe they didn't."

They had planned on shopping in Dalby the next morning and Bernard had decided to take the dagger and envelope to an old jeweller that he knew in Dalby. He had been a patient of Bernard's and was quite friendly, he had repaired Bernard's Rolex Oyster watch and had told Bernard to look after it as it would be very valuable in years to come.

Rather than take the gun, as it was illegal to own a concealable firearm, Matilda had used tracing paper and a pencil to produce a facsimile of the wording and crest on the chamber slide of the pistol.

Alois Pfeiffer was a jeweller by trade, and he was German. He had learned his craft in Pforzheim, the renowned "City of Gold," where generations of master craftsmen had perfected the art of fine watchmaking and jewellery design. His skill with metals and gemstones was unparalleled, but it was his keen eye for detail and meticulous precision that had led him down a very different path, one far removed from the quiet, dignified world of jewellery.

During the war, Alois had worked undercover in Germany for the American OSS, the Office of Strategic Services, the forerunner of the CIA. He had been recruited not only for his fluency in multiple languages but for his ability to forge documents, alter engravings, and craft near-perfect replicas of official seals and insignias, a skill that had proven invaluable for smuggling intelligence operatives in and out of occupied territories.

Under the guise of a jeweller, he moved through high society, mingling with Nazi officers who sought custom pieces for their mistresses or insignia rings for their units. His work earned him access to circles that most spies could only dream of infiltrating. But every transaction, every handshake, every polished gemstone was a carefully calculated move in a game where the stakes were life and death.

By the time the war ended, Alois had vanished from official records, slipping into obscurity like so many others who had served in the shadows. It was far too dangerous for him to remain in Germany, too many people knew his face, and too many loose ends could mean a quiet, sudden death at the hands of those who still had scores to settle. The OSS, recognising the risk, had given Alois three options for relocation: Britain, the United States, or Australia.

While the US and Britain both promised safety and opportunity, it was Australia that caught his attention, not for what it offered, but for who might be there. He had an older brother, a sailor who had jumped ship in Melbourne just before the war. Though he had no concrete information on his whereabouts, Alois clung to the slightest hope that he might track him down. With that in mind, he chose Australia and left his old life behind.

For several years, Alois lived in Melbourne, working in various jewellery shops and trying in vain to locate his brother. He placed ads in the Salvation Army's "War Cry" weekly publication, hoping his brother might see them or that someone might recognise the name. But weeks turned to months, and months into years, with no response. The trail had long gone cold.

Then, in 1947, while scanning the classifieds, he saw an advertisement that would change his course yet again, a jeweller in Dalby, Queensland, was looking for a business partner. The idea of settling in a smaller town, away from the bustle of the city, intrigued him. It was a fresh start, an opportunity to practice his trade in peace.

And so, he made the journey north, from Melbourne to Dalby, from a wartime forger to a respected small-town craftsman. The transition was more than just geographical; it was a shift from a shadowed past to a future built on skill and honest work.

Alois quickly grew to love Dalby, its slower pace, its friendly faces, the sense of community that felt a world away from the chaos he had once known. More than anything, he found great satisfaction in his work at the local jewellery shop. His craftsmanship, honed through years of meticulous precision, earned him a solid reputation among the town's residents.

The partnership deal had been straightforward, a fifty-fifty split with a modest buy-in price. It seemed like the perfect opportunity, a fresh start. However, it didn't take long for Alois to realise that his business partner lacked the same level of expertise.

He began noticing an unsettling trend, watches he had not personally repaired were being returned by dissatisfied customers. Time and again, pieces that had supposedly been 'fixed' needed a second examination. Alois would carefully reopen them, only to find sloppy work, misaligned gears, loose screws, a lack of proper lubrication.

Frustration gnawed at him. Reputation meant everything in a small town, and repeat customers were the lifeblood of their trade. Alois knew that if this continued, the shop's name, and his own, would suffer.

It did not take Alois long to realise that his business partner, Bendik Rugaas, a Norwegian man in his mid-fifties, with no family in Australia, had a serious problem, he was an alcoholic.

At first, Alois had tried to give him the benefit of the doubt, attributing his sloppy craftsmanship to age or failing eyesight. But as time passed, the truth became undeniable. The smell of alcohol clung to Bendik at all hours, and there were days when he barely managed to steady his hands enough to work on delicate timepieces. Alois had also found Bendik's hiding place for the bottles of gin that seemed to be his favourite drink.

It was a frustrating predicament. The jewellery shop depended on precision, reliability, and reputation, qualities that Alois prided himself on. Yet, time and again, he found himself redoing Bendik's botched repairs, smoothing over customer complaints, and worrying about the shop's future.

Finally, Alois decided to address the matter directly. One evening, as they locked up the shop, he made an offer.

"Bendik, I'd like to buy out your share of the business," Alois said, keeping his tone measured. "You could take the money and retire, live comfortably, and not have to worry about the pressures of running a shop anymore."

But Bendik's response was immediate and unwavering. His eyes, bloodshot and weary, locked onto Alois with a stubborn intensity.

"I will never sell," he declared, his voice thick with defiance. "Not now, not ever."

Alois felt a sinking feeling in his gut. He had hoped for a pragmatic resolution, a clean break, but instead, he found himself locked in a stalemate with a man who refused to let go, whether out of pride, desperation, or the false courage found at the bottom of a bottle.

As the days passed, an uneasy tension settled over the workshop. Alois knew that his new life in Dalby, the stability he had sought, was at risk of crumbling. Bendik's refusal to sell meant that Alois was trapped in a partnership that was growing more dysfunctional by the day. Worse still, Bendik's precarious financial state meant that he had neither the means nor the interest to buy back Alois's share, making any exit strategy nearly impossible.

Alois, however, was not one to surrender easily. If there was no straightforward way out, he would find another path.

He devised a plan.

With careful preparation, he scheduled an appointment with a local doctor, Bernard Collins. At their consultation, he spoke with conviction, detailing a war injury that affected his legs. The treatment, he explained, had been prescribed by his doctor in Germany, regular massaging with pure alcohol to relieve muscle stiffness and pain.

Dr. Collins listened thoughtfully, considering both the practical and psychological aspects of such a treatment. While there was no real medical advantage to rubbing alcohol into Alois's legs, Collins understood the power of belief and routine in managing chronic conditions.

With little hesitation, he reached for his prescription pad and wrote out an order:

500ml of pure alcohol.

Alois took the prescription, his mind already working ahead. The plan was in motion.

With careful precision, he began executing his scheme. Each day, he would tip out approximately 100ml of gin from Bendik's hidden stash, a bottle that was always within reach yet never under scrutiny. In its place, he would pour an equal measure of pure alcohol, its potency far beyond what even a seasoned drinker like Bendik could tolerate.

At first, Bendik seemed no different, his usual self, teetering between drunken cheer and sluggish incompetence. But over the next few days, subtle changes began to emerge. His face grew paler, his hands less steady, and his usual grumbling was replaced by spells of laboured breathing and disorientation. Alois watched with quiet detachment as the man unwittingly consumed his own demise, sip by sip.

It didn't take long. Before Alois's 500ml bottle of pure alcohol was even half empty, Bendik was dead.

The cause? Officially, liver failure, an unsurprising fate for a man known to drink excessively. There were no questions, no investigations. Just a quiet funeral, a few muttered condolences, and the swift closing of Bendik's chapter in the business.

With Bendik gone, Alois moved swiftly. He contacted Bendik's surviving relatives in Norway, offering what he deemed a fair valuation for the deceased man's fifty percent share of the jewellers shop. The sum was reasonable, yet not generous, a price that avoided dispute while ensuring Alois gained full ownership of the business without resistance.

With the papers signed and the funds transferred, the shop was finally his alone.

He had come to Dalby seeking a fresh start, a stable future, and a craft to call his own. Now, with Bendik out of the picture, Alois could finally run the business as he had always intended, efficiently, professionally, and without the burden of a drunken liability dragging him down.

He locked the shop's door that evening and poured himself a drink, not gin, not poison, just a quiet toast to a future he had secured with his own hands.

Of course Bernard knew nothing of this, he knew him only as a German jeweller who happened to be a patient of his.

Leaving Matilda at the grocery store, Bernard crossed the street to visit the jeweller. The small shop had an air of quiet precision, with gleaming watches and delicate pieces of gold and silver displayed behind polished glass. As he stepped inside, he was warmly greeted by the shop assistant, a young woman who handled most of the jewellery and watch sales.

"Good morning, sir. How can I help you?" she asked with a pleasant smile.

"I'm wondering if I might have a brief word with Alois," Bernard replied politely.

"Of course, I'll let him know you're here," she said before disappearing into the back of the shop. Moments later, Alois Pfeiffer emerged from a workbench cluttered with tools and tiny watch components, wiping his hands on a jeweller's cloth. His sharp eyes, accustomed to examining the finest details, immediately took in Bernard's expression.

"Ah, Doctor! What brings you in today?" Alois asked, his German accent still noticeable despite years in Australia.

Bernard handed him the traced facsimile of the pistol engraving, watching as Alois adjusted his spectacles and examined it closely. Almost instantly, his face lit up with recognition.

"Ah! This is a 9mm Vis," he exclaimed. "A Polish pistol, very fine craftsmanship. Here, you see?" He pointed to the crest etched into the slide. "That is the Polish National Emblem, an eagle wearing a crown." He nodded approvingly. "These were far superior to the Luger, in my opinion. Much simpler, much smoother action."

Bernard noticed a faraway look in Alois' eyes, as if the weapon had stirred some deep memory. His fingers traced the outline of the engraving with an almost reverent familiarity.

"Unlike the Luger with its intricate toggle-lock mechanism, the Vis was a soldier's pistol, quick, reliable, and deadly accurate."

                                    Max Barrington

Alois nodded to himself before murmuring in German, "Ja... das ist besser als die Luger."

Intrigued by his reaction, Bernard then reached into his bag and carefully pulled out the dagger in its scabbard, setting it on the counter. Alois' demeanour changed in an instant, his eyes widened, and he inhaled sharply as if recognising an old ghost.

"Mein Gott," he whispered, reaching out to pick it up. He turned it over in his hands, his fingers running along the smooth black grip before carefully drawing the blade from its sheath. The polished carbon steel caught the light as he studied the etched inscription: 'Meine Ehre heißt Treue.'

"This is a genuine SS dagger," Alois confirmed, his voice now quiet and measured. "Based on the Swiss dagger of the 16th century… but this one… this belonged to someone of rank." His grip on the weapon tightened briefly before he slid it back into its scabbard.

Bernard hesitated, then pulled out the small envelope and carefully peeled back the aged, envelope flap, that revealed the strange celluloid squares, black, thin, and no larger than a 1/16", stuck to the flap.

Alois peered at them with a look of deep concentration. Bernard waited as the jeweller gently tilted the envelope under the light, inspecting the curious objects with a careful, practiced eye. Then, after a long pause, Alois looked up, his voice barely above a whisper.

"Where are you finding these items, mein Herr?"

Bernard studied the jewellers face. The friendly, composed demeanour Alois had worn just moments ago had shifted into something far more serious, his eyes darkened with concern, and the corners of his mouth tightened as if he were weighing something heavy in his mind.

Sensing the change, Bernard spoke deliberately. "Why don't we have lunch across the street at the Commercial Hotel? I'll tell you what I know." He kept his voice light, but there was an unspoken understanding between them now.

Alois hesitated, glancing down at the dagger and the peculiar celluloid squares still resting on the counter. For a moment, he seemed lost in thought, as though the objects had stirred something buried deep in his past.

Without waiting for the jeweller to answer, Bernard added smoothly, "I'll fetch my wife from the grocery store and meet you there in, say… ten minutes?" He gave Alois a pointed look before turning on his heel and stepping back out into the warm midday sun.

As Bernard crossed the street, a nagging feeling settled in his gut, Alois Pfeiffer might be exactly the right person to shed light on the peculiar discoveries they had made. The Polish pistol, the SS dagger, the mysterious celluloid squares, and even the ripped interior of the Ford Pilot, each piece of the puzzle hinted at a deeper story, one that was rapidly becoming more unsettling. Not to mention the strange death of their homes previous occupants.

Reaching the grocery store, Bernard spotted Matilda inside, examining a display of fresh produce. As he pushed open the door, the small brass bell above it jingled, and she turned to him with a questioning glance.

"We need to have lunch with Alois Pfeiffer," he said quietly, his voice low enough that only she could hear.

Matilda frowned. "Why? What's going on?"

Bernard exhaled, glancing briefly over his shoulder before replying. "I think that he might be the right person to tell about the strange things that we are discovering at home."

Matilda found herself captivated by the jewellers easy charm. Despite his accent, which at times made it difficult for her to fully grasp his words, his warmth and enthusiasm made him a compelling storyteller. As he spoke, he offered them both a brief

                    Max Barrington

but vivid history of his time in Germany, particularly his role in the war. Bernard and Matilda listened, fascinated and intrigued, as Alois recounted his exploits against the Nazis. The tales of espionage, resistance fighters, and dangerous close calls painted a picture of a man who had lived through extraordinary times.

And then, he dropped the clanger.

"Those little squares on the envelope are microdots," he announced, tapping the table for emphasis. "That gun you have, it likely belonged to a freedom fighter, possibly Polish, unlikely to be a German as they were forbidden to use Jewish weapons. The dagger? That was definitely, the property of a high-ranking German officer. There are other markings on it that might tell us exactly who it belonged to. Normally, I'd say it's just a war souvenir… but now, I'm not so sure."

Alois picked up his beer, taking a long, thoughtful drink. Bernard and Matilda exchanged uneasy glances as he continued.

"I would very much like to see what's on those microdots. I don't have a reader, but it would be quite simple for me to make one. There is definitely something going on with that house, and the sooner we uncover it, the better."

Matilda shifted in her seat, glancing at Bernard before speaking. "You really think this is something important?"

Alois nodded, his expression serious. "Ja, and I suspect the people who lived there were involved in something far bigger than you might have imagined."

Bernard sat forward. "The names of the previous occupants were Petryczek, Anton Petryczek. And I'm fairly certain the woman's name was Kalina."

Alois's brows drew together as he rolled the names over in his mind. He drained the rest of his beer, then leaned back in his chair, lost in thought. Matilda, sensing the moment, didn't hesitate, she stood and made her way to the bar, returning a moment later with three fresh drinks.

Alois took his glass and exhaled slowly. "I very much doubt those were their real names," he said, swirling the liquid inside the glass. He set it down and straightened in his chair. "Here is what I think we should do."

Without hesitation, he laid out a plan, one that had seemingly formed in his mind within minutes.

First, he would take possession of the envelope with the microdots and construct a reader to decipher their contents. Meanwhile, Bernard and Matilda were to conduct a thorough search of the house, especially for anything that might reveal another name, a hidden document, or a connection to something like an engraved silver plate or cuff links with initials. Also, see if you can find out the date that they moved in there.

Alois took another look at the dagger, this time using his jewellers loupe to inspect it more closely. He jotted down the nearly invisible inscription that had been etched into the blade, murmuring to himself as he studied it.

Finally, he suggested that they all meet at Stanlee over the coming weekend to go over their findings together.

Bernard and Matilda agreed without hesitation. There was an unspoken understanding between them now, this had become more than just an unusual discovery. There was a mystery buried in that house, in the artefacts they had found, and perhaps even in the tragic deaths of its previous occupants.

Alois rose from the table, shaking Bernard's hand firmly before tucking the envelope into the inner pocket of his jacket. He took the address for Stanlee, nodded once, and with a parting glance that held both excitement and concern, strode back across the street toward his jewellers shop.

As Bernard and Matilda finished their drinks, neither spoke for a long moment.

Finally, Matilda exhaled and leaned in. "I don't know about you, but I feel like we've just stepped into something much bigger than we bargained for."

Bernard nodded. "And I have a feeling we're only scratching the surface."

"I'm frightened, Bernie!" Matilda's voice trembled slightly, her wide eyes searching his face for reassurance. "Do you think it's safe to go back to our house? Oh, Bernie... I'm becoming scared!"

She clutched her arms, rubbing them as though warding off a sudden chill, despite the warmth of the afternoon. The discovery of the gun, the dagger, the mysterious microdots, everything was beginning to feel far too real.

Bernard reached for her hand, his grip firm and steady. His deep, soothing voice was calm as he reassured her. "Matilda, listen to me. It's highly doubtful that we're in any danger. If someone wanted something from that house, they had months to take it. The place sat empty for over three months after the Petryczek's died. If anyone was searching for something, that would have been the perfect time, not now."

Matilda bit her lip, her fingers fidgeting with the edge of the tablecloth. "But what if, what if they didn't know something was hidden there? What if they only just found out?"

Bernard sighed, rubbing his chin in thought. "That's highly unlikely, but possible, I suppose… but I think we would have seen some sign if someone had been watching the house. And perhaps, " He hesitated for a moment before continuing. "Perhaps I shouldn't have involved Alois in this."

Matilda frowned. "You think that was a mistake?"

Bernard leaned back in his chair, staring into the distance. "I don't know. The man's smart, resourceful. And let's be honest, if anyone can make sense of all this, it's him. But if there was any risk, I've just put him in the middle of it too."

A silence fell between them. The distant sounds of traffic and the chatter of people passing by the hotel filtered through the open window. Matilda exhaled slowly.

"I suppose there's no going back now," she murmured.

Bernard shook his head. "No. We're in this now, Matilda. And I think the only way forward is to keep going."

She met his gaze, searching for the strength he always seemed to carry. Finally, she gave a small nod. "Alright. But if you so much as suspect something isn't right, we leave."

Bernard squeezed her hand. "Agreed."

For now, they would return home. But something told Bernard that their quiet life in Stanlee had just taken a turn they could never have anticipated.

Bernard and Matilda had been invited to a barbecue at his parents' home in Girraween, a welcome opportunity to step away from the growing mystery that had begun to consume their thoughts. As they prepared to leave, Matilda casually suggested, "You know, this might be the perfect chance to ask your parents about the Petryczek's, without giving too much away, of course."

Bernard paused, considering her words. She had a point. His parents had lived in the area for years and were well-acquainted with the locals. If anyone knew anything about Anton and Kalina Petryczek, it would be them. But caution was necessary. They still didn't fully understand what they had stumbled upon, and the last thing Bernard wanted was to unwittingly put his parents in danger.

"You're right," he agreed. "We need to tread carefully, though. Just casual questions, nothing that would make them suspicious or worried."

Matilda nodded. "Exactly. We don't even know what we're dealing with yet."

With that unspoken understanding, they set off next door for Girraween. The drive was a pleasant one in the Land Rover that they had just acquired, the rolling countryside stretching before them in a patchwork of greens and golds under the late afternoon sun. Matilda seemed more at ease, perhaps comforted by the thought of being surrounded by family, if only for a few hours.

When they arrived at Bernard's parents' home, the warm scent of grilled meat and the sound of easy laughter greeted them. His mother, always the gracious host, ushered them in with affectionate hugs, while his father, ever the storyteller, was already regaling a few guests with a tale from his younger days.

As the evening unfolded, Bernard and Matilda carefully steered the conversation towards local history, mentioning the Petryczek's in passing. "I remember that the Wilson's lived there when I was here and attending school, It wasn't until I came home from Uni that I first noticed them," Bernard remarked casually, watching for any flicker of recognition in his parents' expressions. "Did you ever meet them?"

His mother glanced at his father before answering. "Oh, the Petryczek's? Yes, we knew them, not well, mind you, but enough to exchange pleasantries. They were private people, kept to themselves mostly. Anton was quite handy, used to fix things around town from time to time, from what I heard."

"And Kalina?" Matilda prompted gently.

His mother frowned slightly. "She was... lovely but quiet. Always had this faraway look, as if her mind was somewhere else. You know, now that I think about it, there was always something a little unusual about them."

Bernard leaned in slightly. "Unusual how?"

His father shrugged. "Hard to say, really. But I do remember something strange, when they first moved into the house, a man came looking for them not long after. Foreign-sounding fellow, dark suit, serious type. Your mother answered the door, didn't you, love?"

She nodded. "Yes. He asked for them by name but seemed surprised when I told him that they did not live here, but the adjoining property. He just thanked me and left."

Bernard and Matilda exchanged a glance.

His mother waved a hand dismissively. "Probably nothing, dear. But I do remember thinking at the time that it was odd. The Petryczek's weren't exactly social, so someone turning up out of the blue like that... it stuck in my mind."

Edwin took a slow sip from the cold beer Matilda had handed him, his eyes narrowing slightly as he recalled the memory. "Funny thing, one day," he began, "As I was driving past their place and saw Anton with a car parked beside the gate and the bonnet was up. It was the first time I'd ever seen the Ford Pilot, so I figured it must have been a new car he'd picked up." He paused, shaking his head slightly. "I thought I would do the right thing and I stopped to help. He hadn't heard me pull up, so I got out of the Landy and called out to him by name, but he didn't answer straight away."

Bernard and Matilda exchanged a glance. "Why do you think that was?" Bernard asked, curiosity creeping into his voice.

Edwin shrugged. "Dunno. Maybe he was just deep in thought. When he finally looked up, he seemed... startled, like he wasn't expecting anyone. Turns out he'd lost the keys, or, so he told me. And he was trying to get the ignition switch out to have new keys made. Strange,I thought." He took another sip of his beer before adding, "Odd bloke, Anton. Always seemed to have something on his mind."

                    Max Barrington

Before anyone could comment further, Phyllis chimed in, her expression animated. "Oh, and I saw them both in Dalby that same week, at the butcher and then at the chemist," she said, glancing between Bernard and Matilda. "I walked in just behind them, and Kalina was speaking to Anton in her own language, Polish, I assume. I couldn't understand a word of it, of course, but one thing stuck with me."

Matilda leaned in. "What was that?"

Phyllis pursed her lips for a moment, as if choosing her words carefully. "I heard her say the name Carl, quite a few times, actually. She seemed... tense, like she was warning him about something. It was only two days after that stranger came looking for them, so at the time, I just assumed they must have been talking about him, that his name was Carl."

A heavy silence settled over the group for a moment before Bernard spoke. "You never saw that stranger again, did you?"

Phyllis shook her head. "No, never. But...now I think about it, there is something that makes me think his face might be familiar.....no...it's gone,...don't overcook those steaks dear!" She aimed the last sentence towards Edwin at the BBQ.

Alois arrived on Saturday afternoon as planned, pulling up in his old but well-maintained Vauxhall with three crates of beer in the backseat. As he stepped out, Matilda took one look at the sheer quantity of beer he had brought and insisted that he stay the night.

"You're not driving home after that lot," she declared, hands on her hips.

Alois grinned, clearly not one to argue when hospitality and cold beer were involved. "If you insist, Matilda, I shall not protest."

As they showed him around the house, Alois was visibly impressed, particularly when Bernard led him to the guest room. "This is a fine home," he said, setting his small overnight bag down that he had brought with him on the off chance of an invitation. "Solid structure, beautiful timber work... You chose well."

Once he was settled, Alois wasted no time getting to the reason for his visit. "Did you manage to find anything, anything at all, that might indicate another name?" he asked eagerly.

Bernard nodded. "My mother mentioned that she once overheard the Petryczek's talking in the butcher shop in town. Kalina was speaking in what she assumed was Polish, though, to be honest, she wasn't entirely sure. But she did clearly hear one name, Carl, and more than once, she said Kalina directed it to Anton."

Alois stroked his chin, deep in thought. "Carl, you say?" He seemed to turn the name over in his mind, as if it meant something to him.

"We also learned about a stranger who came looking for the Petryczek's, but we're not exactly sure when that was," Matilda added.

Alois's brow furrowed. He took a slow sip of his beer before suddenly asking, "Do you have an office in the house?"

                                    Max Barrington

Matilda beamed. "Oh, do we ever! And it's a beauty, with an absolute ripper of a eucalyptus, spotted gum, desk." She motioned for him to follow her.

As they entered the office, Alois ran his hands over the smooth, polished wood, nodding in approval. "It is indeed a very fine desk," he said just as Bernard arrived, balancing three freshly opened beers. Alois turned to them both, a sudden intensity in his gaze. "Was this desk here when you moved in?"

Matilda and Bernard both nodded. "Yeah, it was part of the house," Bernard confirmed.

"Did it have a desk blotter on it, by any chance?" Alois asked, indicating with his arms the general three foot by two foot desk blotter size.

Matilda wrinkled her nose. "It was pretty disgusting, so we hoiked it!" she said with a dismissive wave of her hand.

Bernard, however, scratched the back of his head. "Actually… I never got around to tossing it. It's still out in the shearing shed." He cast a wary glance at Matilda, as if expecting a scolding.

Alois's eyes lit up with sudden excitement. "Can you bring it in? I'd like to have a look at it."

Though puzzled, Bernard didn't question him and disappeared outside, returning minutes later with the old desk blotter. It was large, worn, and still encased in its original leather corners. He set it down on the desk just as it had been when they first arrived at the house.

Alois wasted no time. He carefully removed the stack of blotting paper from its base, his fingers deftly sliding away the top layers until he reached the very last one, the sheet that had been pressed directly against the masonite base surface.

"Ah-ha!" he exclaimed. The bottom-most blotter was covered, absolutely covered, in scribbles, doodles, short notes, and phone numbers. The faded impressions of hurried handwriting sprawled across the paper, layered over time like ghosts of old conversations.

Alois looked up at them, his excitement barely contained. "Now," he declared, flattening the sheet across the desk, "we must study this minutely, looking for names, initials, anything that could tell us more."

Bernard and Matilda leaned in, the three of them scanning the markings, their intrigue growing with each passing moment.

After an hour of looking and two bottles of beer each they were pretty certain that they had found the initials of CR in at least three places. They were most impressed, who would have ever thought, they mused and then Alois told them of his research results.

As they settled on the front verandah Alois told them that he had researched the number, CSZ 8887845 that he had found on the dagger and it had belonged to; Hauptmann (Captain) Carl Reimer. He was a decorated officer in the German Generalstaboffiziere (General Staff Officers), specializing in intelligence and counter-espionage. Born in 1906 in Königsberg, East Prussia, Reimer joined the Wehrmacht in the late 1920s and rapidly climbed the ranks due to his sharp tactical mind and unwavering ruthlessness. By 1940, he had transitioned into the intelligence arm of the military, working closely with the Abwehr and later the Sicherheitsdienst (SD), where he played a key role in identifying and eliminating resistance networks within occupied Poland.

In early 1943, while stationed in Breslau Poland, Reimer was assigned to dismantle a Polish underground resistance cell. During a raid on a suspected safe house, he captured Anton and Kalina Petryczek, high-ranking Polish operatives involved in smuggling intelligence and microfilm to Allied contacts in Switzerland. Reimer, ever the opportunist, saw a way out of the collapsing Reich as Germany's war effort was beginning to falter.

Instead of merely executing them, he extracted valuable intelligence from the couple through brutal interrogation. Once he had what he needed, Reimer and his wife, Elsa, executed Anton and Kalina in the cellar of a remote hunting lodge. Carefully forging documents, they assumed the Petryczek's' identities and used Polish resistance escape networks to travel south, eventually crossing into Croatia under the guise of Polish refugees.

By 1944, as the Eastern Front collapsed and the Reich descended into chaos, Reimer and Elsa successfully fled Europe. It is believed they secured passage on a neutral vessel using stolen diamonds, war spoils amassed from Jewish deportations and resistance raids, to bribe their way to safety. Their trail disappears briefly before resurfacing in Australia, where they likely entered under the guise of displaced persons.

Intelligence sources and post-war investigations suggest that Reimer did not leave Poland empty-handed. A considerable quantity of diamonds that had been collected by Reimer's unit went missing at the very time that Reimer and his wife also went missing.

The SS, notorious for eliminating traitors, deserters, and those who knew too much, had placed Reimer on their death list before the war even ended. His military number, CSZ 8887845, appeared in SS archives as an individual slated for "Sonderbehandlung" (special treatment), a euphemism for execution. This meant that he would be tracked across the world to be executed and the diamonds would be returned to the Third Reich.

Alois leaned forward, his voice lowering as if the walls themselves might betray their conversation. "So, it would seem that the Petryczek's were, in fact, the Reimer's," he concluded, lifting his glass and refilling it from the open bottle of beer.

Matilda and Bernard sat frozen in shock. Bernard opened his mouth, about to ask a question, but closed it again as he processed what they had just learned. His mind reeled, this wasn't just a case of mistaken identity or a tragic accident. It was something far more sinister.

"It's my guess," Alois continued, swirling the amber liquid in his glass, "that the SS caught up with Carl and Peta Reimer, here, in this house, and executed them."

Bernard's brow furrowed as he stared at Alois. "But the war ended nine years ago… there are no SS anymore!"

Alois let out a dry chuckle, shaking his head. "That's where you're wrong, my friend. After World War II, many former SS officers and Nazi officials fled Europe to escape prosecution. Paraguay became a key refuge due to its authoritarian government, lax immigration policies, and support from dictator Alfredo Stroessner, who had German ancestry and sympathised with fascist ideologies.

The escape routes, often called the "Ratlines," were organised by networks that included ODESSA (Organisation der Ehemaligen SS-Angehörigen), former Nazis, and sympathetic clergy. Many fled through Spain or Italy, often using Vatican-issued travel documents and forged Red Cross passports. From there, they boarded ships to Argentina, which had already welcomed many Nazi fugitives under Juan Perón's rule. Once in Argentina, it was easy to cross into Paraguay, where they were granted asylum, new identities, and in some cases, Paraguayan citizenship.

Notorious war criminals like Josef Mengele and Eduard Roschmann lived in Paraguay under Stroessner's protection. The country's isolated rural areas and corrupt officials helped them avoid detection for decades.

The SS may have lost the war, but they never disappeared. They went underground, regrouped. Their main base is thought to be in Itatiaia, Rio de Janeiro." He took a sip of his beer before continuing. "The British and Americans knew that high-ranking

                    Max Barrington

Nazi officers and war criminals were hiding in South America. They tried to drag them back to Nuremberg in '45 to face justice, but they couldn't get extradition. Too many powerful people were protecting them."

Matilda's hands trembled slightly as she reached for her own glass. "Are you saying that… someone, an assassin, tracked them all the way here to this house? After all these years?"

Alois nodded grimly. "That's exactly what I'm saying. The SS didn't forgive traitors. If Carl Reimer stole from them, betrayed them, or even knew something valuable, they would have hunted him to the ends of the earth to silence him." He leaned back, exhaling heavily. "And they succeeded."

"But the police said that there were no suspicious circumstances, that it was a double suicide." Added Matilda somewhat questionably.

Alois, with a smile, replied "How convenient for the police, the deceased just popped the capsules into their mouths, bit down on them and died a quite excruciating death. I really don't think so my dear……I am sure that if the police forensic had bothered to look closely around the victims mouths, then they may have found some force marks, fractured teeth, perhaps?"

Bernard and Matilda considered this briefly and Bernard queried Alois. "Right….and the victims simply allowed the killer to place the capsules into their mouths knowing what they were….no way!"

"Was there a tractor here when you bought the place?" Alois asked simply as though changing the subject.

They both returned a strange look towards Alois when he asked this as if in confusion, "Yes…we have a tractor, it was here when we came….but…"

"Let's go and have a quick look at it shall we?" As Alois moved aside to allow Bernard and Matilda to pass in order to follow them outside to where the shed containing machinery and other items, as well as an International Harvester Formal type AV Tractor. "Here she be Alois, we haven't even touched it yet." Bernard held his arm towards the tractor.

Alois approached the tractor with deliberate calmness, his eyes scanning its worn exterior before stopping at the small metal toolbox affixed to the left rear mudguard. With an easy familiarity, he flipped open the lid, the rusty hinges creaking slightly in protest. He peered inside, his fingers moving methodically through the contents before settling on a small, brown, translucent capsule. It was pliable between his fingers, about two inches long and half an inch thick.

Holding it up to the light, he turned toward Bernard and Matilda, allowing them both to get a clear look at the object. A knowing glint flickered in his eyes as he asked, "Do either of you know what this is?"

Bernard, who had been watching closely, immediately recognised it. He stepped forward, his brow furrowing slightly as he examined the capsule from a distance. "It's a cold start cartridge for the tractor," he stated matter-of-factly, his tone laced with the certainty of a man familiar with farm machinery.

Alois gave a slow, approving nod but remained silent for a moment, his fingers turning the capsule over as if he were weighing not just its psychical properties, but the implications it carried. His expression was thoughtful, almost calculating, before he finally spoke.

"Yes… it is," he affirmed, his voice steady. "And did you know that each one of these contains exactly seven cubic centimetres of ether?" He lifted his gaze to meet Bernard's, a knowing look in his eyes. "I think that you, being a doctor, understand precisely what that means."

Bernard's reaction was immediate. His expression shifted from curiosity to realisation in an instant. "Of course!… And how

                    Max Barrington

very convenient," he murmured, his voice carrying an edge of intrigue.

Matilda, however, looked between them, frowning slightly. "Wait, what are you saying? What does that mean?"

Bernard turned to her, his tone calm but firm as he explained, "This small capsule contains enough ether to render a dozen, or more, people unconscious for hours."

Matilda's eyes widened as the weight of his words sank in. She turned back to Alois, who remained quietly studying the capsule, a small but unmistakable glint of satisfaction in his expression.

Matilda understanding instantly, exclaimed "And, these, capsules, are here, on tap, so to speak." Slowly shaking her head. "But, how would the…the…killer…know about…"

"I presume that he is a German, most of Germany is rural, most of us German's, grew up on farms with equipment such as this and the German climate requires these ether capsules to enable the machinery to start in the cold mornings."

Bernard exhaled sharply, running a hand through his hair. "Christ… and we just walked into this mess without even realising it." he said as they all walked back to the house and settled in the lounge.

Alois leaned back in his chair, his expression calm yet firm. "You have nothing to worry about," he reassured Bernard, his voice steady. "They got their man, or man and woman, in this case. Their mission here is finished. I highly doubt you'll ever hear or see anyone from the SS again. There should be nothing left in this house that would interest them."

Bernard wasn't entirely convinced. He cast a glance at Matilda, who still looked uneasy. "What about the microdots?" he asked, his tone carrying a weight of apprehension.

Alois sighed, rubbing his chin before responding. "Ah, yes… the microdots," he murmured, reaching for his beer. "They were peculiar, I'll admit. One of them was a map of Breslau in Poland, with a particular building circled. Another microdot contained a close-up image of that very building. The third was a photograph, an open bag filled with diamonds. And the fourth?" He paused, setting his glass down. "It showed the same bag of diamonds, but now sealed and inside the box alongside the dagger."

Matilda's eyes widened. "So, the diamonds,…were once in the box that we found the dagger in?"

Alois nodded. "It also suggests that the significant portion of the stolen diamonds were hidden somewhere in that building in Poland. But here's the catch, I checked historical records. That building was destroyed in 1944."

Bernard exhaled, shaking his head. "So they might be lost forever?"

"Possibly," Alois admitted, "or… maybe they were moved before the building was destroyed. Who knows?"

Matilda's eyes flicked between Alois and Bernard, a spark of realisation dawning on her. "The diamonds… they could still be in this house somewhere!" she said, her voice rising with excitement. Then, turning quickly to Bernard, she added, "The car, that must be why someone tore the seats apart! They were searching for the diamonds!"

Alois, however, remained unconvinced. He slowly shook his head from side to side, his expression thoughtful. "I very much doubt there are any diamonds left," he said, his tone measured. "Most likely, they were used to finance their escape, false papers, safe passage, bribes. Then there's this house, their living expenses for the past nine years… it all adds up. But…" He hesitated, rubbing his chin. "Yes… the car. That is peculiar."

Matilda leaned forward, determined. "So why didn't the murderer, or, the executioner, as you called him, find the gun and the box with the dagger?" She directed the question straight at Alois, her gaze sharp, challenging.

Alois smiled softly at her, as if amused by her persistence. "I believe the executioner did search the house," he said, glancing at Bernard. "And I suspect he did find the gun."

Bernard frowned. "But we found the gun, wrapped in that old tea towel."

"Half wrapped," Alois corrected. He tilted his head slightly. "Didn't you tell me it was only partially covered?"

Bernard nodded slowly. "Yeah… the towel was kind of bunched around it. Like someone had picked it up and then set it down again."

"Exactly," Alois said, tapping his fingers on the table. "That suggests whoever searched the house found the gun but left it. Maybe he didn't want it. As for the box with the dagger, perhaps he simply never found it." He took another sip of his beer before continuing. "And the torn upholstery in the car? That is still a mystery, but show me where you found the box."

Matilda and Bernard took Alois to the rear of the house where the laundry is located on the closed in verandah. Matilda opened the door and walked into the room with Alois following as Bernard stayed back. Entering the laundry Matilda turned and facing Alois told him to turn around and look above the door. Alois thought it was a strange place to put a cupboard and one that you would not notice unless you were actually looking up, "I'd say that whoever was searching did not see this cupboard," commented Alois, "as with the Public Trustee when they went through the house, although, as you say, the gun was not overly hidden."

A heavy silence settled between them as they each considered the possibilities. If someone had searched the car after the execution, then it meant someone else besides the SS had been looking for something. And if that something wasn't the gun or the dagger… then maybe, just maybe, it was the diamonds after all.

They dined that night on roast lamb from their paddock with roast vegetable's that were mostly from their garden. As the night wore on the drinks flowed freely and they solved the problems of the world, but they didn't solve the mystery at 'Stanlee' that would be for another weekend.

BRRRRINNNGG! BRRRRINNNGG! ... a brief pause ... BRRRRINNNGG! BRRRRINNNGG!

The harsh, metallic ring of the old black Bakelite telephone shattered the silence of the house. The sound echoed through the hallway, urgent and relentless.

Bernard jolted awake, disoriented, his heart pounding from the sudden intrusion. Half-asleep, he stumbled out of bed, his feet barely finding their way to the small wooden table where the phone sat. The cool night air made him shiver as he reached for the receiver, his fingers fumbling over the smooth, curved handle.

He had not been in bed long, perhaps an hour or two at most, but he had been in a deep, exhausted sleep. Matilda was at Dalby Hospital's maternity ward. He had stayed with her until 2 AM, watching over her as she drifted into peaceful rest. Everything had indicated that the birth was still some time away. Her doctor had reassured him, urging him to go home and get some rest so he would be ready for the big moment later in the day. Bernard had reluctantly agreed.

He cleared his throat, trying to shake off the fog of sleep. "Hello?" His voice was hoarse, barely above a mumble.

A crisp, cheerful voice cut through the receiver. "Doctor Collins?" The caller didn't wait for confirmation. "You need to come to the maternity ward immediately..." A short pause. "Actually, Doctor, there's no rush. Congratulations! You're a father. Both mother and baby are doing just fine. See you soon."

The line went dead.

For a moment, Bernard stood frozen, the words sinking in. A father. The weight of it settled over him, a mix of exhilaration, relief, and disbelief coursing through his veins. Then, as if suddenly snapped back into reality, he sprang into action.

Still groggy, he shoved his feet into his shoes, realising he had never changed out of his clothes. He grabbed a jumper, pulled it over his head, and rushed out into the crisp early morning air.

The Ford Pilot roared to life, its engine grumbling as he sped off into the night. The drive to Dalby felt both endless and fleeting, his mind racing with anticipation. By the time he arrived, breathless and wide-eyed, he was met with the sight that would change his world forever, his beautiful daughter, Alison, cradled in Matilda's arms.

Three years after Alison's arrival into the world, history nearly repeated itself with the birth of their son, Lindsay. His arrival was met with just as much joy and wonder, though this time, Bernard and Matilda felt more prepared for the whirlwind that came with a newborn.

As they embraced the busy reality of parenting two young children, their lives naturally shifted into a new rhythm, one filled with sleepless nights, first steps, and the sweet chaos of raising a family. The once-consuming mysteries of the house, which had lingered in their minds for so long, gradually faded into the background. The enigmatic past of the Petryczek's, or whoever they were, the hidden secrets, and even the lingering questions about the house itself became distant thoughts, overshadowed by the demands and excitement of everyday life.

Their home was no longer defined by its past but by the present, the laughter of children, the warmth of family, and the steady comfort of a life they had built together.

It was three days before Lindsay's first birthday, a crisp Monday morning with a lingering chill in the air. Bernard had been called into the hospital in Dalby, where he still maintained his practice twice a week. One of his regular patients had suffered an injury after a horse fall over the weekend, and his expertise was needed.

At home, Matilda was easing into the morning routine. She had taken little notice of the thin veil of smoke that clung to the air, assuming it was simply the remnants of a controlled burn or a distant bushfire, common enough for the season. She had just finished preparing breakfast for the children when,

BRRRRINNNGG! BRRRRINNNGG! … a brief pause … BRRRRINNNGG! BRRRRINNNGG!

The sharp, jarring ring of the telephone made her wince. With Lindsay balanced on her hip and Alison tugging insistently at the hem of her dressing gown, Matilda made her way to the hallway, silently wondering if there was a way to make that dreadful telephone ring a little softer.

She reached for the handset and lifted it to her ear, barely opening her mouth to say "Hello" before the words on the other end sent an icy chill through her.

"Mum and Dad are dead!"

It was Bernard. His voice was frantic, barely coherent, words tumbling out in a distraught mess.

Matilda froze. Her grip tightened around the phone, her mind struggling to process what she had just heard. "What?!" The single word was all she could manage as a wave of shock and disbelief crashed over her.

Bernard kept talking, but his words blurred into a jumble of panic and sorrow. Matilda swayed slightly, holding Lindsay closer as she felt the ground shift beneath her, as if the world itself had suddenly tilted off its axis.

Bernard arrived home late that evening, his face drawn and his shoulders heavy with exhaustion. The weight of the day hung on him like a leaden cloak. He had spent the entire day at his parents' property in Girraween, or rather, what was left of it.

The fire had not spared a single thing. The once-familiar homestead, the place that had echoed with laughter, shared meals, and childhood memories, was now nothing more than a smouldering ruin. Charred beams jutted from the blackened ground like broken bones, and the air was thick with the acrid stench of burned timber and ash. Nothing recognisable remained.

The authorities had ruled it a tragic accident, likely a spark from the old fireplace, or perhaps an electrical fault, but Bernard wasn't convinced. Something about it didn't sit right with him. The timing. The completeness of the destruction. His parents had been careful, meticulous people, not ones to leave a fire unattended or allow a dangerous oversight.

As he stepped inside his own home, Matilda met him at the door, worry etched deep into her face. She had put the children to bed hours ago, though she had barely taken her eyes off the clock, waiting for him. Now, as she took in his haunted expression, she braced herself.

Without a word, Bernard pulled her into an embrace. He smelled of smoke, of loss, of grief too heavy to put into words.

"It's all gone," he murmured, his voice thick with exhaustion.

Matilda swallowed hard. There was nothing she could say to make it better, so she simply held him tighter.

Bernard had dropped that morning's newspaper onto the kitchen table with a dull thud. It had been his first source of information about the fire, about the unimaginable loss of his parents. The stark black headlines had leaped off the page, cutting through the haze of his morning routine like a blade:

"Tragic Blaze Destroys Homestead, Elderly Couple Perish in Overnight Inferno"

His hands had trembled as he read the details, his mind struggling to process the cold, impersonal words that now defined the final moments of his mother and father. A neighbour had reported seeing the glow of flames in the early hours, but by the time help arrived, the house was already lost. Fire crews had worked through the night, but there had been no survivors.

Despite the proximity of Girraween to Stanlee, only a few miles as the crow flies, the rolling hills and dense eucalyptus forests that lay between the two properties made them feel worlds apart. Communication was limited, and unless someone made the effort to ride or drive the distance, news often travelled slowly. Girraween sat on the Dalby side of the Dalby-Chinchilla Road, while Stanlee was positioned on the Chinchilla side. It was only by chance that Bernard had seen the paper that morning; otherwise, he might not have known until much later.

The thought made his stomach turn. His own parents, gone. And he had learned about it from a newspaper article.

Matilda, having difficulty reading the report through her tears put down the newspaper report;

Tragic Fire Destroys Rural Homestead – Two Lives Lost

Authorities Investigating Blaze Near Dalby

Dalby, Monday – A devastating fire tore through a rural property near Dalby in the early hours of Sunday morning, completely destroying a homestead and tragically claiming the lives of two occupants.

The property, known as Girraween, located off the Dalby-Chinchilla Road, was already engulfed in flames when neighbours first spotted the glow on the horizon shortly after midnight. A call was placed to emergency services, but by the time fire crews arrived, the house had been reduced to smouldering ruins.

Dalby Fire Brigade Chief Robert Callahan described the scene as "one of the most intense house fires we've seen in recent years." He stated that the blaze spread rapidly, leaving little chance for escape. "The structure was fully involved when our crews arrived. Given the remote location, it was impossible to contain before complete destruction occurred," he added.

Authorities have confirmed the recovery of two bodies from the ruins, believed to be the occupants of the home. Their identities have not yet been officially released, pending further investigation and notification of next of kin.

Neighbours and locals who knew the residents of Girraween have expressed deep shock and sadness over the tragedy. "They were well-respected and had lived here for many years," said one local farmer. "It's hard to believe they're gone just like that."

At this stage, the cause of the fire remains unknown. Fire investigators and police are working to determine whether the blaze was accidental or if other factors were involved. Authorities are urging anyone with information to come forward.

Further updates are expected as the investigation continues.

If you have any information regarding this incident, please contact Dalby Police or the Rural Fire Service.

The following Thursday Bernard, Matilda and their children drove the Ford Pilot into Dalby;

The newspaper reported: Somber Farewell for Edwin and Phyllis Collins in Dalby

The small rural town of Dalby fell silent on Thursday morning as family, friends, and community members gathered to pay their final respects to Edwin and Phyllis Collins, whose lives were tragically lost in the devastating fire at their Girraween homestead earlier this week.

The funeral service, held at St. Joseph's Church, was solemn and dignified, with mourners filling the pews to capacity. A hush settled over the congregation as the two simple wooden coffins, adorned with wreaths of native Australian flowers, were carried inside by pallbearers, including close family members and long-time friends of the couple.

The service was led by Reverend Thomas Gallagher, who spoke warmly of Edwin and Phyllis, recalling their generosity, resilience, and strong ties to the community. "They were the kind of people who never hesitated to lend a hand, who welcomed everyone with kindness, and who built a life founded on hard work and love," he said.

Tears were shed as Bernard Collins, their only son, stood to deliver a heartfelt tribute to his parents. His voice, though steady, carried the weight of grief as he spoke of childhood memories at Girraween, of his parents' unwavering support, and of the devastating loss their absence now left behind.

Following the service, the mourners made their way to the Dalby Cemetery, where Edwin and Phyllis were laid to rest side by side. The sound of the priest's final prayers was accompanied by the distant cry of currawongs in the nearby gum trees, a solemn reminder of the land they had called home for so many years.

As the last handfuls of earth were gently placed over the graves, Bernard stood with his wife, Matilda, and their two young children, clutching each other tightly. The townspeople, many of whom had known the Collinses for decades, lingered quietly, offering whispered condolences and silent support.

Though the tragic circumstances of their passing have left unanswered questions, what remains undeniable is the legacy Edwin and Phyllis Collins leave behind, a legacy of love, community, and a life well lived in the heart of the Darling Downs.

In Loving Memory of Edwin and Phyllis Collins

"Forever in our hearts, forever part of this land."

Bernard and Matilda made the difficult but practical decision not to rebuild the homestead at Girraween. The fire had taken more than just a house, it had consumed a lifetime of memories, leaving behind only ash and sorrow. Though the land remained, the heart of Girraween had been lost.

Fortunately, the manager's cottage and the two workers' cottages had been spared from the blaze. After much discussion, they agreed that operations could continue without the main homestead, with Bernard managing the property from Stanlee. It was not an easy choice, but it was the most sensible one. The sheep and cattle still needed tending, the land still needed working, crops sowing and life, despite its tragedies, had to move forward.

In the months that followed, Bernard settled into the rhythm of overseeing both Stanlee and Girraween. The arrangement, while initially challenging, soon proved workable. With the help of the station hands, the day-to-day running of Girraween continued much as it had before.

After three months of relatively smooth operation, Bernard felt the time had come to make a symbolic change, one that would honour the past while acknowledging the future. Early one crisp morning, he took a set of tools and carefully removed the gate sign at Stanlee. In its place, he erected a new sign, freshly painted and boldly inscribed with a single word:

"Girraween"

It was more than just a name; it was a tribute, a declaration that the land would endure despite the loss, and a commitment to ensuring that Girraween, at least in spirit, would live on.

The Fire Brigade had conducted an extensive search through the ruins, rubble, and ash of the Girraween fire. Though three months had passed, the investigation remained ongoing, and no official findings had yet been released to the coroner. The uncertainty weighed heavily on Bernard and Matilda, who longed for answers but had resigned themselves to the slow pace of official inquiries.

BRRRRINNNGG! BRRRRINNNGG! … a brief pause … BRRRRINNNGG! BRRRRINNNGG!

The sharp, jarring ring of the telephone shattered the quiet afternoon. Matilda, caught off guard, jumped involuntarily, her heart pounding as she steadied herself against the kitchen counter. From down the hallway, Lindsay, startled by the sudden noise, began to cry. His distressed wails echoed through the house, adding to Matilda's growing unease.

She hurried to the telephone and picked up the receiver.

"Hello!" she answered, trying to mask the tension in her voice as she attempted to soothe Lindsay from a distance.

A firm yet polite voice responded. "Good afternoon. I'm Senior Constable Damien Rhodes from the Dalby station. Could I please speak to Doctor Collins?"

Matilda stiffened at the mention of the police. A thousand possibilities raced through her mind, each one worse than the last.

"I'm sorry, he's not here at the moment," she replied cautiously. "Can I help?"

There was a brief pause before the officer answered.

"No, I'm afraid it's Doctor Collins that I need to speak with. I can call back later when he is home, perhaps?"

Matilda hesitated, her pulse quickening. Whatever this was about, it was serious. Suddenly, she thought of Bernard's surgery.

"You could reach him at his practice," she offered quickly, giving the constable the number.

"Thank you," he replied, his tone giving nothing away. Then, with a click, the line went dead.

Matilda remained standing there, the receiver still in her hand, staring at nothing in particular. A heavy sense of unease settled over her. What could this be about? Was there news about the fire? Had something else happened?

She knew one thing for certain, she would spend the rest of the afternoon anxiously waiting, dreading whatever it was that the police needed to tell Bernard.

Matilda was feeding the children when Bernard arrived home that evening. The scent of warm food filled the kitchen as Alison chattered happily about her day, and Lindsay, still in his high chair, clumsily gripped his spoon, more interested in making a mess than eating.

After a round of hellos and affectionate kisses, Bernard reached into the icebox, pulled out a cold beer, and settled into a chair at the kitchen table, where Matilda stood, wiping Lindsay's sticky hands. But she was far too preoccupied to focus on the usual evening routine.

She turned to Bernard, her voice edged with impatience. "Did the police call you at the office?"

He took his time, pouring the beer into two glasses, one for himself, one for her, before answering. His tone was measured, careful, as if trying to soften the impact of his words.

"The fire brigade found an item in the ashes of Mum and Dad's house that may be... extraneous."

The deliberate way he said it only made Matilda more anxious. Her instincts flared, and she was on full alert.

"What sort of item?" she asked immediately, her hands pausing in mid-motion.

Bernard sighed, knowing there was no point in easing her into it. She would demand the full truth, and she would want it now.

"A fuse igniter," he said, watching her closely. "A Nobel fuse igniter, to be specific."

Matilda frowned, the term unfamiliar. "And that means?"

"It's used to light the fuse of gelignite." Bernard set his glass down and rubbed his forehead. "The police wanted to know if Dad ever kept gelignite on the property."

A chill ran through Matilda. This was no accident. A fuse igniter in the ruins of the house? That meant someone had deliberately set the fire.

Her voice was barely above a whisper. "And did he?"

Bernard shook his head slowly. "Not that I ever knew of. But I need to check with the workers. If Dad ever had gelignite, it would have been for clearing tree stumps or breaking up rock. Still, that doesn't explain why there would be an igniter left behind in the house."

Matilda swallowed hard. She had already been uneasy about the fire, but now, for the first time, true fear settled into her bones.

Bernard knew it was going to be a long and restless night for Matilda, and, by extension, for himself. Once she had something on her mind, there was no shaking it loose, and he could already see the tension in her shoulders, the way she twisted her wedding ring absentmindedly, deep in thought.

He sighed and took another sip of his beer, running a hand through his hair in frustration. This entire ordeal, the fire, the police inquiry, and now the discovery of a fuse igniter in the ashes, was starting to wear on him. And what irritated him most was the nagging feeling that this was somehow connected to the tangled mess of German and Polish espionage nonsense that had been hanging over them for far too long.

"I'm getting bloody sick of all this spy bullshit," he muttered under his breath.

Matilda shot him a sharp glance. "What do you mean?"

Bernard exhaled heavily, leaning back in his chair. "I mean, I'm tired of it. I'm tired of the secrets, the paranoia, and whatever the hell we got tangled up in before we ever set foot in this house. If someone deliberately started that fire, then I want to know why. I want to know who. And more than anything, I want it to be over."

Matilda nodded, her lips pressed into a thin line. "So do I."

The next morning, after speaking with the manager at Girraween and confirming that no explosives had ever been stored or used on the property, Bernard wasted no time driving into Dalby. His mind churned with frustration as he pulled up outside the police station, barely bothering to shut the car door properly before striding inside.

Constable Rhodes looked up from his desk as Bernard entered, his expression shifting from neutral to mildly wary. The doctor wasn't in the mood for pleasantries. He stepped up to the desk, placed his hands flat on its surface, and fixed Rhodes with a steely glare.

"I checked with my manager. There have never been any explosives at Girraween, none. So I'm going to ask you again, Constable: just what the fuck is going on here? Because we don't need this shit."

Rhodes blinked, clearly taken aback by the outburst. He straightened in his chair, choosing his words carefully.

"Do you mean about the fire?" he asked, almost reflexively.

The second the words left his mouth, he regretted them.

Bernard's eyes flashed with anger. "Are you kidding me? Of course, I mean the fire! You call me, tell me you found a fuse igniter in the ashes of my parents' home, and now you're acting like this is just some routine investigation?"

Rhodes exhaled sharply, rubbing a hand over his chin as he gathered his thoughts. He hadn't intended to sound dismissive, but he understood why Bernard was furious. Hell, if it were his parents who had died in that blaze, he'd be demanding answers too.

Bernard's patience was wearing thin, and it showed. His voice was sharp, his words cutting through the tense silence in the small police office.

"Well, isn't that why you contacted me in the first place? The fire? Are you not implying that it may have been deliberately lit?"

He was trying to keep his composure, but the weight of the past few months, losing his parents, the unanswered questions, the gnawing uncertainty, was pressing down on him. Bernard had little tolerance for hesitation, and right now, Constable Rhodes was dancing around the subject like a man afraid to speak his mind.

"You need to tell me what you're thinking, what you know, and you need to stop fucking around!" His voice was controlled but firm, laced with a barely contained fury that made it clear he wouldn't accept anything less than the full truth.

Bernard pulled out a chair and sat opposite Rhodes, arms crossed, jaw set, waiting.

Rhodes hesitated for only a moment before exhaling deeply. Without a word, he stood, walked to the door, and quietly closed it, making sure it latched before returning to his seat. The gesture wasn't lost on Bernard, this was about to get serious.

The constable leaned forward, resting his forearms on the desk. His voice, when he finally spoke, was low and measured.

"Alright, Doctor Collins… here's what we do know. There were four distinct areas in the fire debris that tested positive for traces of zirconium potassium perchlorate. It's a compound found in fuse igniters, used primarily for setting off controlled explosives."

Bernard's brow furrowed. He knew enough about chemicals to understand that this wasn't something naturally occurring.

Rhodes continued, choosing his words carefully. "These fuse igniters aren't exactly easy to light. From what I've recently been told, it takes at least three matches held together, with the end of the igniter pressed firmly against the emery paper on a matchbox, to get it started. Once ignited, it burns intensely, almost like an oxy-acetylene torch, and it lasts for about ten minutes."

He paused, letting the information settle before dropping the real bombshell.

"And here's the thing, a break-in was reported at the council quarry just north of town. It happened about two weeks before the fire. Nothing appeared to be stolen or disturbed, except for one item, a bundle of ten fuse igniters, taken from an open box. That's it. Nothing else was touched."

Rhodes let the words hang in the air, watching Bernard's reaction.

The room suddenly felt smaller, the weight of the revelation pressing down on them both. Bernard swallowed hard, his mind racing. This wasn't just a tragic accident. Someone had set that fire, on purpose. Bernard sat frozen, his mind a tangled mess of thoughts. He didn't know what to think, let alone what to do next. If he told Matilda, she would fall apart, he was sure of it. This was more than just devastating news; it was something dark, something sinister.

He swallowed hard, lifting his gaze to Constable Rhodes. "What do we do now?" His voice was quieter than before, the initial frustration now replaced with a deep, unsettling uncertainty. He felt adrift, completely at a loss. The logical part of his mind searched for a solution, a course of action, but nothing came.

Rhodes met his eyes with a steady, measured look. "With all due respect, Doctor Collins… we do nothing."

Bernard blinked. Nothing?

The constable continued, his tone firm but not unkind. "There are detectives actively working on this. That's why there's been no official report yet. This isn't something that can be rushed, we need to be thorough."

Bernard exhaled sharply, running a hand through his hair.

"I have to ask you to keep this to yourself for now," Rhodes added. "I understand how difficult this is, but I promise, you will be the first to know when we have anything concrete. You have my word."

Bernard wanted to argue, to demand more answers, but what good would that do? He nodded slowly, his mind still reeling. He had walked into this office looking for clarity, but he was leaving with more questions than ever.

Bernard stared at the constable for a few moments, his mind still fogged with shock and uncertainty. Finally, he gave a slow nod, acknowledging the officer's words. He barely remembered murmuring a word of thanks before turning on his heel and walking out of the station, his thoughts spiralling. He needed to talk to someone, someone who could help him make sense of all this. But who?

As he stepped onto the street, his feet moved almost instinctively toward a familiar destination, Alois, the German jeweller. He had always been a man of quiet wisdom, someone who saw the world through a different lens. Perhaps he could offer insight.

But just as Bernard reached the corner, he stopped abruptly, his pulse quickening.

Can I trust Alois?

The thought struck him like a slap. His mind raced, weaving through the events of the past few months, the strange occurrences, the suspicions. Could he be involved? Could he be the arsonist? Could he even, God forbid, be the murderer in the case of the Petryczek's?

He clenched his fists, staring down at the pavement as if the answer could be found there. It was absurd… wasn't it? But how could he be sure? How well do I really know him?

The weight of doubt pressed down on him, yet another layer of unease settling in his gut. He took a deep breath, exhaling slowly. He had two choices, turn back, keep this to himself, let the police handle it. Or he could confront Alois head-on, lay it all out in front of him, and see how he reacted.

Bernard straightened his shoulders. Damn it, he thought. Let's do it.

As Bernard stepped into the jeweller's shop, the soft chime of the doorbell rang out, a delicate, almost musical sound that momentarily cut through the heavy thoughts clouding his mind. A young shop assistant, startled by the interruption, emerged from the back room and approached the counter, smoothing down the front of her blouse.

"Good morning," she said with a polite smile, then cast a quick glance at the delicate marquise wristwatch on her wrist. "Oh, just past twelve, actually. Good afternoon, then."

Before Bernard could respond, movement from the back of the shop caught his attention. Alois had looked up from his workbench the moment Bernard entered, his sharp eyes narrowing with recognition. The German jeweller had been meaning to reach out, to offer his condolences, but in the whirlwind of grief and investigation, their paths had not yet crossed. Now, here he was.

Alois wiped his hands on a cloth, stood, and approached with his usual air of warmth. "Gutes timing, mein Herr!" he declared, clasping Bernard's hand firmly in greeting. "It's my shout for lunch, and it's good to see you!"

With a gesture as smooth as it was casual, he reached for the door and pushed it open, holding it wide in invitation. There was no hesitation in his demeanour, no flicker of unease in his expression. If Alois was hiding something, he was doing a damn good job of it.

Bernard hesitated for the briefest of moments, his gut still twisting with uncertainty. Then, exhaling slowly, he nodded.

"Alright," he said. "Let's get lunch."

Seated in a quiet corner of the saloon bar, away from the midday patrons nursing their beers and discussing the latest town gossip, Bernard leaned in slightly, lowering his voice. The rich scent of aged timber and old ale lingered in the air, mixing with the distant clatter of glassware from behind the bar.

Despite the constable's explicit instructions to keep the information to himself, Bernard found the weight of it unbearable. It pressed on him like an unseen force, demanding to be shared, analysed, understood. And so, with a deep breath, he recounted everything the police had told him, word for word.

Across from him, Alois listened intently, his expression unreadable, his hands wrapped around his beer glass but otherwise motionless. Bernard watched him carefully, searching for the slightest flicker of surprise, guilt, or recognition. Yet, there was none.

As he spoke, any reservations he had held about Alois, the suspicions lingering in the back of his mind, melted away. Something in the jewellers steady gaze and quiet focus reassured him. This was not a man playing a part or feigning interest.

When Bernard finally finished, exhaling as though he had just set down a heavy load, Alois remained silent for a moment. Then, slowly, he leaned back in his chair, his fingers tapping lightly against the side of his glass.

"You trust me with this?" he asked, his voice measured, thoughtful.

Bernard nodded without hesitation. "I do," he said. And he meant it.

Alois returned from the bar, setting down fresh drinks with a steady hand. He took his seat across from Bernard, leaning in slightly. "I think whoever is behind this wants to scare you away from your house," he said, his voice low but firm. "And if I'm right, there will be a follow-up… soon."

Bernard stiffened. His fingers tightened around his glass. "Follow-up? In what way?" His tone was sharp, edged with alarm.

Alois hadn't intended to rattle him, but he could see the worry flash across Bernard's face. He immediately softened his approach, offering a measured response. "I don't know for certain, and I could be wrong," he admitted, raising a hand slightly as if to ease Bernard's concern. "I didn't mean to alarm you. But I do think you need to be careful."

Bernard exhaled sharply, trying to steady himself.

Alois continued, his voice thoughtful. "The police are investigating, which means that whoever did this, whoever the suspect is, knows they're under scrutiny. And if they know the police are watching, you can bet your bollocks they'll be watching, too. Moving carefully. That's probably a good thing for you, it means they won't act recklessly."

Bernard's gaze remained fixed on Alois, searching for reassurance.

Alois took a slow sip of his drink before adding, "I'll make a few calls. I have some old colleagues, men I trust, who are here in

Australia. Maybe they can help. Maybe not. But either way, this has turned into a chess game." He paused, studying Bernard carefully before finishing, "And now, it's their move."

Bernard's face dropped at the mention of their, and Alois caught it immediately. He placed a firm hand on Bernard's shoulder and gave him a reassuring pat.

"I mean a move," he corrected quickly. "Could be one person. A him or a her, not necessarily a group." He forced a small smile. "No need to start imagining a conspiracy."

Bernard let out a long breath, but the unease in his gut remained.

Bernard had made up his mind, he wouldn't tell Matilda about his conversation with Alois, just as he and Alois had agreed. Nor would he share the full details of his discussion with the police. At least, not yet.

She was already on edge, and the last thing he wanted was for her to become paranoid. Matilda was naturally cautious, and in her current state, any mention of arson, investigations, or potential threats would only heighten her anxiety. If anything, she needed reassurance, not more reasons to worry.

Alois had been right, this was now a waiting game. "It's their move," he had said. And until something happened, all Bernard could do was stay vigilant and patient.

For the next seven weeks, life had settled into a comfortable rhythm. Everything had been running smoothly, no unexpected dramas, no lingering shadows from the fire. Both Bernard and Matilda had gradually put the tragedy behind them, focusing on their daily routines, their work, and their family.

Then, just as complacency had set in,

BRRRRINNNGG! BRRRRINNNNGG! … a brief pause … BRRRRINNNGG! BRRRRINNNNGG!

The sharp ring of the telephone shattered the quiet.

Bernard had been on his way out the front door when the call came through. With a swift pivot, he grabbed the receiver. "Bernard speaking."

From the kitchen, Matilda flinched at the sudden noise, muttering under her breath, "Fucking telephone." She despised the jarring, intrusive sound, always bracing for bad news whenever it rang.

"Oh! Doctor Collins…" A smooth yet businesslike voice filled the receiver. "It's Dennis Marshall from Richie & Marshall Real Estate. I hope I'm not disturbing you?"

Bernard frowned slightly, shifting his stance. "Yes, Mr. Marshall, what can I do for you?"

"I'd like to arrange a meeting with you, if possible, Doctor Collins."

There was something about Marshall's tone, polite yet insistent, that aroused Bernard's curiosity. "Is this a medical matter?" he asked.

"Oh! No, no… nothing like that," Marshall said hastily. "It's something else entirely, but I'd rather not discuss it over the phone."

Bernard hesitated. His initial instinct was to brush it off, he had no interest in real estate dealings or whatever else Marshall was selling. But then, Alois's words echoed in his mind.

"Their move."

His grip on the phone tightened ever so slightly.

"Alright," Bernard said finally, keeping his tone casual. "I'll be in Dalby tomorrow. Meet me at the Commercial Hotel at midday, you can buy lunch."

Marshall agreed without hesitation, and the call ended.

Bernard hung up the receiver and turned back toward the door, only to find Matilda watching him, drying her hands on a tea towel.

"Who was that?" she asked.

He didn't miss a beat. "Just a patient needing an appointment tomorrow."

Matilda nodded and went back to her kitchen chores, none the wiser.

Bernard, however, felt a subtle tension creeping into his shoulders.

Tomorrow, he would find out if this was just business, or the next move in a game he hadn't asked to play.

"I have a client, Doctor, who is extremely interested in purchasing your property, both of them, actually…"

Dennis Marshall paused deliberately, watching Bernard's reaction. As expected, Bernard immediately put down his drink, ready to interrupt. But before he could speak, Marshall held up a hand in a polite yet firm 'stop' gesture.

"The offer my client is making is exceptional," he continued. "Far beyond the market value of your properties, both of them. If you'll allow me, I'd like to present it to you."

Bernard raised an eyebrow, leaning back slightly in his chair. "Please, Dennis, call me Bernard. Every time you say 'Doctor,' half the people in the room turn to look at me." He smirked, then took a slow sip of his drink before continuing.

"To be perfectly honest with you, I, we, have never had the slightest inclination to sell. Never even thought about it, really…" He trailed off, studying Marshall carefully. "But since you've brought it up, what kind of money are we talking about?" Then, as an afterthought, he added, "And who exactly is your client?"

Marshall's response was calculated. He revealed the offer, a sum so substantial that Bernard had to stop himself from visibly reacting. It was, without a doubt, a staggering amount.

"As for my client's identity," Marshall continued smoothly, "I'm afraid I can't disclose that at this stage. However, their name will be listed on the sale contract should you decide to proceed."

Bernard set his glass down, his mind working rapidly. Something about this didn't sit right. The secrecy. The urgency. The sheer scale of the offer.

Still, he maintained his composure, offering Marshall a polite nod. "I appreciate the offer, and the lunch," he said. "I'll need to discuss this with my wife before making any decisions."

Marshall extended a hand. "Of course. Take your time, but I would encourage you to consider it carefully."

Bernard shook his hand, then left the hotel, his thoughts spinning.

Glancing behind him to make sure the estate agent wasn't following, Bernard turned the corner and made his way straight to Alois' shop. As soon as he stepped inside, he wasted no time recounting his conversation with Dennis Marshall.

Alois listened carefully, stroking his chin with his right hand, his expression contemplative. "Hmm… so he wouldn't reveal the buyer's name, eh?" He murmured, his gaze narrowing slightly. His fingers tapped against his chin as he thought.

"Ritchie & Marshall Real Estate, you say? That would be the one up past the Commonwealth Bank, I think?"

Bernard shrugged. "No idea. Never been there. Couldn't say." He watched Alois closely, curious about what the old German was thinking.

Alois was silent for a few moments, then suddenly looked up. "Are you in town tomorrow?"

Bernard gave a short nod.

"Good. Call in and see me in the morning if you can." Alois hesitated for a beat, then shook his head. "No, no… actually, let's make it lunchtime at the Railway Hotel. Just for a change." He gave a little chuckle, his eyes twinkling mischievously.

Bernard smirked. "Right then. Lunch at the Railway Hotel it is."

As he left the shop, he couldn't shake the feeling that Alois had already started piecing something together.

That evening, after dinner, Bernard retreated to his office, pretending to be busy with the Girraween day books and stock registers. He flicked through the pages aimlessly, his mind elsewhere. He knew that if he sat down with Matilda and started talking, he'd risk giving away his little secret. And right now, that was the last thing he wanted.

Matilda, however, was in good spirits. With the children finally settled for the night, she strolled into the office carrying a bottle of American bourbon and two glasses. "This is the last of the wedding presents," she announced with a playful grin. "Looks like we'll have to do it all over again!" She giggled as she poured two rather generous drinks, handing one to Bernard.

He took the glass with a smile, watching as she settled into the chair opposite him. Her laughter was infectious, and for a moment, he felt a pang of guilt for keeping things from her. But he pushed the thought aside. There was no need to worry her, not yet, anyway.

Lifting his glass, he clinked it lightly against hers. "To doing it all over again," he said with a smirk, taking a long sip.

Matilda chuckled, curling her legs beneath her on the chair. "You'd be so lucky," she teased.

Bernard laughed, the tension of the day momentarily slipping away as they enjoyed the warmth of the bourbon and the comfort of each other's company.

The next morning seemed to drag on endlessly. Bernard found himself glancing at the clock every few minutes, willing the hands to move faster. Finally, as the clock rolled onto midday, he grabbed his hat and strode purposefully toward the Railway Hotel.

Stepping into the dimly lit saloon bar, he scanned the room. Alois hadn't arrived yet, so Bernard made his way to the counter, ordering two schooners of beer. He preferred to have the drinks ready rather than waiting. Taking both glasses, he found a quiet corner bench and settled in, drumming his fingers on the wooden table as he waited.

Just as he took a sip, the door creaked open, and in walked Alois. The German jeweller spotted him immediately and made his way over, his usual friendly grin in place.

"Cheers!" Alois said, raising his glass before taking a long draught. He studied the tall glass in his hand and smirked. "These are big ones."

"I figured they'd last longer," Bernard replied, watching as Alois took another deep sip. "But by the looks of yours, they won't."

Alois placed his glass down, leaned in slightly, and lowered his voice. "It's a company called 'Green Pastoral.'"

Bernard furrowed his brow. "Sorry?"

"The company trying to buy your property," Alois clarified. "It's called 'Green Pastoral.' A Queensland-registered company." He drained the last of his beer as Bernard stared at him, stunned.

Bernard, still gripping his half-full glass, shook his head in disbelief. "How on earth, "

Alois raised a hand to cut him off, a mischievous glint in his eye. "Let's just say that most 'good' jewellers are also 'good' locksmiths." He chuckled, clearly enjoying Bernard's bewildered expression. "Please don't ask."

Bernard exhaled, still amazed at how quickly Alois had uncovered the information. He pushed his glass aside and stood up. "Well, in that case, I'm getting us two more. I have a feeling I'm going to need it."

                    Max Barrington

Alois laughed, nodding approvingly. "Ja, my friend, that is an excellent idea."

Alois leaned in slightly, keeping his voice low as he explained what he had done the previous night.

"I paid a visit to the real estate office," he said, his tone casual but with a hint of mischief. "Long after it had closed, of course." He took a sip of his beer before continuing. "Inside, I found the contract of sale sitting in the 'in' basket on one of the desks. Convenient, ja?" He smirked. "I didn't take it, of course, too risky. But I copied the name on the front page using a pencil. Old habits."

Bernard's eyes widened. "You're serious?"

"Always," Alois replied with a wink. "This morning, I sent the company details to a colleague via my telex machine. He has access to certain records, useful ones. If I'm lucky, he will have found the names of the company's directors by now."

Just as their meals arrived, steaming plates of grilled steak and thick-cut chips, so did Alois's shop assistant. She stepped into the saloon bar, scanning the room before spotting them. With a purposeful stride, she approached and handed Alois a plain white envelope.

Alois gave her an appreciative nod. "Danke, mein liebling." She smiled before heading out, leaving the two men staring at the envelope resting on the table between them.

Bernard felt his pulse quicken. He wanted to tear it open right then and there. But Alois, ever composed, simply picked up his knife and fork and began cutting into his steak.

"So, mein Herr," Alois said between bites, "after lunch, we shall find out who this person is."

Bernard, gripping his beer glass, exhaled sharply. "You're killing me, Alois."

Alois chuckled. "Patience, my friend. Enjoy your meal. The truth isn't going anywhere."

Finally, after much prodding from Alois and one final beer that Bernard suspected was more about testing his patience than quenching thirst, Alois opened the envelope. He unfolded the telex message with deliberate care, scanning its contents before laying it flat on the table between them.

The message was stark, no pleasantries, no date, no sender or recipient details, just three names with corresponding addresses:

William Cole, 16/243 Roma Street, Brisbane.

Dirk Van Hoosan, 87 Roberts Street, Dalby.

Christopher Graham, Level 6, CML Building, East Street, Brisbane.

Alois read it quickly and passed it to Bernard, who studied the names and addresses but found they meant little to him. He shook his head, looking at Alois for clarification.

Taking the telex back, Alois tapped a finger thoughtfully against the paper. "It's most likely a ghost company," he said. "A front. A shell. The real decision-maker won't be easy to trace."

Bernard frowned. "Then what good is this?"

Alois gave him a knowing smile. "Because our man is almost certainly the one with the Dutch-sounding name, Dirk Van Hoosan."

"Dutch?" Bernard echoed, still not seeing the connection.

"Yes," Alois confirmed. "A Dutchman would attract far less scrutiny than, say, a German or Polish person. After the war, Dutch nationals were generally seen as allies. No one questions them the way they might someone of German descent." He took another sip of his beer, then pointed to the other two names. "The Brisbane addresses? Likely accountants or clerks.

Paper pushers keeping the company's books tidy while the real operation happens elsewhere."

Bernard exhaled, leaning back in his chair. "So, what now?"

Alois placed his empty schooner glass firmly on the table. "Now, mein Freund, we have our man." He tapped the telex. "And, more importantly, we have his address, right here in Dalby, our next task is to get some photographs of him, both frontal and profile and then his fingerprints."

Bernard's face remained expressionless as he stared at Alois, shaking his head in disbelief. "I have two questions," he said slowly. "First, why, in God's name, would you want photographs and fingerprints of this man? And second, how on earth do you propose to get his fingerprints?"

Alois leaned back slightly, rubbing his chin before responding. "The photographs and fingerprints will be sent to the War Criminals Documentation Centre in Vienna," he explained. "They maintain a complete record of every enlisted member of the Wehrmacht, down to the last cook and mechanic. If we provide them with good-quality information, they may be able to tell us whether Dirk Van Hoosan is, or rather, was, a German soldier. And more importantly, whether he is a war criminal."

Bernard's skepticism began to waver, his mind turning over the implications. "And if he is a war criminal?" he asked, his voice quieter now, the gravity of the situation beginning to settle in.

Alois's eyes darkened slightly, and when he spoke, his tone carried an unshakable certainty. "If he is a war criminal, our job is finished. The Nazi Hunters will come for him." He took a measured sip of his beer before continuing. "If he is not a war criminal but simply a former Wehrmacht soldier, then we will receive further details about him. And from there, we will decide our next move." Alois looked sternly at Bernard, Alois leaned forward, his expression grave, his fingers laced together as he chose his words carefully. His voice was low but steady.

"Bernard, I have given this a great deal of thought, considering everything we've discussed and all that has happened in this area over the past few years. And I may be wrong..." He hesitated for a moment, as if weighing the enormity of what he was about to say. "But I believe this man, Dirk Van Hoosan, is the one who murdered the Reimer's…and your parents."

Bernard stiffened, his breath catching in his throat. Alois let the words settle before continuing, his gaze locked onto Bernard's.

"I also believe that there is something in your house that this man wants, something important enough for him to kill for. And whatever it is, he hasn't found it yet."

Alois's bluntness had hit Bernard like a freight train. Though he had begun to suspect something along these lines, Alois had just driven the nail straight into the timber, crystallising the thoughts Bernard had been struggling to piece together. Suddenly, everything made more sense, far more than he was comfortable admitting.

Alois leaned back slightly, giving Bernard a moment to process before continuing. "You have two choices here," he said, his voice measured. "The first option is to sell the property and move elsewhere. It would be the safest, simplest course of action. But make no mistake, if you do, the criminal element wins Whoever is behind this will have succeeded in driving you away, and you'll never know the truth." He paused, letting the weight of that settle.

"The second option," he went on, "is to stand your ground and expose whoever is behind this. To take the risk and see this through. But be warned, Bernard, this path is dangerous. Your life may be at stake. And there will be no great reward at the end, no riches, no medals, just the satisfaction of knowing that you brought to justice the man who murdered your parents."

Alois met Bernard's gaze, his expression unreadable. "No one can make this decision for you. If we move forward from here, there's no turning back. You need to be certain." He exhaled slowly, then added, almost as an afterthought, "You see, for me, this is just an adventure. I have nothing to lose."

Bernard sat in silence for a moment, deep in thought before finally speaking. "I think it's best to keep all of this from Matilda. If she remains unaware of the deliberate arson at my parents' home and the attempt to purchase Girraween, then she, and the children, will be safer. There's no need to burden her with this, not yet." He took a deep breath, steadying himself. "But yes, I'm in. I want to expose this murderer."

Alois nodded approvingly, a hint of satisfaction in his expression. "Gutes. Then it is our move on the board to start lining up a checkmate," he said, his voice carrying a quiet determination. "We need to secure the necessary items, the fingerprints, the photographs, and get them to the Embassy of Israel in Canberra. That is our priority now."

He leaned in slightly, lowering his voice. "There is nothing for you to do at the moment. I will take care of obtaining the prints and photographs. For now, you must play your part, tell the estate agent that you are considering the offer and will get back to him by the end of the month. That gives us just over three weeks, ja?"

Bernard nodded in agreement, recognising the logic in the plan. He drained the last of his beer and rose from the table, shaking Alois's hand firmly before leaving the hotel. As he walked back to his practice, his mind was already racing ahead, contemplating what lay before him. Fortunately, he had recently brought in another general practitioner, Dr. Stephen Robb, to help manage the workload. That, at least, was one thing he wouldn't have to worry about.

Now, all that remained was to wait, and to prepare.

For the next month, life at Girraween carried on as usual, with one small exception, Bernard introduced a pair of Doberman Pinschers to the property. The dogs quickly became part of the household, much to the delight of the children, who adored them. Fortunately, the feeling seemed mutual, as the dogs took to the children with natural affection. Beyond that, Bernard kept up appearances, tending to his practice and maintaining a façade of normalcy while, beneath the surface, the wheels of a far more serious matter were in motion.

Meanwhile, Alois had tracked down 87 Roberts Street and begun discreet surveillance of its occupant. His patience and meticulous nature, honed by years of working with the OSS, proved invaluable. After carefully studying the man's habits, Alois identified a reliable window of time, just over an hour each day, when the occupant would leave the house. This provided the perfect opportunity to discreetly acquire an item that would hold clear fingerprint impressions.

Choosing his moment wisely, Alois entered the premises and carefully selected a drinking glass, ensuring it had been well-handled by its owner. Using his jewellers expertise, he applied black graphite powder to the surface, skilfully lifting a set of clear prints. To further strengthen their case, he also managed to capture high-quality images of the man using his Konan-18 camera with a 50mm lens as he left the house each day.

With the necessary evidence secured, Alois packaged the fingerprints and photographs and sent them via priority mail to the Israeli Embassy in Canberra. From there, the materials were transferred using a diplomatic courier bag to Israel and then forwarded to the War Criminals Documentation Centre in Vienna. Once received, the fingerprints and photographs were analysed using the centre's cutting-edge imaging equipment.

Exactly twenty-one days later, the reply arrived, delivered in reverse order through the same secure channels. Alois now had his answer.

Max Barrington

Alois relaxed with his favourite drink, a beer, in his one bedroom unit above his little jeweller shop as he read the dossier he had just received

Dossier: SS-Oberführer Axel Emmerich

Full Name: Axel Heinrich Emmerich
Date of Birth: August 12, 1902
Place of Birth: Hamburg, Germany
Rank: SS-Oberführer (Senior Colonel)
Service Number: 287 561
Affiliations: Schutzstaffel (SS), Gestapo, Reich Main Security Office (RSHA)
Special Assignments: Einsatzgruppen Operations, Reich Plunder Division
Status: Presumed Deceased (Unconfirmed)

Background & Wartime Activities

Axel Emmerich was a high-ranking SS officer deeply involved in intelligence operations, asset confiscation, and extermination programs. Rising through the ranks of the SS, he was known for his ruthless efficiency in carrying out special missions assigned by Heinrich Himmler. By 1942, he had become a key figure in the Reich Main Security Office (RSHA), overseeing operations targeting those deemed "enemies of the Reich," particularly wealthy Jewish families and resistance figures suspected of holding valuable assets.

During the latter years of World War II, Emmerich played a pivotal role in the Reich Plunder Division, an elite unit tasked with confiscating gold, artwork, and precious stones from occupied territories. It was during this time that he became aware of a vast cache of diamonds intended to fund the Nazi war effort. These diamonds, valued at approximately fourteen million Reichsmarks, (Au£12.8m) were last traced to a German family, the Reimer's, who had fled Europe and were believed to have smuggled the fortune with them to Australia.

Post-War Escape & Exile in South America

With the fall of the Third Reich in May 1945, Emmerich, like many high-ranking SS officers and Gestapo operatives, sought refuge in South America, utilising the clandestine escape networks known as the 'Ratlines'. Fleeing first to Spain, he later secured passage to Rio de Janeiro, Brazil, where he established a new identity under the protection of pro-fascist sympathisers. His presence in South America was confirmed through declassified intelligence reports, which placed him among a network of ex-Nazi officials in Argentina, Paraguay, and Brazil.

By 1950, he had assumed a leadership role within a covert network of former SS officers still operating in exile. Reports suggest that Emmerich maintained ties to **ODESSA**, the secretive post-war organisation dedicated to the protection and relocation of Nazi fugitives. It was through these connections that Emmerich was assigned a mission in the mid-1950s, to eliminate the Reimer family and recover the diamonds they had taken from the Reich.

Mission to Australia: The Reimer Assassinations

Sometime in 1954, under a new alias, Emmerich travelled to Australia using forged documents issued in Buenos Aires. The specifics of his operation remain murky, but intelligence sources and survivor accounts indicate that Emmerich was to organise and execute the murder of the Reimer family. It is not know if this mission was completed as there have been no reports back from Emmerich.

Emmerich is not considered a war criminal at this stage but reporting of all sightings of Emmerich is encouraged by this agency.

Alois had called Bernard at his practice, requesting an urgent meeting. They later convened at The Sovereign Hotel, where Alois slid the dossier across the table towards Bernard. The look of the document alone suggested its significance with an official Jewish stamp on the covering page.

Bernard took his time reading through its contents, his eyes widening at each revelation. When he finally set it down, he exhaled deeply, running a hand through his hair.

"Herr Emmerich is not classified as a war criminal," Alois remarked, shaking his head in mild disappointment. "Such a shame."

Bernard, still processing the information, latched onto a single, staggering detail.

"Twelve million pounds worth of diamonds…" he murmured in disbelief. "In my house… somewhere?"

Alois, visibly agitated, leaned forward. "Did you not hear what I said, Bernard?"

"Sorry, Alois… it's just, do you really think that's correct? Twelve million, "

Alois cut him off sharply.

"You need to listen, Bernard!" His voice carried across the room, drawing curious glances from a few nearby patrons. Realising his outburst, he lowered his tone and leaned in closer. "The 'Nazi Hunters' are not interested in taking him. So, we will have to do it ourselves."

Bernard's expression shifted from shock to something more thoughtful, almost calculating. He searched Alois's face for any hint of jest, but there was none. Finally, in a quiet voice, he spoke the words softly, testing them.

"You mean kill him, don't you?"

Alois held his gaze without flinching.

Bernard's mind raced, his initial instinct being to recoil from such a drastic course of action. But then, slowly, the weight of justice settled over him. The fire that had been simmering beneath his grief, his anger, his frustration, it all suddenly aligned into a singular, determined focus. His voice steadied.

"Yes… but how? This is new to me."

Alois, sensing Bernard's resolve, smiled warmly, a stark contrast to the deadly intent behind his words.

"It would be my pleasure and honour to kill this murdering bastard on your behalf," he said with quiet conviction.

But Bernard would not hear of it. This was his fight, his burden to carry. What had begun as an investigation had now transformed into something far more personal. After a heated exchange, each man insisting on taking the responsibility, it was ultimately decided.

It would be a joint effort and now it was just a matter of how, when and where?

"Well, time is of the essence," Alois said firmly, eager to bring their plan to fruition. He leaned forward, his eyes gleaming with a mix of determination and anticipation. "We, no, I, will shoot him while he sleeps in his bed… using the gun you found at your house. The Vis. Do you still have the bullets for it?"

Bernard's mind raced as he tried to recall. "Yes, the ones that were in the magazine. I can't remember exactly how many there are."

"I will only need one." Alois smirked. "A single, well-placed shot through a pillow to suppress the sound. We'll leave the body where it will be, in the bed, with the gun resting in his lifeless grip?" His voice dropped to a near whisper, his tone cold and calculated. "The weapon will trace back to Poland or Germany. When the authorities investigate, they'll quickly realise that our man was from Germany and conclude that this was some kind of 'spy vs. spy' affair." His smirk widened as he sat back, clearly satisfied with the plan.

Bernard nodded, his pulse quickening. "And when?"

"Tonight." Alois didn't hesitate. "You will go home and tell Matilda that you have a meeting at the hospital in Brisbane tomorrow morning and that you have to leave for Brisbane tonight and that you will be home on Thursday evening. This will give us all day tomorrow, and the evening, if we need it to dispose of his body

Bernard swallowed hard. The suddenness of it all, the rapid shift from discussion to execution, the word itself made him pause. "Execution…" he thought. The weight of what they were about to do pressed down on him, but with it came something else, a fierce resolve.

"Yes! Yes… why not? Why not indeed…" His voice, hesitant at first, steadied. He met Alois's gaze head-on. "What time shall we meet? And where?"

Alois watched him carefully, sensing the transformation taking place within Bernard. A knowing smile crossed his lips. "Calm down, mein Freund. Take it easy. Just act normal. Go about your afternoon as you usually would and prepare for your trip to Brisbane and come to my shop after it has closed so that Gwen, my shop assistant will not see you. Then, when the clock strikes one in the morning,….Don't forget to bring the gun."

He raised his glass in a silent toast, eyes gleaming with satisfaction. "Cheers!" He took a slow sip before adding, almost playfully, "Perhaps some diamond hunting on the weekend, mein Herr… ja wohl?"

It was a cool Thursday morning at one o'clock, and the light drizzle did little more than add to the discomfort, making the streets glisten under the dim glow of the streetlights. The moisture in the air carried a chill that clung to their clothes. "Straight ahead, second left," Alois murmured, though even he wasn't sure why he was whispering. A moment later, he added, "Turn right here, it's three houses down… Good… Now just pull over quietly. We'll walk from here."

The street sloped gently downward as they advanced toward number 87. Their footsteps were nearly silent against the damp pavement, but suddenly, the moon broke through the clouds. A silver glow illuminated the street, casting long shadows, making them feel exposed.

They froze.

For a few tense moments, they lingered by the driveway of number 87, blending into the darkness beneath the branches of an overhanging tree. A Morris Minor was parked in the driveway, a small but significant confirmation that Emmerich was likely inside.

The clouds, moving sluggishly across the sky, once again shrouded the moon. The world returned to shadows. Taking advantage of the renewed cover, they crept forward, silent, precise.

Alois reached into his pocket, retrieving a single lock pick and a tension tool. He crouched before the door and, with practiced ease, inserted them into the Eta lock cylinder. A few subtle movements of his wrist, a barely audible click, and the door yielded.

He replaced the tools in his pocket and turned to Bernard, gesturing for the gun.

Bernard hesitated only for a fraction of a second before slipping the Vis 35 from his coat pocket and handing it over. Alois took the weapon with a careful grip, cradling it as if reacquainting

                    Max Barrington

himself with an old friend. With meticulous precision, he pulled back the slide, his sharp eyes watching as a 9×19mm round slid from the magazine into the chamber.

The gun was hot.

A phrase from his OSS days echoed in his mind, a weapon primed and ready.

Without another word, Alois pushed the door open.

The darkness inside was absolute.

They both paused, standing motionless in the inky void, giving their eyes time to adjust. The hallway was still, untouched by time or movement. Then, slowly, deliberately, they advanced.

Alois had been inside before. He knew the way.

The bedroom door was open. Wide open. That was unexpected.

Alois stepped through first, Bernard just behind him. He already knew that the bed was positioned directly ahead, but as they entered, the moon once again broke through the clouds, its pale light cutting through the darkness.

The glow revealed the unmistakable outline of a man lying in bed. Asleep.

Axel Heinrich Emmerich was right in front of them.

Alois, in his condition of anticipation through what was about to happen had forgotten to find a pillow to muffle the gunshot sound. But now was not the time for hesitation.

Alois quickly dismissed the creeping sense of unease and refocused. His sharp eyes flicked toward Bernard, who stood frozen just inside the doorway, barely breathing. There was no time to second-guess their plan.

Turning back toward the bed, Alois took a silent step forward. The rhythmic, steady rise and fall of the sleeping man's chest was unmistakable in the quiet room. His breathing was deep, untroubled. Oblivious.

Alois brought the Vis 35 down toward the man's temple, the cold steel pressing gently against his skin. He exhaled slowly, steadied himself. His finger tightened on the trigger.

And then, a sharp, distinct click.

The sound shattered the silence like a gunshot in its own right.

Misfire.

Alois reacted instantly, his movements fluid. With a well-practiced motion, he racked the slide, ejecting the useless shell and chambering another round.

Click.

Another dud.

But this time, the man in the bed stirred.

It wasn't the noise that had woken him, it was the pressure of the gun barrel against his temple. The momentary confusion in his half-conscious mind gave way to instinct. Survival.

His hand was already beneath the pillow.

Before Alois could react, before he could chamber yet another round, the sleeping man wasn't sleeping anymore.

Axel Emmerich's fingers found the grip of his Walther **PPK**.

With the speed of a man who had survived more than his fair share of close calls, he whipped the small semi-automatic from under the pillow, pivoted his wrist, and fired, twice.

The first shot tore through the air, the muzzle flash momentarily illuminating the room. The second round followed a fraction of a second later, aimed directly at the dark silhouette looming above him.

Without pausing, Emmerich's instincts took over again. A second assassin.

He snapped the pistol toward the doorway and squeezed the trigger twice more.

Boom. Boom.

The gunfire thundered through the house, deafening in the enclosed space.

In the same breath, he rolled sharply to his left, using the momentum to slide out of bed and drop low, vanishing from sight. In a smooth, practiced motion, he tucked himself beneath the bed frame.

Now, he listened.

The silence returned, thick and oppressive, broken only by the distant ringing in his ears. Holding his breath, he strained to detect the slightest movement, the faintest shift of weight on the floorboards above.

He was in his element now, hunting or being hunted.

Seconds passed, each one stretching unbearably long. His pulse slowed, his breathing measured. Still nothing.

Axel Emmerich knew better than to assume his enemies were gone without confirmation. But his years of survival had honed his instincts to a razor's edge, and his gut told him the fight was over. If they weren't already dead, they were close enough to it that it wouldn't matter.

First things first.

Moving with the precision of a man who had done this before, he slid out from under the bed in a fluid motion. No hesitation. No wasted movements. His Walther PPK remained firm in his grip, ready for the slightest sign of life.

Nothing.

He rose to his feet, keeping his body low as he crossed the room to a wooden chair. A pair of shorts lay draped over its backrest. He slipped them on swiftly, tucking the pistol into the pocket before grabbing the shirt beside them. As he buttoned it with quick, practiced fingers, he was already moving toward the front door.

His mind worked just as fast. There would be noise. Neighbours. Questions. He needed a story.

Just before stepping outside, he flicked on the front porch light, bathing the damp pavement in a dim glow. He didn't hesitate as he crossed the threshold and strode towards the front gate.

His neighbours were already gathering. A few stood in their doorways, peering into the night with wary curiosity. Others, bolder, had stepped onto the street, murmuring amongst themselves.

He joined them with ease, blending seamlessly into the scene.

"Christ, did you hear that?" he called out, his voice carrying just the right mix of surprise and irritation. "Sounded like someone tearing through here at sixty miles an hour."

He exhaled sharply, shaking his head.

"I was just letting the damn cat back in when I saw the headlights. Then the backfiring nearly made me jump out of my skin!"

The gathered neighbours nodded, their own theories forming. Someone mentioned a reckless teenager. Another grumbled about the state of the roads.

Misdirection. A classic tool of survival.

Axel played his part well. He listened, nodded, chuckled in agreement where necessary. Within minutes, the energy dissipated. Satisfied with their shared speculation, the neighbours began retreating to their homes, their curiosity dulled by exhaustion.

Axel lingered just long enough to make it seem natural before heading back inside.

Locking the door behind him, he turned immediately for the bedroom, switching on the light.

Now, he could inspect the carnage.

The room smelled of gunpowder, blood, and something else, a faint metallic tang that lingered in the damp air. Axel took a slow breath, steadying his nerves. He had been here before.

His instincts had been whispering to him, warning him that something felt off. A premonition. He was being watched. Talked about. Perhaps even played with.

That feeling had first surfaced days ago, when the real estate agent had casually mentioned that the owner of the house, needed three weeks to think about Axel's offer.

Three weeks? No one needed three weeks to decide whether to sell a house unless they were stalling.

"Well… checkmate," Axel muttered under his breath, his lips curling into a wry smile.

He turned his attention to the second body, the one sprawled near the doorway. His own shots had landed high, both in the chest, just below the collarbone. Likely a result of the man's tall frame. One bullet may have torn through his heart. If not, he wouldn't have lived long enough for it to matter.

Axel crouched down, his movements efficient, methodical. No hesitation.

Reaching into the dead man's back pocket, he retrieved a wallet. Inside, his eyes fell on a small, passport-sized photograph, an attractive woman with two young children. Something about her face tugged at his memory. He flipped to the driver's license and felt the corner of his mouth twitch.

The name. The address.

"Well, fuck me," he chuckled, shaking his head in disbelief.

This was the man who owned the house. The very house Axel had wanted to buy, he placed the wallet on the bed.
Small world.

Axel turned his attention to the first body, the one collapsed at the edge of the bed, the shooter.

Unlike the second target, this one had jumped back as if to escape the projectiles from his Walther. His hand still gripped the useless pistol, he had two massive exit wounds blasted through his skull. Blood had splattered onto the bed, seeping into the sheets, the metallic scent thick in the air.

Axel crouched again, patting down the corpse with quick, practiced hands.

No ID. No wallet. Nothing personal.

Just a small set of tools, a lock pick and a tension wrench.

Axel turned them over in his palm, examining the craftsmanship.

"Hmm… a professional," he mused aloud. Then, glancing at the ruined remains of the man's skull, he smirked.

"A dead professional."

Rising to his feet, he stepped over the body and moved toward the kitchen.

Before flipping on the light, he pulled the curtains shut.

Just in case someone was watching.

He took a bottle of Johnny Walker from the cupboard and a glass from the draining board. He needed to think of a plan to get rid of these bodies….just another fucking nuisance that he didn't need.

He remembered seeing a sign at the end of the street yesterday that was advertising the Dalby Show an annual event, each April. He smiled to himself "perfect."

Show Day in Dalby was a much-anticipated event, a special occasion that brought the town to life each year. Held on a Friday, it granted the locals a welcomed day off, turning an ordinary weekday into a celebration of community, excitement, and spectacle. From the moment the first posters were pinned to shop windows and telephone poles, the air buzzed with anticipation.

The travelling showmen and their caravans usually began arriving in town early in the week, their presence marking the unofficial start of the festivities. These shows, many of them family-run businesses passed down through generations, had been making their way across Australia for decades, bringing with them a sense of nostalgia and wonder. For the young men and women who joined these travelling carnivals, life on the road promised adventure, an escape from the mundane and a chance to see the country in a way few others could.

But not all who followed the circuit were seeking excitement or a fresh start. Some were drifters, passing through with no intention of staying beyond a single season. Others had nowhere else to go, taking up temporary work before disappearing into the next town. Among them were those with hard pasts, men and women worn down by life, some simply victims of circumstance, while others carried the weight of former crimes. It was no secret that a handful of the show's workers had spent time behind bars, their tattoos and wary gazes betraying stories of regret, desperation, or perhaps a defiant refusal to conform.

Yet, when Show Day finally arrived, none of that seemed to matter. The town square transformed into a kaleidoscope of flashing lights, the scent of fried food and spun sugar filling the air. Laughter and shrieks of excitement echoed from the rattling rides, and crowds gathered around the games of skill and chance, hoping to win oversized stuffed animals or pocketfuls of cheap trinkets. For one day, Dalby was a different place, a place of illusion, where fortunes could be made or lost at the roll of a dice, and where, for better or worse, strangers blended seamlessly into the crowd.

The local pub where these sorts of men gathered, the roughest pub in town, was the perfect place for Axel Emmerich to find the help he needed. It was a dimly lit, smoke-filled establishment where the beer was cheap, the floors were sticky, and the regulars were the kind of men who had seen better days. It was here, amid the clatter of pool balls and the murmur of half-hearted conversations, that Axel spotted his targets.

Two men stood near the pool table, drinking and playing a lazy game, their expressions vacant but their eyes sharp. They looked like the kind who had little concern for the law and even less concern for where their next dollar came from. Axel approached them casually, his posture relaxed but his intent clear.

"You boys with the show?" he asked, keeping his tone light.

The taller of the two nodded, taking a swig from his beer. "Yeah. Why?"

"I need a hand with something. A bit of heavy lifting." Axel paused, lowering his voice slightly. "I've got two dead llamas at my place. Need to get rid of 'em before they start stinking up the joint."

The men exchanged a glance, their interest aroused.

Axel leaned in a little closer. "I've got a spot near the council quarry where I can dump them. Problem is, it's illegal. Very illegal." He let that last word hang in the air before reaching into his pocket and pulling out two crisp twenty-dollar notes.

Twenty dollars was no small sum, back then, it was nearly two weeks' wages for an honest labourer. But these men weren't exactly honest labourers, and Axel knew they'd recognise easy money when they saw it. He waved the bills slightly, watching their eyes follow the movement.

"That's why I'm paying so well," he continued. "This job has to be done quickly and quietly. No questions. No screw-ups. We do it now, and we're back before the pub closes at ten."

The shorter man scratched at his stubble, considering the offer. "How heavy are they?"

"Not too bad. Between the three of us, it won't take long."

The taller man smirked. "You're payin' cash, right?"

Axel flicked the twenties toward them. The men caught the bills without hesitation, shoving them into their pockets.

"Alright, let's get it done," one of them muttered, draining the last of his beer before setting the glass down on the pool table.

Axel nodded, suppressing a satisfied grin. "Good. Let's go."

Axel had the hired 1959 FC Holden ute parked just across the road from the pub, its dull paintwork blending into the dimly lit street. As soon as the two labourers stepped outside, beers in hand, he gestured toward the ute.

"Hop in," he said, nodding toward the passenger side.

The men didn't need to be told twice. They climbed into the cab, clutching the tall bottles of beer Axel had bought them, an unspoken bonus for the job ahead. The taller of the two twisted the cap off his bottle with a practiced flick of his wrist, taking a long swig as he settled into the seat. The other did the same, letting out a low grunt of appreciation.

Axel slid behind the wheel, his movements precise and methodical. He started the engine, the old Holden grumbling to life, and eased it away from the curb. A glance in the rearview mirror confirmed what he already knew, Dalby's streets were quiet at this hour.

As they approached his house, he slowed, rolling the ute into the driveway. Earlier that evening, he had moved his Morris onto the street, clearing space to manoeuvre the ute as close to the front door as possible. He needed to minimise the distance they would have to carry the bodies.

Bringing the ute to a stop, he shifted into reverse, carefully backing it up until the tailgate was mere inches from the threshold. The positioning was deliberate. Every second counted, and he wanted this done with as little effort, and as little noise, as possible.

Switching off the ignition, he turned to the two men, who were still drinking, oblivious to the weight of what they were about to do.

"Alright, boys," Axel said, his voice low but firm. "Let's get to work."

As expected, the moment the two men realised the so-called "llamas" were, in fact, human bodies, their enthusiasm for the job evaporated. The shorter of the two took a step back, his expression shifting from drunken bravado to unease.

"Ah, hell no," he muttered, shaking his head.

Axel, anticipating their hesitation, remained calm. He reached into his pocket and pulled out a neat stack of notes, sixteen crisp twenty-dollar bills. Holding them up, he let the offer linger in the air.

"Are you sure, fellas?" he asked, his tone almost casual. "This makes it a hundred bucks each, for half an hour's work. Most of that just sitting in the car."

The short one, 'Spratt,' rubbed a hand over his face, clearly spooked. "But they ain't llamas, mister. That's a big difference!"

The taller man, however, wasn't nearly as concerned. He eyed the cash, weighing his options. He was no stranger to doing things best left unspoken, and this, well, this was just another job with a bigger payout.

"They look like fucking llamas to me," he finally said, stepping forward. Without hesitation, he bent down and grabbed the first body, Bernard. He grunted with the effort. "Come on, Spratt, give us a hand, or the pub'll be shut by the time we get back."

Spratt hesitated for only a second longer before caving. The money was too good to walk away from, and his mate was already committed. With a reluctant sigh, he grabbed the second body by the legs, as he pulled on the legs, the gun slipped from the hand of the dead man. "Wow" said Spratt, "can I keep the gun?"

Axel could not see why not, "It's yours my friend, but let's get going huh!"

In no time, both corpses were loaded into the back of the ute, hidden under the taut tonneau cover. The two men climbed into the front, swigging the last of their tall bottles as Axel slid into the driver's seat and started the engine.

The journey to the dump was silent, except for the occasional slosh of beer in glass and the quiet hum of the ute's tires against the road. Axel's mind, however, was anything but quiet.

He had thought ahead. A heavy-duty tarp, freshly purchased from the local hardware store, lined the ute's tray. It would take care of the immediate mess, easy to remove and dispose of later.

But the house… that was a different story.

A quick glance in the rearview mirror, and Axel exhaled slowly. Cleaning up that mess, replacing the carpets, stripping the bed, making sure there wasn't a trace left, would take a solid week at best.

He did not need this shit.

As the ute rolled up to the locked quarry gate, Axel put the vehicle in neutral, rubbing his temples. He was already calculating the next steps.

Axel muttered the words to himself as he reached under the front seat of the ute, fingers closing around the cold, heavy steel of the bolt cutters. He had found them in the house he rented, one of the few useful things left behind. With a swift, practiced motion, he positioned the cutters around the chain securing the gate and applied pressure. The metal links resisted for only a moment before snapping apart with a sharp clink.

He pushed the gate open just wide enough to drive through, easing the ute forward with a slow, deliberate pace. As soon as he cleared the entrance, he killed the headlights for a moment, sitting in the darkness, listening. The night was still. Good.

Climbing out, he moved back to the gate and swung it shut, looping the broken chain through the posts to make it appear undisturbed. If someone happened to pass by, he didn't want an open gate catching their attention and inviting curiosity.

Satisfied, he walked back to the driver's side, slid into his seat, and restarted the engine. The only sounds now were the low rumble of the ute and the dull clinking of the empty beer bottles the two men had carelessly discarded in the footwell.

At the very top of the quarry, Axel manoeuvred the ute carefully, inching it backward toward the edge. One of the labourers stood behind, waving his arms and calling out instructions, ensuring he got as close as possible without going over himself. The night air was cool and carried the scent of dust and dry earth, but there was no wind, just silence, thick and expectant.

As soon as the ute was in position, the two men set to work, dragging the bodies out from under the tonneau cover. Bernard's lifeless form hit the ground with a dull thud, followed quickly by the second corpse. The taller of the two men let out a chuckle as they each took hold of a body and heaved it over the edge. They stood there, watching, as the bodies tumbled down the sheer rock face, bouncing off jagged ledges before finally slamming onto the quarry floor far below with a sickening thud.

The shorter man, "Spratt," let out a sharp bark of laughter. "Bloody hell, that was louder than I thought!"

His companion grinned. "Yeah, bet they didn't see that coming."

Axel smiled faintly. "Nice work, boys."

As they wiped their hands clean with the towels he'd handed them, Axel reached into his pocket, not for money, but for his pistol. With practiced ease, he raised it and fired twice, each shot finding its mark in the side of their temples. The taller man went down first, his body crumpling in a heap. Spratt barely had time to register what had happened before the second shot took him, his expression frozen in shock as he dropped to the ground.

The gunshots echoed briefly, swallowed by the vast emptiness of the quarry.

Axel stepped forward, crouching down to retrieve the crumpled twenty-dollar notes from their pockets. No sense in letting good money go to waste.

Then, with the same methodical efficiency, he grabbed each man by the arms, dragged them to the edge, and sent them tumbling into the abyss. He listened, smirking as the bodies hit the ground below with the same satisfying thump as the first two.

"Goodnight, boys," he muttered, before turning back toward the ute.

Matilda stirred in the night, reaching out instinctively across the bed, only to find Bernard's side cold and empty. Blinking against the darkness, she glanced at the bedside clock. The red numbers glowed 12:30 AM. Just after midnight, she thought groggily. He did say he'd be late.

Rolling onto her side, she pulled the blankets up to her chin and drifted back into sleep.

The next time she woke, a sense of unease settled over her before she even opened her eyes. Something felt off. She turned her head toward the clock again, 3:45 AM. Matilda frowned. Surely, he's home by now? Perhaps he was in the bathroom. She listened for movement but heard nothing. Sleep tugged at her again, and she let herself sink back into the warmth of the blankets.

It was the children's morning chatter that fully roused her, their voices carrying from the next room. The familiar sound brought a small smile to her lips, until she turned to Bernard's side of the bed. His pillow was untouched. Her stomach clenched. He never came home.

A cold wave of panic surged through her, chasing away the last remnants of sleep. Throwing back the covers, she sat up, heart pounding as a dozen scenarios rushed through her mind. Had there been an accident? Had something happened at the meeting?

Barefoot, she hurried to the window, pulling back the curtain, expecting, hoping, to see his car in the driveway. But the space remained empty.

Matilda paced the bedroom, her breath coming in shallow gasps. Think rationally… think rationally… everything has a logic… think logically, she whispered to herself, pressing her hands to her temples.

Had Bernard decided to sleep in the sick bed at the surgery? That made sense, especially if he'd had a few drinks after his meeting. Yes, that must be it…

But then… why hadn't he called?

Her gaze snapped to the clock. Oh, God.

"It's eight-forty. It's eight-forty!"

Her hands trembled as she grabbed the phone from the bedside table and frantically dialled the Brisbane community hospital where he said his meeting was.

"Brisbane Community Hospital, Marion speaking."

"Marion, is Doctor Collins there, please?" Matilda's voice was laced with desperation, though she fought to keep it steady.

"I don't think so, let me see, I don't have an internal listing for a Doctor Collins, but have you tried his office, or surgery?" the receptionist asked, her tone professional but unconcerned.

"I have tried his surgery," Matilda replied, forcing herself to stay calm. "But there's no answer."

A brief pause. "I can see if we have any stand by after-hours or emergency number for a Doctor Collins, but I don't think he is on our call list either , "

Matilda cut her off, panic rising like a tidal wave. "This is his after-hours number! This is his wife, I can't find him!"

And then, the floodgates broke.

"Please… .Please help me find him!" Her voice cracked as sobs tore through her.

The receptionist hesitated, then quickly placed Matilda on hold. Seconds later, she contacted the Brisbane metropolitan police, relaying what she had just heard.

She switched the line over for the police to speak to Matilda.

The line was dead.

The Women Police Officer (WPO), Sergeant Sharna O'Donnell, wasn't scheduled to start her shift until 10:00 AM. A note was left in her in-tray, marked URGENT, from Brisbane Metro instructing her to contact Dr. Collins' wife as soon as she arrived. The message included the phone number provided by the hospital.

Meanwhile, Matilda sat by the phone, gripping the receiver with white-knuckled fingers. She had already called Bernard's practice multiple times, but each attempt went unanswered.

It's nine-thirty, she thought, glancing at the clock. They open at eight-thirty. Why isn't anyone picking up?

Her stomach twisted with unease.

Who else could he be with?

Alois.

She quickly found the number for his jewellery shop and dialled. The line rang and rang. No answer.

Matilda's heartbeat pounded in her ears. This doesn't make sense.

Even if Alois wasn't there, his shop assistant should have opened by now. It was nearly ten o'clock, far too late for the store to still be closed.

She hung up and stared at the phone in front of her, dread creeping up her spine.

Finally, the police. Of course! Why hadn't she thought of them sooner?

Matilda scrambled to find their number in the Teledex, flipping through its worn pages with shaking fingers. Where is it? Where is it? She flipped through again. Nothing.

Frustrated, she grabbed the heavy phone book from the shelf under the desk, her hands fumbling clumsily through the pages.

The numbers blurred together. Her breath came in short, panicked gasps.

Where the hell is it?!

With a cry of frustration, she threw the book to the floor. The loud thud startled the children, and they began to cry.

Matilda closed her eyes and pressed her palms to her temples. Slow down. Slow down! She had to think clearly.

First things first, feed the children. Then she would figure out what to do.

She placed a bowl of Rice Bubbles in front of Alison, who was watching her mother with wide, worried eyes. Lindsay had just finished his bottle and was making a mess of his Weet-Bix, his tiny hands slapping the mushy cereal as Matilda tried to guide the spoon to his mouth.

She forced herself to slow down, to be patient. The phone. She needed to call the,

BRRRRINNNGG! BRRRRINNNGG!

BRRRRINNNGG! BRRRRINNNGG!

Matilda jolted so hard that the spoon flew from her hand, splattering milk and cereal onto the table. Lindsay immediately burst into tears.

Her heart pounded as she snatched up the receiver.

"Hello?!"

She just knew it was Bernard. It had to be. He would have a perfectly reasonable explanation for not coming home. She could already hear herself yelling at him in relief.

"Where on earth have you been?" Her voice cracked, teetering on the edge of tears.

There was a pause.

A long, dreadful pause.

Then, finally,

"Hello... is that Mrs. Collins?"

It was a woman's voice.

Not Bernard's.

Matilda's breath caught in her throat.

"Hello? Mrs. Collins?"

The voice was patient but firm. Matilda swallowed hard.

"Oh... I'm so sorry! I thought you were Bernard... who is this?" She struggled to steady her voice.

"This is Sergeant Sharna O'Donnell from the police station, Mrs. Collins."

Matilda's grip tightened around the phone. "Oh, thank God! I was just trying to call the police, but I couldn't find your number," Matilda blurted out, her words tumbling over each other in relief.

Sergeant Sharna O'Donnell could hear the strain in her voice, the sharp edge of fear, the wavering tension just beneath the surface.

"What is it you need to contact the police for, Mrs. Collins?" she asked, keeping her tone calm and measured.

Matilda was trembling now, clutching the phone so tightly her knuckles had turned white. She was losing control, and she knew it. But why? Bernard would have a perfectly reasonable explanation for his absence. Surely, there was a logical reason for all of this. Any moment now, he would walk through the door, smiling at how worked up she had gotten over nothing.

That thought gave her strength.

She took a deep breath, steadied herself, and forced a sense of control into her voice. "My husband has gone missing," she stated firmly.

Matilda quickly relayed the facts, how Bernard had gone to a meeting last night and never returned home. How she had assumed he had slept at the surgery, but there was no answer when she called. How she had also tried the jeweller's shop, but no one had picked up there either.

A pause.

Then Sharna's voice, calm but firm.

"Mrs. Collins, you said you called the surgery and the jeweller's, but… it's Show Day today. Almost everything in town is closed."

Matilda's breath hitched.

Show Day.

She had completely forgotten. "Oh..of course,..but….that doesn't change the fact that he is still missing." And the concern and anguish again started to appear.

"Look, Mrs. Collins, how about I come out to your place and get some more information? Can you tell me your address?" Sergeant Sharna O'Donnell kept her voice steady, though she could clearly hear the distress creeping into Matilda's tone.

Matilda took a shaky breath. "It's Girraween, on the Dalby-Chinchilla Road. That's the only address I know."

There was a pause on the other end of the line before Sharna spoke again, a note of hesitation in her voice. "But I thought that property burned down a few months ago?"

Matilda quickly shook her head, even though the officer couldn't see her. "No, no… that was Bernard's parents' place. You keep going past there, and you'll see the new sign for our Girraween."

Satisfied, Sharna assured her she was on her way.

Hanging up the phone, Matilda immediately set to work, she had to pull herself together. The police were coming, and she needed to be in control. She dressed Alison and Lindsay, wiped their faces, and tried to tidy up the kitchen as best she could, though her hands trembled as she moved. The morning dragged on, every minute feeling like an hour.

It was nearly an hour and a half after her call when she finally heard the faint rumble of an engine approaching. She looked up from the kitchen window just in time to see the police car pull up at the gate to the house yard, then come to a complete stop.

The two Dobermans were at the fence, their muscular bodies tense, ears pricked forward, their deep, menacing growls carrying across the yard.

Matilda quickly slipped on her shoes, stepped outside, and called the dogs back. With a sharp whistle, she led them to their kennels and secured the latch before making her way to the gate. She pulled it open, gesturing for the officers to drive through.

The police car rolled forward, coming to a stop near the house. The doors opened, and two officers stepped out.

The woman was in her late thirties, dark-haired, with an air of quiet authority about her. She took the lead, offering a small, professional smile. "Good morning. I'm Sergeant Sharna O'Donnell, and this is Senior Constable Damien Rhodes."

The younger male officer, fair-haired and broad-shouldered, nodded politely.

Sharna studied Matilda for a moment, taking in her pale complexion, the slight redness around her eyes, the way she stood, upright, but tense, as though holding herself together by sheer force of will.

"And you must be Mrs. Collins?"

Matilda gave a stiff nod before correcting her. "Hello… and please, call me Matilda. Come inside."

Her voice was brave. But Sharna could see the fear lurking just beneath the surface.

After listening to everything Matilda could tell her about Bernard's unusual behaviour, Sergeant Sharna O'Donnell offered a reassuring smile. "I agree, Matilda, it certainly seems out of character. But I'm sure there's a simple explanation for your husband's whereabouts. We'll maintain contact with you throughout the day, and please, if Doctor Collins returns, let us know right away."

Matilda nodded, though the tightness in her expression betrayed her lingering unease.

Sharna placed a gentle hand on her arm. "I have a feeling he'll be home before long."

With that, the officers took their leave, driving back toward Dalby.

The morning was bright, the sky cloudless, and the town was alive with the buzz of the annual show. As they neared the show grounds, Sharna glanced at Rhodes. "We'd better check out the show while we'er near, she grinned!"

Rhodes smirked. "Not a bad idea. I could go a hot dog."

They parked near the entrance and strolled into side show alley, weaving between the clusters of families, teenagers, and farmers enjoying the day out. The air was thick with the scent of deep-fried food, popcorn, and livestock.

As they passed the arena, Sharna spotted a familiar face in the ring. Her niece, Hunter, was competing in the horse jumping event, guiding her bay gelding over a set of crisp white rails. They paused to watch for a few minutes, Sharna quietly proud as the young rider cleared each jump with precision.

Afterward, they grabbed a hot dog each, eating as they made their way back to the station.

That afternoon, Constable Rhodes sat at his desk, entering the details of their visit to the Collins property into the system. His fingers hesitated over the keyboard as a vague sense of unease settled over him. Something about this situation didn't sit right.

His mind flicked back to the doctor's recent visit to the station, just a week or so ago.

What was it Collins had been here for?

Rhodes frowned, scrolling through the logbook. A strange feeling crept into his gut, a whisper of intuition telling him that something about this was very, very wrong.

Axel Emmerich had spent the night in the spare bedroom of his rented house at 87 Roberts Street. He hadn't slept well, but it was enough to dull the exhaustion from the previous day's events. Now, after a quick breakfast, he stood in the doorway of the master bedroom, staring at the mess that awaited him.

The dreaded cleanup.

In the harsh morning light, it didn't look quite as bad as it had in the dead of night. The blood had congealed, dark and tacky, and the metallic stench that had filled the air yesterday had faded somewhat. The bedroom's only carpet, a small mat beside the bed, was completely soaked through, the once-muted pattern now a deep, crusted brown. There was no salvaging it. That, along with the bloodstained tarp from the utility, would go straight into the garbage bins along with the wallet that had been on the bed. Garbage collection was on Tuesday, which meant that he put the bins out on the nature strip in front of the house on Monday night "nice timing" he thought.

At least the polished mango timber floors were easier to deal with. He had expected a nightmare, but as he knelt down, damp cloth in hand, he realised the slick surface made the job more manageable. A few buckets of hot, soapy water and a bit of elbow grease would take care of the worst of it.

Still, the weight of what had happened lingered in the room, heavy and inescapable. As he scrubbed, Axel's mind drifted.

This hadn't been the plan.

None of it had.

By midday, Axel had finished the painstaking task of cleaning and was finally able to relax with a cold beer. He sat back in his chair, letting the condensation from the bottle cool his fingers, and exhaled slowly. The house was in order again, at least on the surface.

As he took another sip, something caught his eye through the front window. Parked three doors up from number 87 was a Ford Pilot. Not just any Ford Pilot. He knew that car. Knew it well.

A slow smirk crept across his face, though there was no humour in it.

It was the same car he had once torn apart, methodically searching for the diamonds, the diamonds that Carl Reimer, alias Anton Petryczek, had thought he could take with him into the next life. Axel had made sure he didn't.

The memory came back in sharp detail, as vivid as if he were living it all over again. The isolated property, the cold efficiency with which he had exterminated Reimer and his wife, the endless search for the stash they had been foolish enough to think they could keep hidden.

He leaned back, resting the beer on his thigh, and let his mind drift back to that day at Szansa.

He had them both bound tightly with baling twine, their wrists and ankles secured just as he had learned to do with the SS

He had visited their shed before going to the house in search of baling twine and seeing the tractor, that was identical to the one back at the orphanage farm near Ottenhofen, thirty kilometre's outside of Munich, a sudden thought had struck him then, a memory from long ago.

The tractors at the orphanage had relied on these capsules to fire up on bitterly cold mornings. He could still recall the distinct metallic click as the capsules were punctured, releasing their volatile contents to aid combustion. But that wasn't the only memory they stirred.

As boys, they had played cruel games with them, piercing the fragile casings with a needle and directing the fine mist of ether into each other's faces. It had been their version of mischief, watching as the unwitting victim's eyes rolled back, their legs giving out as they crumpled to the ground in a momentary daze.

Now, standing over his captives, Axel was growing impatient. They had refused, point-blank, to share any knowledge about the whereabouts of the diamonds, stubborn in their silence despite the threats, the pain, and the inevitability of their fate. No matter, he would exterminate them both and search the house himself. He had all the time in the world.

Turning the ether capsule between his fingers, he savoured the moment. He knew exactly how potent it was, how quickly it would work, and how much easier it would make his task. Once they were unconscious, he would slip the glass cyanide capsules into their mouths, thin, fragile things designed to shatter at the first clench of teeth, releasing death in an instant.

A slow grin crept across his face as he crouched down.

"Time for some old tricks," he murmured, piercing the capsule and directing the fine mist of ether towards Carl.

Carl squeezed his lips shut, holding his breath, his body rigid with resistance. His wife, Peta, did the same, their survival instincts kicking in. But Axel had seen this before, fear could delay the inevitable, but it could never stop it.

He sprayed again, closer this time, letting the ether cloud hang around Carl's face. Within seconds, the tension in Carl's body faded, his head drooping, his muscles giving way to unconsciousness. That was all Axel needed.

He pried Carl's jaws open just enough to slip the cyanide capsule between his clenched teeth. Then, with a sharp, calculated uppercut to the jaw, he forced Carl's mouth shut. The brittle capsule shattered instantly, the lethal cyanide flooding his system. There wasn't even time for a gasp, Carl slumped forward, dead before he hit the ground.

Axel turned to Peta. Her eyes were wide with terror, her breath coming in short, panicked bursts. She tried to twist away, but the baling twine held fast.

"Your turn," he said softly, as he brought the ether capsule to her face.

She thrashed, desperate to resist, but the vapour was already working its way into her system. Her struggle weakened, her eyelids fluttering, her body betraying her. Axel slipped the cyanide capsule between her lips, pressing it against her teeth.

Then, just as he struck her jaw to finish the job, her last breath escaped in a desperate, gasping cry.

"Car!"

Her voice was cut short as the poison took hold. Her body convulsed once, then went still.

Axel stood over the two corpses, frowning.

Car?

Axel studied the car intently, his sharp eyes tracing over every inch of its worn exterior. It was a Ford Pilot, pommy garbage, he thought with a sneer. He had never been fond of British engineering, preferring the precision and efficiency of German craftsmanship. Still, the car had its advantages. Its large, boxy frame and heavy construction made it sturdy, and more importantly, it provided plenty of places to hide something valuable.

His mind worked quickly, piecing together the possibility. If Carl and Peta had been desperate enough to keep the diamonds from him, they wouldn't have hidden them in the house. No, they would have chosen a place less obvious, a place they could access quickly if they needed to leave in a hurry.

The car.

Yes, he had thought, that made sense. It would be the perfect hiding spot and he had spent hours ripping the leather upholstery apart to no avail. He had even ripped the roof lining in search for the treasure….nothing.

He had commenced a methodological search of the house on the very day of their deaths and had returned each day to continue his search in a manner that would not miss anything and also leave no trace of his search. It was getting late one afternoon on the third day of searching that he had thought he was close when he had found the hand gun that was wrapped in a tea towel in one of the laundry cupboards. The gun was of no use to him so he had returned it back to the cupboard. The next day he was to continue searching the laundry but as he arrived at the property he saw the police car and a Land Rover. That had meant no more searching, another plan would now be required.

And now as he looked across the street to where the Ford Pilot was parked, he wondered if Bernard, its new owner, had ever had the upholstery replaced. He decided not to find out.

On Monday, Axel would put pressure on the real estate agent, Dennis Marshall, to expedite the purchase of Girraween. The unexpected loss of Matilda's husband could work in his favour, grief often clouded judgment, and with the right approach, he might be able to secure the property at a reduced price. A distressed widow, burdened with uncertainty, might be more inclined to sell quickly rather than haggle over every last pound.

Money was getting low. The bounty Axel had received for eliminating Reimer was dwindling, now down to £150,000. While still a considerable sum, he knew better than to let it slip through his fingers without reinvestment as he no intention of returning to Europe. Land, especially a secluded property like Girraween, offered more than just stability. It provided cover, legitimacy, and a secure base of operations, far removed from prying eyes.

As he sat nursing a cigarette, Axel reflected on the original price placed on Carl Reimer's head: 4,000 Deutsche Marks, courtesy of ODESSA, Organisation der Ehemaligen SS-Angehörigen. While ODESSA's primary mission was to assist former SS officers in escaping Europe, it also enforced a strict code of loyalty among its members. Betrayal, whether in the form of theft or insubordination, was met with a single, inescapable consequence: death.

Axel had been paid a premium, nearly double the standard bounty, because he was not the first to be assigned the task. Two years prior, Oberleutnant Otto Klein had been sent to eliminate Reimer. But Klein had disappeared without a trace. No body. No final report. Nothing.

That alone had made Axel cautious when he had approached the Reimer's.

Had Klein failed and simply gone into hiding? Had Reimer somehow turned the tables on his would-be assassin, Klein?

Axel had pressed both Carl and Peta Reimer for answers about Otto Klein's whereabouts, but his inquiries had been met with nothing but contempt and silence. Neither of them flinched, neither betrayed the slightest hint of recognition. If they knew what had happened to Klein, they were determined to take that secret to their graves.

Axel studied them carefully, weighing the possibility that they were bluffing. But something about their unwavering composure unsettled him. Either they were exceptionally good liars, or Otto Klein had truly vanished without a trace.

He exhaled slowly, watching the smoke from his cigarette coil toward the ceiling in lazy, twisting tendrils. Whatever had happened to Klein, one thing was certain: Axel would not make the same mistake.

At least, not yet.

Yes, Monday would be a busy day indeed. He would return the hired utility first thing in the morning, ensuring there were no loose ends. Then, on his way back, he would pay Dennis a visit and gently remind him to push the sale through. If persuasion didn't work, well, Axel had other methods of encouragement.

It had been the worst weekend of Matilda's life. Every hour seemed to stretch endlessly, filled with worry, fear, and an overwhelming sense of helplessness. She had considered calling Bernard's brother, Bruce, and his wife, Dawn, but hesitation held her back. The relationship between them had fractured years ago when Bernard's parents, Phyllis and Edwin, had gifted the property Stanlee to Bernard and Matilda as a wedding present. Bruce and Dawn had never forgiven them for that, and their resentment had only deepened over time. They had even refused to attend Phyllis and Edwin's funerals. What comfort could she expect from them now? None.

The only other person Matilda could turn to was her sister, Kathleen, who lived on the Gold Coast. But they had lost touch. The last time she had seen or even spoken to Kathleen was on her wedding day, where Kathleen had stood by her side as Matron of Honour. It had been years since then, and Matilda had no idea what her sister's life was like now. Would she even want to help? Would she even care?

Still, she had decided to wait until Monday before reaching out. Maybe, just maybe, by then everything would be fine. Maybe Bernard would walk through the door with an explanation, some ridiculous, foolish reason for his absence that would make her both furious and relieved.

Oh God, how she hoped for that.

The not knowing was the worst part. Every time the phone rang, her heart lurched. Every shadow outside made her rush to the window, only to feel crushed by disappointment. She tried to prepare herself for the worst, but how could she? How could she condition herself to accept that Bernard might never come home?

No. She refused to believe that. Not yet.

If Kathleen were here now, it might help. But calling her would feel like admitting defeat, like surrendering to the possibility that Bernard was truly gone. And Matilda wasn't ready to do that.

On Saturday morning, Matilda had tried calling Alois's jeweller shop, but there was no answer. She frowned, staring at the silent receiver in her hand. That was strange.

Alois had always insisted that Saturday mornings were his busiest trading hours. He had once told her that the sales he made on a single Saturday morning often matched the total earnings from the five preceding weekdays combined. It made no sense for the shop to be closed or unattended.

She tried the number again, listening as the call rang out with no response. A feeling of despair crept over her. There was nothing that she could do but wait, wait until Monday, at this stage.

Monday morning brought torrential rain, driven sideways by fierce winds sweeping across the open plains. The storm made driving treacherous, with visibility reduced to almost nothing as sheets of rain pounded the roads.

At the intersection near the town bypass, a Holden utility approached a stop sign. Whether the driver had come to a full stop before proceeding was unclear, but in the blinding rain, the vehicle pulled forward, straight into the path of a fully laden tipper truck hauling stone from the quarry.

The collision was catastrophic. The impact sent the utility spinning before it erupted into flames, the force of the crash rupturing the fuel tank. The blaze raged violently, fed by the wind and rain that hissed uselessly against the inferno. By the time emergency crews arrived, there was nothing they could do. The fire had consumed everything, leaving only a charred shell of twisted metal.

The occupant inside never stood a chance.

This incident marked the second major call-out for the police station that morning.

The first had come just after dawn, a grim report from the quarry. Workers arriving for the early shift had stumbled upon a horrifying scene: four bodies sprawled across the rocky floor of the excavation site. The rain had already begun to wash away some of the evidence, but there was no mistaking the signs of violence.

Before officers had even finished processing the details of the first call, the second emergency came through, the fiery collision at the bypass. The already stretched police force now had two major investigations unfolding simultaneously.

On the corner of the main street, outside Alois' jewellery shop, Gwen Noble, the shop assistant, huddled under the awning, trying to stay dry. The rain was relentless, drumming against the pavement and pooling in the gutters. She glanced at her watch, 8:15 a.m. Alois was usually punctual, opening the shop promptly at eight each trading day, yet the doors remained locked, and there was no sign of him.

Meanwhile, over on Roberts Street, the occupants of number 84 had grown increasingly frustrated with the abandoned Ford Pilot parked in front of their house. It had been sitting there since Thursday, unmoved and unnoticed by anyone except them. After waiting days for the owner to reclaim it, they had finally called the council offices that morning to report the vehicle.

At the show ground, the owner of the dodgem cars was in no better mood. He muttered curses under his breath as he worked alone in the downpour, dismantling the track and loading the heavy steel sections onto the transport trucks. The labourers he had picked up from the Bundaberg Show, useless, unreliable drifters, had vanished without a word, leaving him to do the backbreaking work himself. They hadn't even bothered to show up for work on the biggest trading day, Show Day, and now he was paying the price. He spat into the wet dirt, cursing his own bad luck, as the rain continued to fall.

Senior Constable Damien Rhodes and Constable Peter Praxoulus had returned from the quarry, their faces set in grim expressions. The scene they had left behind was nothing short of a nightmare, and now it was up to Forensics to piece together what had happened. They had left Constable Verity Wright at the sealed-off quarry floor, tasked with maintaining a watch until the forensic team arrived.

Verity, drenched from head to toe despite her raincoat and umbrella, stood in the relentless downpour, shifting her weight from foot to foot to keep warm. The station had promised to send out a car for her to use as shelter, but for now, she had no choice but to endure the miserable conditions. The rain had turned the quarry floor into a thick, muddy mess, and visibility

Max Barrington

was poor. She glanced around, half expecting the shadows to shift, her nerves were on edge.

Meanwhile, the forensic unit from Brisbane had been contacted and was scheduled to arrive later that morning to examine the grisly scene at the quarry. Another forensic officer from Toowoomba had been dispatched to investigate the fatal car accident, the second major incident of the day. The roads were treacherous in this weather, and with visibility near zero, it wasn't surprising that a tragedy had occurred.

As Rhodes and Praxoulus pulled into the station, shaking off the rain, they both knew that this was only the beginning of what promised to be a long and exhausting day.

By late that night forensic had cleared the quarry scene for the bodies to be removed and taken to the hospital mortuary for autopsies pending identification. A preliminary forensic report was submitted to the OIC at the police station.

Summary of Findings:

At approximately 11:56, forensic officers arrived at the Dalby Quarry following the discovery of four deceased individuals on the quarry floor. The bodies were examined on-site before being transported to the coroner's office for further analysis. Preliminary findings indicate all four individuals suffered fatal gunshot wounds before sustaining extensive secondary injuries from a fall of approximately 160 feet.

Victim Descriptions and Wounds:

Victim 1: Male, Charles Timothy Scott, 114 Albert Road, Lakes Entrance Vic. DOB 16/09 1935, identity; from Victorian drivers licence P:887645C3.

Single gunshot wound to the right temple, entry wound approximately 7mm in diameter.

Bullet trajectory suggests close-range execution-style shooting.

Recovered projectile consistent with a 7.65mm caliber round.

Secondary injuries: multiple fractures to the skull, ribcage, and extremities consistent with high-velocity impact from a significant fall.

Victim 2: Male, Rodney Stewart Baker, 26 Codd Street, Lakemba NSW. DOB 03/06 1934, identity; from NSW drivers licence A887G9982. There was a firearm wedged in the belt of this body. The firearm is a Radom Vis 35 calibre 9x19mm Par. Serial Number 15567. Details have been sent to Polish Police Ballistics. The weapon had not been recently fired..

Single gunshot wound to the left temple, similar in characteristics to Victim 1.

Recovered projectile also consistent with a 7.65mm caliber round.

Secondary injuries include extensive skeletal fractures and soft tissue damage from quarry floor impact.

Victim 3: Male, estimated 50s-60s. identity unknown

Two gunshot wounds: one to the torso (entry wound approximately 7mm) and one to the head.

Ballistic analysis confirms both wounds caused by 7.65mm rounds.

Severe trauma to the cranial region and multiple broken bones from fall impact.

Victim 4: Male, estimated 30s-40s. identity unknown

A set of three car keys were found on a single key ring in the right hand side trouser pocket. Two of the keys are embossed 'Ezy Cut' and the third key is 'Dalson C26'.

Two gunshot wounds: one to the body and one to the head.

Wound patterns and recovered projectiles consistent with a 7.65mm firearm.

Extensive internal injuries, including a ruptured spleen and lung collapse, in addition to skeletal fractures from the drop.

Additional Observations:

The victims exhibited no signs of defensive wounds, suggesting they were incapacitated prior to falling.

Positioning of bodies indicates they were likely dropped from the quarry edge post-mortem.

Blood spatter analysis at the drop site suggests the shootings occurred at a different location, with bodies transported and disposed of at the quarry.

The evidence strongly indicates a homicide involving execution-style shootings followed by body disposal via a high drop into the quarry. The recovered projectiles will undergo further ballistic testing to identify potential weapon matches. Law enforcement investigation is ongoing.

Detective Inspector Leonard Campari from Brisbane Homicide was formally assigned to lead the investigation into what appeared to be a brutal, execution-style murder at the Dalby quarry. With four bodies discovered at the scene, each bearing gunshot wounds consistent with a close-range attack, the case had quickly escalated into a high-priority matter. Campari, known for his meticulous approach and sharp investigative instincts, wasted no time in coordinating with forensic teams and local law enforcement to piece together the sequence of events that led to the killings.

Meanwhile, Sergeant Clive Dagmar of the local police branch was tasked with identifying the sole occupant of the vehicle involved in that morning's fatal crash. The circumstances surrounding the incident raised immediate concerns, was it an unfortunate accident, or was there a connection to the homicides at the quarry? Dagmar was also responsible for determining the probable cause of the crash, working closely with traffic investigators and forensic specialists to examine the wreckage for any evidence that might shed light on the driver's identity and the events leading up to the collision.

With two major investigations unfolding simultaneously, tensions ran high at the Dalby police station. The morning's grim discoveries had cast a shadow over the town, and for those involved in the case, it was only the beginning of what promised to be a complex and deeply unsettling inquiry.

Relatives of the two identified victims were promptly contacted by police and interviewed at their respective locations. In the case of Charles Timothy Scott, his family revealed that he had been working with a travelling showman, moving from town to town across Australia. They described him as a restless soul who had always been drawn to the transient lifestyle of show grounds and carnivals. His involvement with the show circuit explained why he had been in the area, though it offered little insight into how he had ended up murdered in such a brutal manner at the Dalby quarry.

The response from the relatives of the second victim, Rodney Stewart Baker, was markedly different. When informed of his death, his family showed little reaction, with some members admitting that they had not known his whereabouts for some time. Their indifference suggested a history of estrangement, and when questioned further, they provided no useful information about his recent activities or possible associates. If Baker had been involved in anything illicit, his family either didn't know or didn't care to find out.

With one victim having loose ties to the travelling show community and the other seemingly disconnected from his family, investigators were left with more questions than answers. The challenge now was to uncover what had brought these men together and what had led to their violent deaths at the bottom of the quarry.

By the time this information had surfaced, most, if not all, of the travelling show community had already moved on, making their way toward Miles, the next stop on the circuit, located approximately 80 miles from Dalby. However, a portion of the group had opted to stay in Chinchilla, planning to set up for the show there after Miles. Given the transient nature of the show people, police determined that the most effective approach would be to conduct interviews at Chinchilla first before travelling on to Miles to question the remaining individuals.

The second person interviewed at Chinchilla provided the first significant lead. When shown photographs of the two victims, he immediately recognised them by name. He confirmed that both men had been working at the Dalby show and had finished their shift on Thursday afternoon. According to his account, after knocking off work, they had headed straight to the Winston Hotel, the nearest pub to the show grounds. That was the last time he had seen them.

With this information, detectives now had a clearer timeline of the victims' last known movements. The next step was to establish if they had been in the Winston Hotel on that Thursday and when they had left there.

At the Winston Hotel, detectives approached the bar staff, hoping to confirm whether the two young men had indeed been there on Thursday afternoon. The woman behind the bar glanced at the photographs they presented but shook her head apologetically.

"I'm not sure," she admitted. "When the showies are in, it gets pretty busy. I don't really have time to look at people closely, let alone remember faces."

Just as the detectives were about to move on, the duty manager happened to walk past. Catching sight of the photographs, he paused.

"Hang on," he said, leaning in for a better look. "Yeah, I do remember these two."

The detectives exchanged a glance. This was the first concrete confirmation that the victims had been at the hotel.

"Are you certain?" Detective Inspector Campari pressed.

"Absolutely," the manager replied. "I saw them leave around eight-forty-five that night. They were with a well-dressed bloke, mid-forties, I'd say, driving a Holden Ute."

"Anything else you can tell us about him?"

The manager nodded. "Yeah. I remember because I was working in the bottle shop at the time. The guy drove into the driveway, got out, and bought two tall bottles of Fosters Lager. Had an accent too. European, maybe?"

"Have you seen him around before?"

The manager shook his head. "No, I didn't recognise him, sorry. He paid cash, took his beer, and left with those two fellas in his Ute."

"The numberplate, did you get the rego number by any chance" it was a long shot.

"Aww come on!" Responded the manager, looking at the detective as if he wasn't the full quid.

The detectives now had a new lead, an unidentified, well-dressed man with an accent, driving a Holden Ute. They needed to find out who he was and why he had left with the victims. Now where to look?

The photographs of the two unidentified bodies were displayed in the muster room, where officers gathered to discuss ongoing cases. As the detectives continued their briefing, Constable Damien Rhodes studied the images closely. A jolt of recognition struck him. He took a step closer, scrutinising the features of one of the men, then turned to the duty sergeant.

"Sergeant!" Rhodes said, his voice measured but firm, "I'm ninety-nine percent sure that this man is Dr. Bernard Collins."

The duty sergeant's expression shifted immediately. The name was familiar, too familiar. Dr. Collins had been reported missing only days ago, and his wife, Matilda Collins, had been desperately awaiting news.

"Are you certain?" the sergeant asked, leaning in to examine the photograph himself.

"As certain as I can be without official confirmation," Rhodes replied. "I spoke to the man only a week, or so ago when he came into the station."

"We'll need a positive identification," the sergeant said. "Get a car organised to visit Mrs. Collins."

Rhodes hesitated. "Sir, maybe we should wait until morning. Sergeant Sharna O'Donnell will be on duty then. She's already familiar with Mrs. Collins and this case."

The sergeant considered this for a moment before nodding. "Good call. First thing tomorrow, O'Donnell and a team will go to Mrs. Collins and request a formal identification."

The weight of the task ahead was evident. If the identification was confirmed, Matilda Collins would no longer be waiting for news, she would be facing a tragic reality.

BRRRRINNNGG! BRRRRINNNGG!
BRRRRINNNGG! BRRRRINNNGG!

Matilda jolted awake, her heart pounding as the shrill ringing of the telephone cut through the quiet of the morning. She turned her head toward the bedside clock, 8:30 AM. The children were still asleep. Thank God, she thought, as she flung back the covers and hurried to the phone.

"Hello!" she answered, her voice sharp and abrupt, not out of rudeness, but because that was simply how she spoke these days, always on edge, always expecting the worst.

"Matilda, it's Sergeant Sharna O'Donnell," came the familiar voice on the other end. "Good! you're home? I'd like to come by and give you an update on Bernard."

Matilda's breath caught in her throat. An update. The word alone sent a chill down her spine.

"Yes, of course," she said quickly, her voice barely above a whisper. But before she could ask anything, before she could demand to know whether this was good news or bad, Sharna had already hung up.

Matilda stood there, gripping the receiver, staring blankly at the wall. An update. It could mean anything. Was Bernard alive? Was he hurt? Or was this the moment she had been dreading?

She swallowed hard, glancing toward the hallway where her children still slept peacefully, before going outside and locking the Doberman dogs into the kennels and opening the gate to the house yard, then returning the house to put on the coffee percolator in preparation for the police visit.

Matilda already knew what the police were going to tell her. She had been preparing herself for days, conditioning her mind to accept the inevitable. It was now Tuesday, six nights since Bernard had left for his meeting in Brisbane on Wednesday night. Six nights of silence. Six nights of waiting, of unanswered calls, of hope fading into dread. From everything she had

Max Barrington

managed to piece together, it seemed that Bernard had never even made it to the Brisbane hospital.

Still, knowing was one thing. Hearing it spoken aloud was another.

The knock at the door made her stomach clench. She took a deep breath, smoothing down the front of her blouse with trembling hands before she opened it.

Standing on the doorstep was Sergeant Sharna O'Donnell, her expression unreadable but her presence alone enough to confirm Matilda's worst fears. Beside her stood Constable Damien Rhodes, whom Matilda recognised, and a young woman in uniform, someone she had not met before.

"Good morning, Mrs. Collins," Sharna said gently. "You remember Damien, and this is Constable Verity Wright… May we come in?"

Matilda nodded stiffly and stepped aside.

As they entered, Sharna cast a quick glance at Verity before speaking again. "Verity will be staying with you this afternoon, or for as long as needed, until we can arrange for any additional support."

Matilda's throat tightened. Support. The word made her feel as if she were being propped up on crumbling ground.

She had been expecting the worst, bracing herself for it, but now, standing here in her own home with these solemn-faced officers before her, she realised something, no amount of preparation could truly ready her for the moment someone said the words aloud.

Her heart pounded in her chest as she waited, barely breathing.

And then, Sharna spoke, though in truth, the words weren't necessary. Matilda had already understood what was coming the moment she opened the door. Sharna had a way of handling difficult conversations, of softening the impact without diminishing the weight of the news. There was no need to say the word dead.

"We don't have a lot of details yet, Matilda," Sharna began gently. "But we'll keep you updated as more information comes to hand. For now, you won't be required for a positive identification, so there's no need for you to leave home."

Matilda nodded numbly, her fingers gripping the edge of the hallway table for support.

Sharna glanced briefly at Verity, then continued, her tone measured and practical. "If there's anything urgent you need, Verity can take care of it. She can do some shopping, run any errands, you'd just need to lend her your car. And she's great with kids, so if you need some time to yourself, she can help with that too."

Matilda blinked, barely processing the words. Shopping? Errands? Kids? It felt surreal, this conversation about everyday necessities while the foundation of her world was crumbling beneath her feet.

She wanted to say something, to ask a question, but her throat felt thick, clogged with emotions she wasn't ready to face. Instead, she swallowed hard and forced a small, shaky nod.

Sharna placed a reassuring hand on her arm. "Take your time, Matilda. We're here for you."

Matilda exhaled slowly, knowing that while they were there now, soon enough, they would leave. Soon enough, she would be alone with her grief. She had been in touch with Kathleen, her sister, who would be with her by tomorrow, Matilda just had to be able to drive to the station to collect her. Perhaps the police, could do that for her. That would be a big help.

Ken Brooks, the owner of Dalby Car & Truck Hire, had contacted the police regarding a vehicle that had not been returned. In response, Constable Peter Praxoulus was dispatched to obtain a full statement and details from Ken.

As the constable took notes, Ken leaned against the counter and asked casually, "What was the number plate on yesterday's burnout? I have a feeling it might've been my utility."

Peter shook his head, maintaining protocol. "I'm sorry, sir, but we can't release that information."

Ken exhaled sharply, clearly frustrated, but didn't argue. Instead, he provided the details of the missing vehicle along with a photocopy of the hirer's license. "Here's what I've got. If it's my ute, I want to know."

Back at the station, Praxoulus compared the provided registration number with the records from Monday's fatal collision. A chill ran down his spine as he realized they were a match. Wasting no time, he reported his findings to his sergeant.

Sergeant Clive Dagmar took the photocopy of the license, adjusting his glasses as he read aloud, "Anton Petryczek, 87 Roberts Street, Dalby." He looked up at Praxoulus. "You'd better head over there and see if this guy has any family. You know the drill, tread softly, young feller."

As an afterthought, he added, "Take Constable Brett Croker with you. He's been under my feet all morning, might as well make himself useful."

When the two officers arrived at 87 Roberts Street, they immediately spotted a Morris Minor parked in front. Given that no other cars were in the driveway, they assumed it didn't belong to the house.

They knocked on the front door. No answer.

Circling to the back, they found the door unlocked. That in itself raised a flag, but what caught their attention even more was the unmistakable, putrid stench wafting from the garbage bins nearby.

Croker wrinkled his nose. "That's rank."

Praxoulus nodded, already feeling uneasy.

Cautiously, Croker lifted the lid of one of the bins. A thick cloud of flies erupted into the air, buzzing furiously as if disturbed from a feast.

Swallowing back the bile rising in his throat, Croker turned to Praxoulus. "This isn't good."

The second bin yielded the same result, though the smell, while awful, wasn't quite as overpowering.

Praxoulus exhaled, stepping back. "We need to call this in." Without another word, he strode over to the patrol car and picked up the radio, his tone measured but firm as he contacted VKR base.

After a brief wait, the response crackled through the speaker. "Maintain a watch. Detectives will be en route shortly."

Returning to where Croker stood near the garbage bins, Praxoulus muttered, "We hold tight."

Minutes ticked by as they waited in the driveway of 87 Roberts Street. The wind carried the sickly stench from the bins, making it difficult to ignore the unpleasantness of their discovery.

A voice interrupted their thoughts. "Morning, officers."

They turned to see a middle-aged man approaching from across the street, three houses back from their position. He gestured toward the curb in front of his house. "You blokes here about that abandoned car?"

Praxoulus and Croker exchanged a glance before following the man across the road.

Parked in front of 84 Roberts Street was a Ford Pilot. The vehicle looked as though it had been sitting there for some time, its dusty exterior streaked with dried rain marks.

"We called the council about it," the man continued. "It's been here since Thursday. No one's come back for it."

Croker leaned down, peering through the window. The interior was empty, but something about the vehicle felt off. He straightened up and walked back to the police car and again called VKR.

"VKR, this is Constable Croker. We've got an abandoned Ford Pilot in front of 84 Roberts Street. Requesting a check on the registration."

The reply came swiftly. "Noted, Constable. Hold position and relay the information to Detective Inspector Leonard Campari upon his arrival."

Inspector Leonard Campari arrived a few minutes later, accompanied by Detective Sergeant Phillip Gibson. As they stepped out of their vehicle, Constable Croker immediately briefed them on the abandoned Ford Pilot parked across the street.

Campari glanced over at the car, his sharp eyes taking it in before mumbling something to Gibson. Without hesitation, Gibson turned to Croker. "Call VKR. Have them send out a tow truck and get that vehicle taken to the station."

Croker nodded and walked briskly toward the patrol car to radio it in.

Meanwhile, Campari strode toward the garbage bins. Without flinching, he lifted the lids on both and let them drop to the ground with a loud clatter. A foul stench billowed up, thick and putrid. His face remained impassive as he surveyed the contents.

He turned his gaze to Praxoulus, his voice calm but firm. "Get onto VKR. We need the SOCOs (scene of crime offices) out here. And tell them today… now."

Praxoulus didn't need to be told twice. He grabbed his radio, stepping away from the overwhelming stench as he relayed the urgent request.

Later that day at Police HQ;

Dalby Police Briefing – Summary of Events

Inspector Leonard Campari – End of Day Briefing

Monday Morning: Two Major Incidents

Fatal Motor Vehicle Accident

A single-vehicle crash involving a Holden utility resulted in a fatality.

The vehicle exploded on impact, incinerating the occupant.

Discovery of Four Bodies at the Local Quarry

Bodies were found on the quarry floor, showing evidence of gunshot wounds.

Preliminary forensic findings suggest an execution-style killing.

Established Link Between Incidents:

The driver of the crashed vehicle was identified via a Queensland driver's license (A6755492) as Anton Petryczek, residing at 87 Roberts Street, Dalby.

Further investigation into the license revealed:

License originally issued in 1954, cancelled upon the death of the original holder.

Reissued in 1955 with a change of address.

Raises questions regarding identity fraud or alias usage.

Search & Forensic Findings at 87 Roberts Street:

The SOCO team conducted an extensive search, uncovering the following evidence:

Carpet/mat in the rubbish bin

Heavy blood staining detected.

Blood type matches one of the yet-unidentified quarry victims.

Poly tarpaulin with bloodstains

Matches two victims:

Bernard Collins (positively identified victim).

Unidentified quarry victim.

Bloodstains on bed base and floor

Blood found on the bed base and timber flooring beneath a bed leg.

Matches Bernard Collins.

A single 9×19mm Parabellum cartridge

Live round with a primer strike, indicating a failed discharge ("misfire").

Additional Firearm Findings

A Vis 35 handgun was recovered from Rodney Stewart Baker (quarry victim).

The weapon contained a misfired round still chambered, suggesting a potential malfunction or an attempt to execute the victim that failed.

Next Steps & Investigative Priorities

Verification of Anton Petryczek's true identity.

Examination of the circumstances surrounding the reissued license.

Further forensic analysis on recovered evidence.

Tracing the ownership and origin of the Vis 35 handgun and its ammunition.

Establishing a timeline linking Petryczek, the victims, and their last known movements.

Inspector Campari concluded the briefing by emphasising the complexity of the case and the need for coordinated efforts moving forward. The investigation remains ongoing, with further updates expected following forensic reports and witness interviews.

The unidentified body was finally identified as that of Alois Pfeiffer, a local jeweller and known associate of Doctor Collins.

The police could only reconstruct the events before that fateful Monday following the show day of 1959 by meticulously piecing together forensic evidence, witness statements, and logical deductions. What had unfolded in Dalby, a usually quiet rural town, was nothing short of shocking. The sheer scale of the violence, with multiple homicides and a fatal car accident all seemingly connected, had sent ripples of fear through the tight-knit community.

Through their investigation, the police believed they had arrived at a plausible explanation of the sequence of events, at least as much as could ever be known. The evidence strongly suggested a brutal execution-style killing, followed by an attempt to cover up the crime, which ultimately led to the fiery demise of the key suspect. But despite their best efforts, some questions remained unanswered.

In the end, no arrests were made, no charges were laid. There was simply no one left to prosecute. Those responsible were either dead or beyond the reach of justice, leaving the case effectively closed, if not entirely resolved.

Girraween 1977

In 1977, Queensland experienced a series of significant events that shaped its political, cultural, and social landscape.

The state held its general election on November 12, 1977, resulting in a victory for the National-Liberal Coalition under Premier Joh Bjelke-Petersen. The Coalition secured 59 out of 82 seats, marking their fourth consecutive win since 1957. A major campaign issue was law and order, particularly the controversial law requiring permits for street marches, which were seldom granted. This legislation sparked debates over civil liberties and governmental control.

In 1977, Queen Elizabeth II visited Queensland as part of her Silver Jubilee celebrations. The state government commemorated this milestone by commissioning the Queen Elizabeth II Silver Jubilee Fountain, symbolising the enduring relationship between Queensland and the monarchy.

The Swedish pop group **ABBA** toured Australia in March 1977, but notably excluded Brisbane from their itinerary, leading to disappointment among Queensland fans.

Overall, 1977 was a year of political reaffirmation, cultural milestones, and social activism in Queensland, reflecting the state's dynamic and evolving identity.

It was also the year that Lindsay Collins turned 19 and his sister Alison Collins celebrated her 22nd birthday. Both siblings were proudly serving in the Australian Armed Forces, and by a stroke of luck, they were home at Girraween on leave at the same time.

Normally, the homestead at Girraween was a quiet and peaceful retreat, occupied only by Matilda Collins and her sister Kathleen Simmons. However, with the return of Lindsay and Alison, the once-tranquil household was suddenly bursting with activity. Their homecomings had a way of transforming the property into a lively hub, as neither of them ever seemed to return alone.

Alison, true to tradition, had brought a close friend along to share in her time off. Lindsay, never one to be outdone, arrived with not just one but two companions from his unit. The farmhouse, which was usually filled only with the soft sounds of rustling leaves, the distant call of livestock, and the occasional clatter of Matilda and Kathleen's daily routines, was now alive with conversation, laughter, and the heavy footsteps of young soldiers moving about.

For Matilda and Kathleen, the change was both overwhelming and welcome. While they cherished their peaceful existence, there was something undeniably heartwarming about having the house filled with youthful energy once again. The kitchen table was now surrounded by hungry, talkative young men and women, stories from military life were exchanged over steaming cups of tea, and the once-quiet evenings were now filled with the occasional bursts of raucous laughter.

Though it was only temporary, these were the moments that Matilda and Kathleen treasured most, the rare occasions when their family was whole, the house was full, and the echoes of laughter, camaraderie, and home-cooked meals created memories that would linger long after the last goodbyes were said.

Both of Matilda's children seemed to have the same urge as their father. And that was to get away from the farm just as soon as they were able. Alison had followed in her father's footsteps and was to graduate as a doctor this year with the Australian Defence Force Academy and the University of New South Wales.

Both Matilda and Kathleen were eagerly looking forward to their trip to Canberra later in the year for Alison's graduation. It was a momentous occasion, one that filled them both with pride, and they had decided to turn it into more than just a simple visit, they would make a holiday out of it.

Rather than flying, they agreed that the journey itself should be part of the experience. A long road trip gave them the opportunity to explore the countryside, visit old friends, and reminisce about days gone by. To ensure they travelled in both comfort and style, they decided it was time to buy a new car, one suitable for long-distance touring.

Kathleen had already set her heart on a Holden Statesman Caprice, believing it to be the perfect vehicle for the journey, spacious, luxurious, and smooth on the open road. Matilda, though perfectly content with her sister's choice, would have personally preferred a Ford Fairlane, a car she had always admired for its refined design and reliable performance. However, she was more than willing to compromise, knowing that Kathleen's enthusiasm for the Holden was unwavering.

With the decision made, they began making plans for the trip, mapping out stops along the way and looking forward to the freedom of the open road.

Lindsay, on the other hand had opted to join the navy and was studying mechanical engineering through The University of New South Wales and the Australian Defence Force Academy.

Since Bernard's unexplained and untimely death in 1959, Kathleen had made a significant shift in her life to join her sister at Girraween. Once a dedicated Detective Senior Constable in the Federal Police, she had chosen to leave behind the world of law enforcement, a career she had once been deeply committed to, in favour of a completely different path.

With a determination to reinvent herself and take control of her future, Kathleen turned her attention to cattle and sheep production and general grazing. It was a bold move, but one she embraced wholeheartedly. The land had always held a certain pull over her, and with Bernard gone, she felt a deep-seated need to dedicate herself to something more tangible, more grounding.

Kathleen approached her new venture with the same discipline and sharp analytical mind that had served her well in law enforcement. However, this time, instead of investigating crimes, she was investigating soil health, breeding techniques, and efficient grazing systems. The transition wasn't easy, life on the land demanded long hours and relentless hard work, but she thrived in the challenge.

Since being at Girraween she had spent two full years working with the Girraween Agricultural Manager on a full time basis, introducing new technologies in beef and cattle production and regenerative systems for the continuous production of livestock feed.

With her children grown and pursuing their own careers, and Kathleen fully immersed in the operations at Girraween, Matilda found herself at a crossroads. Always one to keep busy and embrace new challenges, she decided to expand her skill set in a way that would not only benefit the family business but also provide her with a sense of purpose and personal growth.

She enrolled in courses in accounting and bookkeeping, recognising the importance of financial management in both agriculture and business operations. With Girraween's expansion and Kathleen's modernisation efforts, keeping track of expenses, profits, and investment opportunities had become more critical than ever. Matilda took on the responsibility of managing the property's finances, ensuring that budgets were maintained, expenditures were justified, and new projects were financially sustainable.

At the same time, she found herself intrigued by the rapidly advancing field of computing science. The world was entering a new technological era, and she saw an opportunity to stay ahead of the curve. Matilda began learning basic programming, fascinated by the potential applications of computers in both business and agriculture. She explored spreadsheets, database management, and early financial software, recognising that these tools could streamline operations and improve efficiency.

Though she was not yet an expert, Matilda was determined to grasp the fundamentals of computing. She envisioned a future where digital record-keeping, automated calculations, and financial forecasting would replace the old ledgers and manual bookkeeping methods. Her forward-thinking approach reflected the same resilience and adaptability that had carried her through the many challenges of life since Bernard's passing.

With her newfound skills in accounting, finance, and computing, Matilda not only found a renewed sense of purpose but also played a crucial role in securing the financial future of Girraween.

On one of their frequent trips into Dalby to stock up on supplies and take care of various odds and ends, Matilda and Kathleen decided to make a leisurely afternoon of it. The summer heat was unrelenting, shimmering off the pavement as they made their way down Cunningham Street, the town bustling with the usual midday activity.

After ticking off the last few items on their shopping list, Matilda wiped her brow and glanced over at Kathleen. "How about we stop at the Royal Hotel for a cold drink and a counter lunch?" she suggested.

Kathleen, already thinking the same thing, nodded. "Sounds good to me. I could do with something cold."

The Royal Hotel was one of Dalby's most well-known watering holes, a staple for locals and travellers alike. With its solid timber bar, polished brass fixtures, and a wide veranda offering shade from the midday sun, it was a place where farmers, stockmen, and business owners all rubbed shoulders over a cold schooner and a hearty meal.

Stepping inside, the sisters welcomed the cool relief of the air-conditioned lounge, the scent of freshly pulled beer and pub-style cooking filling the space. The room was already buzzing with the lunchtime crowd, men in work shirts and Akubra's discussing the latest cattle prices, shopkeepers on their break, and a few familiar faces from town sharing a laugh over their meals.

Matilda spotted an empty table near the window and led the way. She glanced at her sister with a playful smirk.

"Drink first, Sissy?" she asked as they slid into their seats.

Kathleen picked up a menu and flicked through it absentmindedly. "Sounds good to me!" she replied. "I'll figure out what I'm having while you're up there."

Matilda nodded and made her way over to the bar, where the bartender, a broad-shouldered man with a sun-lined face and an easy smile, was wiping down the counter.

"Two cold ones, please," Matilda ordered, resting her arms on the polished wood.

Just as the bartender reached for the taps, she felt a gentle tap on her arm.

She turned, eyebrows raised in curiosity, and found herself face-to-face with someone she hadn't expected to see today.

"Hello, Mrs. Collins," came a smooth, confident voice.

Matilda turned to see a smartly dressed woman, perhaps a few years younger than herself, standing beside her with an easy yet knowing smile.

"I'm Gwen Noble. I used to work with Alois Pfeiffer."

Matilda blinked, surprised by the introduction. For a moment, she struggled to place the name, but then recognition dawned.

"Oh, wow! I didn't recognise you at first," Matilda admitted, studying Gwen more closely. "It's been quite a while."

She now remembered Gwen as Alois Pfeiffer's shop assistant. Alois, the meticulous and somewhat eccentric watchmaker, had always spoken very highly of her. Matilda could only recall meeting Gwen once, and even then, it had been brief.

Gwen offered a polite, almost knowing smile before glancing past Matilda toward Kathleen. "I see you're with someone, so I won't hold you up. Please don't think I'm being rude, but…" she hesitated for just a second, "did you ever find the diamonds?"

Matilda stiffened. "Diamonds?"

Gwen's eyes studied her, filled with curiosity and something else, something Matilda couldn't quite place. "I know that's what they were talking about the night they went to get Axel Emmerich."

A sudden chill ran through Matilda, despite the warmth of the room. She hadn't heard that name before, not that she could remember anyway.

She hadn't even thought about diamonds in just as long, when she and Bernard had decided there must have only been enough diamonds to get the Petryczek's settled with their property and bits and pieces.

Yet here was Gwen, standing in front of her, speaking about them as if they were still an open-ended mystery.

Matilda could feel the weight of something unresolved pressing down on her, as if a door she thought had been firmly shut had suddenly creaked open again. If Gwen knew something about Bernard and Alois meeting with this Emmerich person, then maybe she knew more, maybe she held the missing piece of a puzzle that Matilda had long given up trying to solve.

And, if she were being honest, she felt something else too.

A stirring of excitement.

The feeling of an adventure looming.

Matilda's lips curled into a slow smile. "Why don't I grab you a drink, Gwen? You can come over and sit with us."

Gwen hesitated for only a moment before nodding. "That would be lovely."

Matilda signalled to the bartender for another drink before leading Gwen back to the table.

"Sissy, this is Gwen Noble. She used to work for Alois Pfeiffer."

Kathleen extended her hand. "Nice to meet you, Gwen."

"Likewise," Gwen replied as she took a seat, her eyes flickering with something Matilda couldn't quite place, curiosity, perhaps, or maybe something deeper.

What started as a lighthearted lunch quickly turned into a conversation laden with intrigue.

Gwen had once worked closely with Alois, but as she admitted, he never truly confided in her. Still, his habit of leaving things lying around had granted her unintentional access to pieces of a much larger puzzle, one that Matilda hadn't even realised they were still trying to solve.

Gwen leaned in, her voice dropping to a near whisper as she recounted what she had come across over the years.

Letters from corporate investigators, detailing a company's persistent attempts to purchase Girraween, as it was believed that the diamonds are hidden there. At Girraween! This information had caused Matilda to snort in her drink and nearly choke

Gwen went on, letters from the War Crimes Documentation Centres in Nuremberg and Venice, revealing something even more startling:

The Petryczek's were not who they claimed to be.

They were, in reality, the Reimer's, a family that had been under investigation for decades. The letters suggested that the Reimer's

Max Barrington

were believed to be in possession of over £12 million worth of diamonds, stolen from the Third Reich in the final days of the war.

And then there was the most chilling revelation of all.

The documents suggested that Waffen-SS SS-Oberführer Axel Heinrich Emmerich had been sent to Australia with a mission, to eliminate the Reimer's and retrieve the stolen diamonds.

Matilda and Kathleen exchanged glances, their meals momentarily forgotten.

But Gwen wasn't finished.

Among Alois's scattered papers, she had also found scribbled notes, seemingly harmless at first glance, but now, in this moment, carrying an undeniable weight.

One note read: "Remind Bernard to bring the gun for tonight."

Another was a hand-drawn map, a simple sketch of the interior of a house.

And on that map, in the first bedroom, a small cross was marked on the bed.

The implications hung heavy in the air.

By the time they finished their last drinks, it was almost five o'clock, but Matilda's mind was racing.

The drive home was unusually quiet. The late afternoon sun cast long shadows across the open fields, the golden hues of the landscape rolling past them in a familiar yet somehow distant blur. Each sister was lost in her own thoughts, contemplating the weight of the revelations Gwen had laid before them.

They had each bought a tall bottle for the journey, the rhythmic clinking of glass the only sound breaking the silence between them.

It wasn't until they were well out of town, the Royal Hotel now just a memory in the rearview mirror, that Kathleen finally spoke.

She turned to Matilda with an enormous grin, eyes twinkling with mischief and knowing.

"Alright, Maddy, what is it that you're keeping from me?"

Matilda had to laugh. She should have known better than to think she could hide anything from her sister.

"You always were a sharp one, Sissy."

By the time they turned onto the long dirt driveway leading to Girraween, the sun dipping low behind the homestead, Matilda had told her everything about how she and Bernard had found the gun and the dagger, and she told of the searches that they had for the diamonds, but had given up believing the diamonds to be just a small amount that was probably just enough for the Petryczek's, or who ever they were, to buy their farm. "But!..Hey!…£12 million….well..fuck me!..that's now twenty four million dollars in Australian!"

She went on talking about every fragment of information that they had now heard today, every whispered clue, every lingering question that had resurfaced over the course of their afternoon with Gwen.

The diamonds. The false identities. The assassination orders. The cryptic map.

As the dust settled behind their car and they pulled up to the house, they exchanged a look.

Tonight wasn't going to be like any other night.

Tonight, they were making plans. Serious plans. But both agreed, the search would have to wait.

With Lindsay and Alison still home on leave, along with their friends, there were too many eyes and too many questions. It would be impossible to keep their curiosity under wraps with a house full of young, sharp-eyed military personnel. Better to wait until next week, once the kids had returned to duty.

In the meantime, they had plenty to do.

"We should go to the library in Dalby tomorrow," Kathleen suggested as she poured herself another drink. "There are books on house searching, you know. We had them for training in the police force."

Matilda raised an eyebrow. "They actually teach you that?"

Kathleen smirked. "Of course. What, did you think detectives just stumble around opening drawers?"

Matilda chuckled, but her mind was already spinning with ideas. There had to be a method to this, some kind of system to make sure they didn't miss anything.

Then, as she swirled the last of her whiskey in her glass, she hesitated before voicing a thought that had been nagging at her.

"Do you think it would be silly to bring in a psychic?"

Kathleen looked up sharply, then surprised Matilda by grinning.

"Actually, I think that's a brilliant idea. The only problem is, where the hell do we find one?"

That, as it turned out, was an easier problem to solve than expected.

Flipping through an old copy of the Courier Mail, they found a few psychics advertising their services. Some sounded like proper mediums, others seemed like charlatans, but it was worth a shot.

Matilda jotted down a couple of names and numbers. Tomorrow, she'd make some calls.

Whether they found anything or not, one thing was certain, things at Girraween were about to get very interesting.

The next morning, after a leisurely breakfast, the kids announced their plans for the day.

"We're heading out swimming," Alison said, tying her hair into a quick ponytail. "All five of us."

Lindsay, already in his swim shorts, tossed a towel over his shoulder. "Yeah, figured we'd make a day of it. The water should be perfect."

Matilda and Kathleen exchanged a glance, both pleased to see how well the group was getting along. There was an easy camaraderie between them, a bond formed not just through family but through shared military life.

Alison grabbed the keys to her mother's Holden Kingswood, flashing a grin as she twirled them around her finger. "We'll be back in time for dinner. And by the way, steak sounds really good."

Lindsay gave a thumbs-up. "Don't overcook mine."

With that, they were off, piling into the car with laughter and the kind of energy that came with youth and a day of adventure ahead. As the sound of the engine faded down the driveway, Matilda turned to Kathleen with a knowing smile.

"Well, that gives us the whole day to ourselves."

Kathleen leaned against the kitchen counter, arms crossed. "Library first?"

Matilda nodded. "Library first. Then, if we have time, I'll make those calls to the psychics."

The library had been a disappointment.

"Nothing useful?" Matilda asked as Kathleen closed yet another book with a sigh.

"Nope. But the book I need is in Toowoomba," Kathleen replied, tapping her fingers on the counter. "They can send it here next week for free, or if I pay $1.20, I can have it on the overnight bag service and pick it up tomorrow morning."

Matilda didn't even hesitate. "Pay the $1.20."

Kathleen smirked and handed over the money, knowing that Matilda was just as eager to get started as she was.

That afternoon, Matilda made the calls to the two psychics she had found advertised in an old copy of The Courier-Mail. The first was polite but uninterested. The second, however, showed some curiosity, though not without conditions.

"If you cover my rail fare each way and provide accommodation, I'll consider it," the woman stated bluntly over the phone. "Hotel accommodation, that is. I do not stay in private houses."

Matilda raised an eyebrow at Kathleen, who was listening in with an amused expression.

"That's fine," Matilda agreed without argument. "I'll book a room for you."

The psychic promptly gave Matilda her bank account details and insisted on a deposit before making any travel arrangements.

As Matilda hung up the phone, Kathleen chuckled. "She sounds charming."

Matilda rolled her eyes. "If she's the real deal, she can be as difficult as she likes."

Kathleen leaned back in her chair, stretching. "Well, between the book and our psychic friend, things are moving along. Now, all we have to do is wait."

"Yes, the kids go back next Monday morning, we'll collect your book in the morning and I will pay the psychics deposit into the bank while we are in town. The psychic will be here next Wednesday….so…it's all happening.

                                                    Max Barrington

Monday morning was a whirlwind of activity. It had taken both cars, Matilda's trusty Kingswood and Kathleen's reliable Falcon, to get all five soldiers to the train station in time for their journey to Brisbane. From there, they would board their respective flights to their final destinations.

The drive to the station had been filled with last-minute chatter, laughter, and promises to write or call when they could. Hugs were exchanged, and Alison gave her mother an extra squeeze before shouldering her bag and following the others onto the platform.

As the train pulled away, Matilda and Kathleen stood for a moment, watching until it disappeared down the tracks. They both felt a sense of pride seeing them off, but as they turned back to their cars, there was also a shared understanding, having the kids home had been wonderful, but the return to normalcy would be welcome too.

By the time they arrived back at Girraween, the house was already beginning to settle back into its usual quiet rhythm. The weekend's chaos faded, replaced by the familiar calm of the homestead. The cattle still needed tending, the books still needed balancing, and now, there were plans to finalise.

Matilda stretched as she stepped out of the car. "Well, that was a hectic few days."

Kathleen grinned. "It certainly was. But now we can finally focus on what's ahead."

Matilda nodded, a glint of excitement in her eyes. "Exactly. It's time to start searching, where is the book?"

They both sat on the plush leather lounge with a beer in one hand as Kathleen read from Chapter 7 in the book

Chapter 7: Conducting a Thorough House Search

When searching a house for a hidden item, whether it be a document, jewellery, cash, or an antique, a systematic and methodical approach is essential. This chapter provides a structured plan to guide your search, detailing both obvious and less apparent hiding places that people commonly use.

1. Preparing for the Search

Before you begin, consider the following:

Gather Necessary Tools: A flashlight, gloves (to prevent leaving fingerprints or disturbing evidence), a small mirror for hard-to-see areas, a magnet for detecting hidden metal objects, and a notebook for recording findings.

Assess the House Layout: Understanding the structure of the home, including rooms, crawl spaces, and potential secret compartments, will make your search more efficient.

Think Like the Owner: Where would you hide something valuable if you were trying to keep it safe or concealed? Consider the most secure yet accessible locations.

2. Common Hiding Places

Certain areas are commonly used to store valuables. Begin your search here:

Furniture and Fixtures:

Underneath and Inside Drawers: Feel underneath drawers for taped or magnetised items. Remove the drawers to check behind them.

False Bottoms or Hidden Compartments: Desks, dressers, and wardrobes often have these.

Inside Chairs and Couches: Check under seat cushions and look for zippers or access panels.

Behind Loose Panels in Bookcases or Cabinets: Tap surfaces to detect hollow areas.

Under or Inside Beds: Look for false bottoms in storage compartments.

Walls and Structural Elements:

Inside Air Vents or Ducts: Use a flashlight to inspect inside.

Behind Electrical Outlets or Light Switch Covers: Sometimes, people remove the cover and create a cavity.

In Attics and Crawl Spaces: These are often overlooked and used for safekeeping.

Inside Wall Safes or Behind Wall Hangings: Feel behind paintings, mirrors, or large wall clocks.

Under Floorboards or Carpets: If there's a suspiciously loose floorboard or raised carpet, investigate further.

Kitchen and Pantry Areas:

Inside Cereal Boxes or Food Containers: Some people store valuables inside sealed food containers.

Behind the Refrigerator or Oven: Move appliances slightly to check behind them.

Inside or Behind the Dishwasher: Some models have removable kick plates that reveal cavities.

Bathrooms:

Inside the Toilet Tank: Lift the lid carefully and check inside.

Behind Tiles or Inside the Medicine Cabinet: Loose tiles may indicate a hiding space.

Inside Rolls of Toilet Paper or Feminine Product Boxes: These can conceal small items.

Unusual and Overlooked Spots:

Inside Vacuum Cleaner Bags or Old Appliances: Old electronics and machinery sometimes contain stashed items.

Inside Books: Check for hollowed-out books or stacks of paper glued together with a cavity inside.

Buried in Potted Plants: Some hide valuables under soil in plant pots.

Taped Behind Large Furniture Pieces: Check the back of heavy cabinets and paintings.

In Ceiling Tiles: If the house has a drop ceiling, lift tiles to inspect above them.

3. Searching the Exterior

If the search inside the house is unsuccessful, move outside:

Inside Garages and Sheds: Look inside toolboxes, behind shelves, and under loose floorboards.

Beneath Decking or Porches: Items might be stashed inside hollow spaces.

Inside Mailboxes or Outdoor Light Fixtures: Small containers may be hidden here.

In Garden Statues or Fountains: Some have removable tops or compartments.

4. Advanced Techniques for Finding Hidden Items

Use a Blacklight or UV Light: This can reveal hidden writing or fingerprints.

Metal Detector: This helps locate metallic items within walls, floors, and outdoor areas.

Listening Devices: Tapping walls and floors can help detect hollow areas.

5. Organising and Documenting Your Search

As you go through the house:

Take Notes: Record where you've searched to avoid repetition.

Photograph Findings: If needed, document compartments or suspicious areas.

Restore the Area: If you move or dismantle anything, put it back as you found it to avoid raising suspicion.

6. When to Call in Professionals

If the item remains unfound and is of significant value, hiring a professional investigator or locksmith might be necessary. They have specialised tools and experience in uncovering hidden compartments.

Conclusion

A well-executed search requires patience, attention to detail, and methodical exploration. By following this structured approach and keeping an open mind to unconventional hiding spots, you increase your chances of successfully locating hidden items within a house.

"Well!... where do we start?" Matilda prompted, glancing around the room with an eager grin.

"At the fridge, I think!..." Kathleen quipped, and they both burst into laughter.

"I think we should photocopy the pages and mark items off as we search them. What do you think?" she suggested, looking toward the kitchen bench where Matilda was opening another bottle of beer.

Matilda paused mid-pour, considering the idea. "That's actually a really good idea. It'll keep us organised, and we won't end up searching the same places twice. Let's do it!"

With their plan set, they began at the front door. Facing the hallway, they turned left into the front lounge room, deciding to work methodically, starting from the left, moving clockwise around the room.

"Okay," called Kathleen, reading from their list of common hiding places. "Underneath and inside drawers... What about the drawers in the stereo cabinet?"

Matilda shook her head. "That wasn't here back then, Kath."

"All right, let's try inside chairs and couches!" Kathleen suggested.

Matilda nodded and immediately tipped over one of the old, worn, but still incredibly comfortable, lounge chairs for a closer inspection.

Following the book's suggested procedures for conducting a thorough search, they carefully examined each item in the lounge room. However, they decided to leave the inspection of the two power points for later, as it would require turning off the electricity, and they preferred to check all of them at once when the time came.

By the time they finished their meticulous search of the room, they felt confident they had covered every possible hiding spot. Their most notable discovery was a delicate gold chain, wedged in a narrow crack beneath the skirting board. It was fine and almost imperceptible, but the glint of gold against the wooden floor had caught Matilda's sharp eye.

Satisfied with their efforts, they agreed that they had done a thorough job in this room. With the psychic due to arrive the next morning, they decided to put the rest of the search on hold until after her visit. After all, who knew? If the psychic was as good as she claimed, they might not have to search at all.

The psychic said that she would be wearing a blue and white long dress, to help Matilda recognise her at the station. She didn't say that she had tattoo's on her face, neck and arms.

Matilda and Kathleen, were standing on the platform at Dalby Station, scanning the arriving passengers as they stepped down from the train. Then she saw her.

The woman stood out immediately, Kathleen muttered softy "fuck me", not just because of her flowing blue and white dress, which billowed slightly in the breeze, but because of the intricate tattoos that adorned her face, neck, and arms. The inked patterns were striking, swirling symbols and delicate geometric designs that seemed to have cultural significance, though

Matilda couldn't place them. The tattoos on her face were the most fascinating, thin, elegant lines tracing along her cheekbones and forehead, accentuating her sharp features.

Her hair was jet black, streaked with silver strands, and tied back in a loose braid that rested over one shoulder. Deep-set, piercing green eyes flickered around the platform before settling on Matilda. She carried herself with an air of confidence, gliding forward with a graceful but purposeful stride. Around her neck hung several beaded necklaces, some adorned with small charms that caught the afternoon light.

"You must be Matilda," the woman said in a low, almost melodic voice.

Matilda nodded. "And you must be, "

"Call me Odette," she interrupted with a slight smile, her eyes glinting as if she already knew what Matilda was about to say.

Matilda, momentarily taken aback by the woman's abrupt manner, quickly recovered and introduced Kathleen. Kathleen, ever skeptical, simply gave a curt nod in Odette's direction and muttered under her breath, "Odd alright," as they made their way to the Kingswood. Matilda shot her sister a look but said nothing.

The drive out to Girraween was quiet, save for the hum of the car's engine and the occasional clatter of gravel beneath the tires. Odette sat in the back seat, gazing out the window, her fingers lightly tracing the patterns of her tattoos as if lost in thought. She hadn't said much at all, until they turned into the driveway.

As the sign bearing the name Girraween came into view, Odette suddenly sat bolt upright. "Fuck me…" she muttered, her voice hushed but unmistakably awed. Then, with more force, she repeated, "Fucking mooneee." The words rolled off her tongue with a strange reverence, as if she had just stumbled upon something significant.

Kathleen raised an eyebrow but kept her thoughts to herself as Matilda pulled the car up to the homestead.

Once inside, Matilda, in an attempt to lighten the mood and bring a sense of normalcy to the situation, offered tea. "How about a cup before we get into anything?" she suggested, hoping to ease Odette into conversation.

Odette's expression shifted slightly, and she gave a small, approving nod. "Do you have pu-erh or chai?" she asked, her voice measured, as if already anticipating disappointment.

Kathleen let out a short, dry laugh. "Just good old Bushells," she replied, unable to hide her amusement.

Odette pursed her lips and, without a word, reached into the folds of her flowing blue-and-white dress, retrieving a small cloth pouch. "No worries," she murmured, as she began preparing her own tea. Kathleen rolled her eyes towards Matilda, who chose to ignore the gesture.

They sat at the kitchen table, the air thick with the mingling aromas of strong black tea and Odette's more exotic brew. The women nibbled at cream cakes filled with raspberry jam, an indulgence they had picked up from the bakery in town earlier that day. It was a surprisingly pleasant moment of quiet, until Odette, in a calm but direct manner, broke the silence.

"So," she said, placing her cup down with deliberate care. "What is it that you're hoping to find in this house today?"

There was something about her tone, something steady and assured, that made Matilda pause for a moment. Odette didn't sound skeptical or dismissive. She sounded as though she already knew something.

Matilda opened her mouth to answer, but barely got as far as "Di, " before Kathleen, with her usual bluntness, finished the sentence for her.

"Diamonds," she said plainly. "A few, in a small bag, we believe. Just a few…" Her words trailed off as Odette abruptly pushed back her chair and stood up.

The movement was so sudden, so unexpected, that both Matilda and Kathleen froze. Odette's posture had stiffened, her hands clenching at her sides as she drew in a slow breath. When she spoke again, her voice was low, measured, but filled with unmistakable urgency.

"It is not a few diamonds," she said gravely. "It is a very large quantity of diamonds. And my advice to you, " she looked directly at Matilda now, her dark eyes unwavering, ", is to leave them alone."

Kathleen scoffed. "And why's that?"

Odette didn't blink. "Because it is not good to look for these diamonds. There is something gravely wrong with them." She took another breath, as though steadying herself, before continuing. "They do not belong to you. They were never meant to be found. I reiterate, you should desist in this search, or they shall bring grief."

The kitchen fell silent. Matilda and Kathleen exchanged glances, neither quite sure what to make of Odette's sudden shift in demeanour.

Then, as abruptly as she had stood, Odette reached into the sleeve of her dress and withdrew a small, coloured handkerchief, dabbing lightly at her forehead. She inhaled deeply, composing herself, and then, in a tone far softer than before, said, "I'm sorry. Please take me back to the station. I cannot help you. This is far too dangerous."

Odette sat silently in the back seat as Matilda drove her toward the railway station. Kathleen had insisted on coming along, unwilling to let Matilda be alone with the peculiar psychic. She simply didn't trust Odette. There was something off about her, the way she had reacted so strongly back at the house, her sudden shift from intrigue to outright fear. It didn't sit right with Kathleen.

Matilda, keeping her focus on the road, finally broke the silence. "You'll return the deposit?" she asked, though her tone made it clear she didn't expect much of an answer.

Kathleen scoffed. "We'll write off the train fare and hotel booking as experience," she muttered, folding her arms. "But she should at least do the decent thing and return the deposit."

Odette remained completely still, her expression unreadable in the rearview mirror. She didn't acknowledge their words, didn't even turn her head. It was as if she had already left the conversation, retreating into some private space within herself.

When they pulled up in front of the station entrance, Matilda shifted the car into park. Without a word, Odette opened the door, stepped out, and, carrying her small bag, walked away without so much as a glance back.

Kathleen watched her disappear through the station doors and then exhaled sharply. "Fucking strange bitch," she muttered, shaking her head.

The drive back to Girraween that afternoon was unusually quiet. The excitement and sense of adventure that had fuelled their search earlier in the day had vanished, replaced by an unshakable heaviness. Odette's abrupt departure and ominous warning lingered in their minds, casting a shadow over their plans.

Kathleen stared out the window, arms folded, deep in thought. After a while, she reached over and placed a reassuring hand on

Matilda's leg. "I think it's time we opened that bottle of Para Port that Lindsay brought home on leave," she suggested, her tone light but purposeful.

Matilda glanced at her, and after a brief pause, a slow smile spread across her face. "If that doesn't make us giggle, then nothing will," she agreed.

Kathleen chuckled softly, and for the first time since leaving the station, the tension between them eased. Whatever lay ahead, at least they could face it with a drink in hand, and, hopefully, a little laughter to chase away the lingering unease.

BRRRRINNNGG! BRRRRINNNGG!

BRRRRINNNGG! BRRRRINNNGG!

The sharp, piercing ring of the telephone shattered the silence of the early morning.

Matilda jolted awake, her heart pounding in her chest. Disoriented and filled with an inexplicable sense of dread, she forced herself to sit up. The shrill ringing continued, relentless and demanding.

BRRRRINNNGG! BRRRRINNNGG!

BRRRRINNNGG! BRRRRINNNGG!

Matilda swung her legs over the edge of the bed, hesitating for a fraction of a second before pushing herself up. Every instinct told her she didn't want to answer that call. Wrapping her dressing gown tightly around her, she stepped into the dimly lit hallway.

Each ring sent a spike of anxiety through her, but she kept moving, her bare feet soundless against the wooden floorboards. Reaching the phone, she hesitated again. The room felt colder. A deep sense of foreboding settled in her chest.

Her fingers hovered over the receiver. Then, just as the phone rang again, she snatched it up and pressed it to her ear.

She opened her mouth to say "Hello," but before she could speak, a voice, crackling with static, cut through the line.

"Mrs. Collins?" The voice was distant, distorted. "Hello? Mrs. Collins?"

Matilda swallowed hard. "Yes… Yes, this is Mrs. Collins. Who's calling, please?"

There was a pause, followed by another burst of static.

"Hello?" she repeated, gripping the phone tighter.

Then the voice came through, clearer this time.

"Mrs. Collins, I am Lieutenant Commander Roland Blakely from Sea Command, Canberra. Look!… We have a situation following an exercise off Nowra, on the New South Wales, South Coast this morning."

Matilda's breath caught in her throat.

"There are a few of the lads missing from an overturned boat. Your son, Lindsay, is one of the men we are searching for."

She clutched the receiver, her knuckles turning white.

"At this stage, it is a rescue mission," he continued, his tone firm but urgent. "I reiterate, it is a rescue mission. We will keep you informed of the mission's progress."

Matilda opened her mouth to respond, but no words came. The room spun. Her legs buckled. The last thing she heard was the Lieutenant Commander's voice still speaking as darkness swallowed her whole.

Much later that day, a navy-blue Ford Fairlane pulled into the driveway at Girraween, its tires crunching against the gravel. The afternoon sun cast long shadows as Captain Vincent Scott stepped out, adjusting his cap before making his way to the front door.

By then, Matilda already knew. She had felt it the moment she had come to, lying on the hallway floor with Kathleen kneeling beside her. She had felt it in the empty silence of the house, in the hollow ache deep in her chest.

When she opened the door, the confirmation came in a steady, practiced voice.

"Mrs. Collins, I regret to inform you…"

The words blurred. The details faded. All she could process was the undeniable, earth-shattering truth.

Lindsay was gone.

Drowned during naval exercises.

Her boy. Her son.

Matilda swayed, her breath ragged. Kathleen caught her just as her legs gave way.

Matilda lay motionless on her bed, staring at the ceiling as if it might somehow absorb the weight of the words she had just heard. The room was heavy with silence, but inside her head, a deafening roar had taken hold, waves crashing, voices echoing, memories flickering like an old film reel.

Captain Vincent Scott had spoken with solemn precision, delivering the news with the detached professionalism expected of a man in his position. Yet, through it all, Matilda had not flinched. She had not nodded, not spoken, not even blinked. It was as if she had turned to stone the moment he uttered the words:

"Lindsay Collins has drowned during naval exercises."

Kathleen stood nearby, watching her sister with growing concern. Had Matilda even heard him? Could she hear anything at all? The news was too vast, too devastating to comprehend. She wasn't crying, wasn't shaking, wasn't reacting.

Kathleen didn't know which was worse, the wailing grief she had expected or this eerie, hollow stillness.

The captain lingered for a moment, as if waiting for some response that never came. Finally, he exhaled softly and turned toward the car.

Kathleen followed him, her emotions a tangled mess of anger, sorrow, and pity. She couldn't fault the man for doing his job, but God, what a wretched job it was. Did he have to do this often? How many doors had he knocked on today? How many mothers had he left broken?

He paused at the car, his voice low and sincere. "I am so sorry."

Kathleen said nothing. There were no words that could make a difference now as she walked towards the front door. She stood there, gripping the doorknob, staring blankly at the floor. Then, with a deep breath, she turned on her heel and strode into the kitchen.

There was only one thing left to do.

Reaching for the bottle of Glenfiddich, she pulled two heavy glasses from the cabinet, filled them with ice, and poured a generous measure into each. If anything could thaw the unbearable numbness settling over the house, it was this.

She picked up the glasses and walked back toward Matilda's room, bracing herself for whatever came next.

Nowra Post :

11 Sailors Missing After Naval Craft Capsizes Near Jervis Bay

Eleven sailors are missing this morning following the capsizing of a naval craft near Jervis Bay late last night. The incident occurred during a routine training exercise, with search and rescue teams deployed at first light to locate the missing crew members.

Naval authorities have confirmed that the craft overturned in rough conditions, and while several personnel were recovered safely, efforts continue to find the remaining sailors.

"The search is ongoing, and we are doing everything possible to locate them," a Navy spokesperson said. "Our thoughts are with the families during this difficult time."

More updates to follow as the situation develops.

The tragic incident near Jervis Bay had sent shockwaves through the Australian Defence Force Academy and the wider naval community. Eleven sailors, all young cadets from the academy, had been aboard the naval craft when it capsized in rough seas during what was meant to be a routine training exercise. The unforgiving waters showed no mercy, and despite an extensive search operation that lasted several days, only four bodies were recovered before authorities were forced to call off the mission.

Among those still missing was Lindsay Collins. The news of the accident devastated his family, who clung to hope even as days stretched into weeks without any sign of him. The ocean had claimed its own, and with no closure, they were left to mourn without a body to lay to rest.

The loss of the young sailors was a stark reminder of the risks that came with service, even during training. The Defence Force conducted a thorough investigation into the circumstances surrounding the capsizing, but no explanation could soften the blow for the families who would never see their loved ones again. Jervis Bay, with its deep blue waters and rugged coastline, would forever hold the unanswered questions and the memories of those who had been lost.

A memorial service for Lindsay Collins was held at Saint Luke's Church in Dalby, drawing family, friends, and members of the local community who came together to honour his life and service. The church was filled with solemn faces, many struggling to come to terms with the tragic loss.

A framed photograph of Lindsey in his naval uniform stood at the front of the church, surrounded by white lilies and the Australian flag draped over a table. His family comprising his mother, sister and aunty sat in quiet grief as hymns filled the air, the weight of her absence felt deeply by all who knew him.

Representatives from the Australian Defence Force Academy attended in full dress uniform, paying tribute to their fallen comrade. A senior officer delivered a heartfelt eulogy, speaking of Lindsay's dedication, courage, and the bright future that had been cut short. Friends shared memories of his warmth, determination, and unwavering spirit, painting a picture of a young man who had inspired those around him.

As the service drew to a close, the Last Post echoed through the church, a final salute to a life lost too soon. Mourners embraced one another, offering comfort in their shared sorrow. Though Lindsay's body had never been recovered, his memory would live on in the hearts of those who loved him, forever honoured in the town he had called home.

Matilda sat at the kitchen table, absently running a comb through her hair, her gaze distant as she spoke.

"Do you think the psychic really knew something?" Her voice was quiet, almost hesitant. "I mean... was what happened to

Lindsay really just an accident? Or do you think there's a connection? A… coincidence, would you say?"

Kathleen, standing at the kitchen bench, let out a sharp breath and shook her head.

"Please, Matilda, stop talking shit," she snapped, though not unkindly. "And for God's sake, stop combing your hair at the kitchen table. You know I hate that."

She pulled a rolling pin from the drawer with a little more force than necessary and placed a ball of dough onto the floured surface. "Besides, you're going to have to move anyway, I need this space to roll out pastry for my pies."

She gave Matilda a pointed look.

"Come on, shift."

Matilda exhaled and set the comb down, pushing herself up from the chair. She moved slowly, as if weighed down by something unseen, but she said nothing more.

The room fell into silence, except for the rhythmic scrape of the rolling pin against the kitchen table.

Matilda drifted into the lounge room, sinking into the well-worn armchair as her mind wandered back to Lindsay's funeral. The memory hit her like a wave, overwhelming and relentless. She could still see the crisp navy uniforms, the solemn faces, the flag-draped table. Parents should never have to bury their children, she thought bitterly, and before she could stop herself, the tears came again, silent but heavy.

From the kitchen, Kathleen's sharp voice cut through the quiet.

"That's enough of that, Maddy!" she called, her tone firm but not unkind. "I can hear you in there. Come on, pull yourself together and stop feeling sorry for yourself!"

Matilda wiped at her face, but the grief clung to her like a second skin.

Kathleen wasn't done. "I mean it, Maddy. We've got a graduation to go to soon, and I am not sitting in a car all day with you if you're going to be like this!"

Matilda took a shaky breath, staring at her hands. Kathleen had always been the practical one, the one who wouldn't let emotions take over. She wasn't heartless; she just refused to let grief steal more than it already had.

With effort, Matilda swallowed back the sob that threatened to escape. She knew Kathleen was right. Lindsay was gone, and nothing would change that. But life, no matter how painful, kept moving forward. And somehow, she had to keep up.

Matilda stood by the car as she spoke to Rob, the new manager at Girraween, who had come around to the house to see Matilda and Kathleen before they headed off.

"Don't forget to feed Gypsy and Spud," she reminded him for the third time. "And make sure they get their biscuits in the evening. I'll call you every afternoon to check in, just to, "

"For fuck's sake, Maddy!" Kathleen's exasperated voice cut through the air. "Leave the poor man alone! He's over twenty-one, I'm pretty damn sure he can survive for two weeks without you Molly-coddling him. Now get in the fucking car before I go without you… and I mean it!"

Matilda sighed but she climbed into the passenger seat of the Statesman. Kathleen, wasting no time, threw the car into gear, Shouted "See yer Rob!" and turned down the driveway, heading toward the Dalby-Chinchilla Road.

"Canberra, here we come!" she shouted suddenly, making Matilda jump in her seat.

"Bloody hell, Kath! A little warning would be nice," Matilda huffed, gripping the door handle.

Kathleen just grinned. "Buckle up, sister. It's a long drive, and I plan on making good time."

The road trip from Dalby to Canberra was a long one, 1,140 kilometres of open highway, winding country roads, and stretches of near-empty landscapes. Rather than pushing through in a single exhausting haul, they had decided to take it slow, breaking the journey into three days and two nights. It wasn't just about making the trip more comfortable; it was also about keeping things light.

Kathleen, ever the practical one, knew that with the big 308 V8 under the hood of the Statesman, they could have easily done it with just one overnight stop. The car had power to spare, and the ride was smooth enough to make the distance bearable. But she also knew that spending too many hours in the car alone with Matilda would eventually lead to the conversation she was trying to avoid, the one about Lindsay. It was inevitable. Grief had a way of creeping in during quiet moments, and Kathleen didn't want to spend the whole trip watching her sister sink into another wave of sadness.

By stretching the journey out, there would be more stops, more distractions, and fewer long silences where Matilda's mind could drift back to the weight of her loss. That was the plan, at least. Whether or not it would work remained to be seen.

Canberra was breathtaking this time of year. The crisp air carried the scent of eucalyptus, and the city's tree-lined avenues were awash with autumn hues, their reds and golds painting a picture of quiet elegance. Matilda and Kathleen had checked into the Hotel Ainslie Rex, one of Canberra's older establishments. Though its décor carried whispers of another era, its charm and sophistication remained intact. More importantly, it was conveniently close to the Australian Defence Force Academy (ADFA), where the upcoming graduation ceremony would take place at the Adams Auditorium.

Kathleen was no stranger to Canberra she had spent many years of her time stationed here during her stint with the Australian Federal Police. It was the place of her recruitment as a female trainee at the Canberra AFP (Australian Federal Police) Training Academy, she underwent a rigorous and structured training program designed to prepare recruits for various roles within the AFP.

She had spent around 24 weeks at the academy, undergoing intensive physical fitness training, firearms handling, defensive tactics, and scenario-based exercises. Classroom sessions covered criminal law, investigation techniques, ethics, and operational safety. She had also trained in communication skills, mental resilience, and cultural awareness to handle the diverse challenges of law enforcement.

Life at the academy was very highly disciplined, with strict schedules, assessments, and teamwork exercises. Kathleen was expected to develop critical thinking, adaptability, and leadership skills. By the end of the program, she had graduated and was deployed to her designated AFP unit, which included general policing, counter-terrorism, cybercrime, and international operations.

That first evening, Alison and her friend Pippa met them for dinner, their excitement palpable. Conversation flitted between the graduation and the girls' much-anticipated holiday to Thailand, their enthusiasm infectious. The restaurant hummed with life, but at their table, the focus was entirely on the milestones ahead.

The following morning was dedicated to exploring the Australian Capital Territory, a chance for Matilda and Kathleen to immerse themselves in the sights before the formalities of the graduation. With an itinerary packed full of sightseeing, celebrations, and quality time with loved ones, their short stay in Canberra was shaping up to be both full and fulfilling.

They couldn't resist the pull of nostalgia, and despite the years that had passed, a journey over the border to Queanbeyan, the town of their birth, felt like a pilgrimage. The first stop was Rutledge Street, a place filled with memories. They parked the car and stepped out, the cool breeze carrying the faint echoes of a time long gone. They walked slowly along the street, their eyes scanning the familiar surroundings, each step stirring the past.

At the spot where their father, Ralph, had once pounded leather, shaping saddles with his skilled hands, they paused. It had been his trade, his craft, and now, it seemed almost like a ghost of his presence lingered in the air. Their mother, Mabel, had worked alongside him, mending and altering clothes, adding her own quiet artistry to the fabric of their lives.

Max Barrington

The small workshop, once alive with the hum of sewing machines and the smell of leather, was now just a memory. The building where it had all taken place had long since changed, but in their minds, it was as vivid as ever. They both stood there for a moment, lost in thought, remembering the countless hours spent in that humble space, where their parents had worked tirelessly to make ends meet and create a life for them.

Next, they made their way to Donald Road, and as they drove, the changes became more apparent with every passing street. The neighbourhood they had once known was unrecognisable. When they finally arrived at number twenty-nine, they were taken aback, what had once been a modest home was now an impressive mansion. It stood tall and imposing, its grandeur a stark contrast to the humble dwelling they remembered.

The sight of the house itself felt distant, almost like a dream. The walls, the garden, the small details that once made it home had faded in their memory. But what really struck them was how unfamiliar the entire area had become. Where once there had been rows of simple homes, now sat sprawling modern residences, many of them far larger and more extravagant than they could have ever imagined.

As they stood there, taking it all in, a wave of emotion washed over them. They paused, reflecting on the past, on the lives of their parents who had once lived in that house. It was here, in this very spot, that their beloved mother and father had both passed away forty-four years ago. Despite the sea of change around them, this was still their parents' home, an anchor to their past, a place where so many memories had been made.

They stood silently for a moment, each lost in their thoughts, honouring the place that had shaped so much of their early lives. The house, now surrounded by a sea of new structures, still held the echoes of their parents' laughter, love, and hard work. It was a bittersweet reminder of the passage of time.

Graduation day was nothing short of spectacular. As Alison stepped onto the grand stage of the Adams Auditorium to receive her doctorate, both Matilda and Kathleen swelled with pride. Seeing her in her academic regalia, the culmination of years of hard work and dedication, was a moment they would never forget. The applause that echoed through the vast hall was well-deserved, and Matilda couldn't help but wipe away a tear as she watched her daughter achieve such an incredible milestone.

That evening, the graduation dinner at Albert Hall was equally magnificent. The historic venue, with its elegant chandeliers and polished wooden floors, provided a perfect backdrop for the celebration. The atmosphere was one of joy and accomplishment, with proud families, distinguished faculty, and newly minted graduates coming together to toast to success. The night was filled with laughter, heartfelt speeches, and the clinking of champagne glasses, a fitting end to such a momentous occasion.

The following morning, however, was far from leisurely. Matilda and Kathleen had promised to take Alison and Pippa to the airport for their connecting flight to Sydney, where they would board their long-haul journey to Thailand. The excitement of their upcoming adventure mingled with the bittersweet feeling of parting, but amidst the flurry of packing, last-minute checks, and hurried goodbyes, there was an undeniable sense of pride.

As they watched the girls disappear through the airport gates, Matilda and Kathleen exchanged a glance, exhausted but happy. This trip had been an emotional whirlwind, but for now, their focus shifted back to the long journey home.

Incredibly, not much had changed at Girraween in Matilda's absence. The sprawling property remained as it had always been, peaceful, steady, and seemingly untouched by time. The familiar scent of eucalyptus still hung in the warm air, and the golden afternoon light stretched lazily across the paddocks, casting long shadows over the homestead.

Rob, the manager, had coped reasonably well without Matilda's watchful eye. Though she had called regularly to check in, perhaps more often than necessary, he had taken everything in stride, ensuring that the daily operations continued without a hitch. The Dobermans, Gypsy and Spud, were well-fed and as lively as ever, greeting Matilda with enthusiastic barks as she stepped out of the car.

Despite her initial concerns, it was clear that Girraween had managed just fine. And while Matilda would never admit it out loud, there was a certain relief in knowing that the world hadn't fallen apart in her absence.

As they lugged their bags through the front door and into the hallway, the sharp, jarring sound of the telephone shattered the quiet afternoon air.

BRRRRINNNGG! BRRRRINNNGG!
BRRRRINNNGG! BRRRRINNNGG!

Kathleen, still lost in thoughts of their trip to Canberra, flinched at the sudden noise. She was almost level with the telephone desk when it rang, the unexpected sound making her heart jump. "I've got it!" she called over her shoulder to Matilda, setting down the bag she was carrying.

Lifting the receiver to her ear, she barely had time to say hello before the voice on the other end spoke. It was the Dalby Police. They had been trying to reach Matilda all morning.

A sense of unease slithered through Kathleen's chest. "What is it?" she asked sharply, gripping the phone a little tighter. She didn't like the tone of the officer's voice, calm, firm, but with a weight behind it. Something was wrong.

"I need to speak to Mrs. Collins," the woman on the line said, unwavering.

Kathleen's jaw tightened. "Can't you tell me first?" she pressed, instinctively trying to shield Matilda from whatever this was.

"I'm sorry, ma'am," came the response, polite but resolute. "I need to speak directly with Mrs. Collins."

Kathleen hesitated for a moment, her stomach twisting. Finally, she exhaled sharply and set the handset down on the table beside the phone. Without another word, she turned and walked outside, where Matilda was retrieving the last few items from the car.

As she approached, Kathleen took a steadying breath. She had no idea what news awaited her sister, but she knew one thing for certain, this wasn't going to be good.

"Who was it!" Matilda called out to Kathleen as she came from the house. Kathleen didn't answer, or couldn't. Matilda saw the tears starting to streak down her sister's face. Matilda rushed to the telephone, there was a scream and the clatter of the telephone's handset as it fell to the timber floor.

Tragic Bus Collision in Thailand Claims Seven Lives, Four Australians Among the Deceased

Phuket, Thailand – March 6, 1977

A horrific crash in northern Thailand has claimed the lives of seven passengers after a tourist bus collided with a truck. The impact caused the bus to plunge down an embankment and burst into flames, trapping passengers inside.

Among the victims were four Australian tourists, who were part of a group on a guided tour of the region. Authorities have confirmed that the others who perished were of various nationalities, though their identities have not been fully released.

The crash occurred on a winding road in the mountainous area of Chiang Mai, a popular destination for tourists. Emergency services rushed to the scene, but the severity of the fire made rescue efforts difficult. Local officials have launched an investigation into the cause of the collision, though preliminary reports suggest that a brake failure may have contributed to the tragedy.

The Australian embassy has been notified, and officials are working to contact the families of the deceased. Our thoughts are with the victims and their loved ones during this devastating time.

Matilda and Kathleen's journey from Dalby to Phuket was one marked by profound sadness, a heavy weight that seemed to settle over them as soon as they received the tragic news. The phone call had been brief but devastating, Matilda's daughter, Alison, was gone. She had been killed in a bus accident in Phuket, in Thailand, along with her friend Pippa, leaving behind a life cut far too short. There were no words that could make sense of the grief that threatened to swallow them whole.

The flight from Australia to Thailand felt long and surreal. Every mile seemed to stretch into an eternity as Matilda and Kathleen sat together, their minds heavy with sorrow and disbelief. The airplane was filled with the hum of life all around them, but to them, everything felt distant, muted by the rawness of their loss.

Arriving in Phuket, the reality of the situation began to sink in. They were met by officials who explained the arrangements, but their words barely registered. It didn't feel real. The bustling streets of Phuket, with their bright colours and tropical warmth, seemed a cruel contrast to the deep, suffocating ache in their hearts.

They were taken to the morgue, where Alison's body had been prepared for transport. Matilda had to summon every ounce of strength to see her daughter one last time, her body still, her face peaceful. Tears flowed freely as she whispered words of love to Alison, hoping that somehow, her daughter could hear them. Kathleen stood beside her, holding her hand, her own grief mirrored in her eyes. It was all they could do in that moment, be there for each other, as they had always been.

The paperwork, the arrangements to bring Alison's body back to Australia, all seemed like a blur. In the whirlwind of logistics, there was no time to process the enormity of what was happening. Every task felt like a mountain they had to climb just to bring Alison back home, to return her to the land where she belonged, where her family could lay her to rest.

The flight back to Australia was equally surreal. It felt like a bad dream they couldn't wake up from. Matilda clutched her daughter's belongings, her heart heavy with the thought that her daughter would never again step foot in Dalby, the town that had shaped so many of their memories. The road ahead was long, both physically and emotionally.

Arriving in Dalby, the quiet town greeted them as it always had, peaceful, serene, and familiar. The contrast between the calm of the town and the storm of grief within them only deepened the sense of loss. They made their way to the cemetery, where the burial had been arranged. As the ceremony took place, Matilda and Kathleen stood side by side, looking on as Alison was laid to rest, a final farewell. The tears that had flowed in Phuket continued here, but now they were joined by family and friends, each mourning the loss of a life that had been taken too soon.

In the silence that followed, Matilda and Kathleen were left alone with their grief. The weight of their loss was too much to bear. Yet, amid the sadness, there was solace in knowing that Alison was home, back in the place where she had been loved, where she would forever remain in their hearts. The journey had been long, and the pain immeasurable, but they knew that, no matter how far she had travelled in life, Alison would always be part of them, part of Dalby, and part of their shared memories.

Life Just Has to Continue

To My Dearest Kathleen,

I don't know how to put this into words, but I need you to know, if not for you, I wouldn't still be standing.

First Bernard, then Lindsay, and now Alison. One by one, my world has emptied, and yet, you remain. You have held me up when I could no longer bear my own weight. You have carried me through the darkest nights, through the kind of grief I never thought possible.

I don't know who I am without them. I don't know how to wake up each morning and keep going when everything feels so hollow. But you, my sister, you remind me that love still exists. That even in loss, I am not completely alone.

Thank you, for your patience, your strength, your unwavering presence. I don't say it enough, but I love you. And though I am broken, I promise to try, for you, but please forgive me.

With all my heart,
Matilda.

Kathleen awoke with a jolt, a dull ache in her head reminding her of the copious amounts of beer she and Matilda had consumed the night before. Their impromptu wake had been, in its own way, a celebration of life, of Alison's, of Matilda's resilience, and of their bond as sisters. Despite everything, Matilda seemed to be finding her way through the grief, piece by painful piece.

As Kathleen swung her legs over the side of the bed, urgency gripped her, a direct consequence of last night's drinks. She hurried toward the bathroom, barely registering the thought that, perhaps, Matilda was stronger than she had given her credit for. But just as she reached for the door handle, a sound cut through the quiet of the early morning.

The unmistakable click of the front door closing.

Kathleen froze. Her mind, still sluggish from sleep, struggled to process it. Too early. It was far too early for Matilda to be up, let alone leaving the house. A prickle of unease crawled up her spine.

Something wasn't right.

Without hesitation, she turned on her heel and rushed toward the front door, her heart pounding with an urgency that had nothing to do with last night's beer.

In the dim pre-dawn light, Kathleen could just make out a lone figure moving toward the dam. The Dobermans stood still, ears pricked, their gaze fixed in the same direction. A chill that had nothing to do with the night air swept through Kathleen as she took off in a sprint, barefoot, the damp grass cold beneath her feet.

Matilda was dressed only in her nightgown, the fabric billowing slightly as she moved with eerie purpose. There was no hesitation in her steps, no sign that she was lost or confused, she was heading toward the water with intent.

Kathleen reached her just in time, gripping her by both shoulders and turning her around. Matilda didn't resist. She didn't fight. She didn't even speak. Like a sleepwalker, she allowed herself to be steered back toward the house without a word, her eyes vacant, her body limp but compliant.

Back inside, Kathleen guided her to the bed and tucked her in, brushing damp strands of hair from Matilda's forehead. There was no protest, no reaction at all. The silence was almost worse than if she had screamed.

As Kathleen stepped back, her eyes flicked toward the bedroom door. A decision formed in her mind, one she didn't even hesitate to act upon. She reached for the mortise lock key, slipped it from the inside, and stepped into the hallway. With a final glance at her sister, she turned the key in the lock, securing the door from the outside.

It was four o'clock in the morning, and the house was still cloaked in the quiet darkness of night. Kathleen had decided to make herself a coffee, a small comfort following the harrowing start to the day. When she flicked on the kitchen light her eyes landed on Matilda's note, left on the counter in her hurried handwriting: "Thank god I heard that door" she thought as she picked up the letter. A cold shiver ran down Kathleen's spine as she read the words. Her heart sank as she thought about what might have happened if she hadn't been awake, hadn't heard the sound in the quiet hours of the early morning. She shuddered at the thought of what she might have discovered later, in the daylight.

In that moment, the comforting thought of a hot cup of coffee seemed insignificant. Kathleen felt the weight of her emotions rise up, her chest tightening as the reality of the situation hit her. With tears welling in her eyes, she turned away from the kitchen, her mind too clouded with worry to focus on anything else. She walked down the hall to her sister's room, her footsteps heavy and uncertain. She unlocked the door softly, as though afraid of waking her, and then slipped under the covers, curling up beside her sister, who was now peacefully asleep. Kathleen's body trembled as she snuggled close to her sister. She would keep her safe, she vowed it!

At 74 years of age, Matilda was doing just fine, as was the property she had tended to with such care over the years, Girraween. The land had stood the test of time, and its manager, Robert, affectionately known as 'Rob', had overseen the property in all its facets for just over thirty years. The house, however, was showing its age. The once vibrant exterior had faded under the relentless passage of time, but Matilda had done everything in her power to maintain it in pristine condition. Inside, the rooms were filled with a quiet charm, a reflection of Matilda's meticulous attention to detail, while the garden outside remained a testament to her love of nature and the land.

Sadly, her beloved Dobermans, Gypsy and Spud, had long since passed. Their absence left an emptiness in Matilda's heart that was never truly filled. The decision not to replace them had been a difficult one. She had been devastated by their loss, their loyal companionship a source of constant comfort for many years. When the pain of their passing was still too raw, the idea of bringing another dog into her life seemed unthinkable. But as time wore on, and the ache of their absence softened, Matilda began to wonder if it might be time to welcome a new four-legged friend.

By the time she had made peace with the idea, however, she found herself grappling with the reality of her age. The thought of training a young dog, of giving it the attention and energy it needed, felt daunting. She had reached the point where she wasn't sure she had the stamina to care for a dog the way she once had. So, with a heavy heart, she chose not to replace them, resigning herself to the quiet solitude that came without the companionship of her loyal pets. It was a decision that weighed on her, but she knew deep down it was the right one, for both her and the life she now led.

Matilda and her sister Kathleen had never stopped searching for the legendary diamonds, which had become a kind of family myth. The elusive jewels were rumoured, by not so innocent or persons of a good calibre, to be hidden somewhere in the house, their exact location a mystery that had captivated them for years. No matter how much time passed, the two sisters remained obsessed with finding them, convinced that the diamonds were not only real but somehow connected to an ancient, sinister past. Strangely, even after all this time, odd pieces of jewellery, and the like, possibly from the Petryczek's, or the Reimer's, or whatever their real name was, would turn up during their searches

Over the years, Matilda and Kathleen had come to a mutual conclusion, those diamonds were cursed. They weren't sure whether the curse had originated from the rich Jewish families from whom the Nazis had stolen the jewels or from the Nazis themselves, who had plundered them during the war. But one thing was certain: the curse was real, and it seemed to follow them, a constant presence in the back of their minds as they combed every corner of the house, searching for the treasure that had eluded them for so long.

Matilda, for her part, had come to believe that she had already paid her dues to the curse. She had endured enough loss, heartache, and hardship in her life that she felt she had borne the brunt of its weight "threefold." The years of searching had not brought her any closer to the diamonds, but they had brought her something else: a growing defiance and inner strength. She was done with the idea of the curse holding power over her. As far as Matilda was concerned, the diamonds, and the curse attached to them, could go and "fuck itself."

Kathleen, ever the pragmatist, had come to the same conclusion. Though the search had once been filled with a sense of mystery and hope, now it was more a matter of stubborn persistence. They were both convinced that the diamonds, if they even existed, were nothing more than a myth, a symbol of the grief and trauma of the past. But that didn't stop them from searching. If anything, it fuelled their resolve. They were no longer searching for the diamonds as much as they were searching for closure, ready to take their fate into their own hands and defy whatever curse may have once lingered over the house. They had, after some very heavy debates, introduced another psychic, this one called herself a clairvoyant, to visit the home in the hope of discovering the whereabouts of the precious stones. Although to no avail, as this woman also had a feeling, so she claimed, of danger and death inside the house. She had also indicated that what was being sought was in, or near, the hallway. "Utter rubbish!" Kathleen had rebuked the clairvoyant, "the location that she described, would cover more than half of the house, with the long hallway."

The clairvoyant had, however, reignited their passion to continue searching for the elusive treasure. The cryptic visions, the tantalising hints, despite their skepticism, Kathleen and her sister couldn't shake the feeling that they were on the verge of something incredible.

As Kathleen mulled over their next steps, a memory surfaced. Years ago, she had come across a bomb recovery company based in Victoria. If anyone had the expertise to conduct a proper underground search, it would be them. Acting on impulse, she reached out to an old colleague from the Federal Police, who, after some digging, provided her with a contact number.

She dialled without hesitation.

The phone rang three times before a gruff voice answered, his greeting abrupt.

"Yellow!"

Kathleen composed herself. "Good morning, I'm looking for a Peter Manning," she said, her tone warm yet professional. "This is Kathleen Simmons speaking."

There was a slight pause, then the voice on the other end responded with wary curiosity.

"This is Peter… do I know you? Or should I?"

Kathleen smiled at the familiar bluntness. "I was with the AFP, many years ago now. You conducted bomb and weapon searches for us back then. I don't suppose you're still active in that field?"

A moment of silence stretched between them, followed by a low chuckle.

"No, Kathleen. I'm much too old and bent up these days to be crawling through rubble looking for trouble," Peter admitted, his voice losing some of its initial gruffness. "But what is it you're after? My grandson does a bit of ground analysis, more of a hobby than a profession, but he's got some decent equipment."

Kathleen hesitated briefly, weighing her next words. She had no reason to trust this man, a near-stranger, yet something told her she had nothing to lose. Taking a breath, she decided to lay it all out.

She told Peter exactly what she and her sister were searching for. Not just a vague idea, but the full story, down to the estimated value.

Twenty-four million dollars. In diamonds.

The silence that followed was palpable. Kathleen could almost hear Peter processing the information. Then, at last, he spoke.

"I see."

Another pause.

Kathleen frowned. "It doesn't sound like you're very interested, Mr. Manning." She was about to hang up when his voice came back, now infused with unmistakable energy.

"Interested?" he sputtered. "Madam, interested?! I'm trying to catch my breath! Did you just say twenty-four million dollars… in diamonds?"

     Max Barrington

His heart was racing. Retirement be damned, this was the kind of opportunity that could rewrite a person's life.

"What sort of… commission, I mean, what sort of deal are you thinking?" he asked, barely containing his excitement.

Kathleen had anticipated the question. Calmly, she laid out her terms. "Five percent of the total value should be more than sufficient."

Peter exhaled sharply, processing the number. "I'd say that's fair, if you're covering all expenses," he countered. "That means travel, equipment transport, accommodation, meals… the whole lot."

Kathleen considered his terms. It was a significant cost, but if the diamonds were really there, it would be a small price to pay.

"Agreed," she said.

Peter grinned on the other end of the line. "Then it looks like I'm coming out of retirement."

Matilda was far from thrilled when she learned that Kathleen had taken it upon herself to make all the arrangements for the search team to come to Girraween. The idea of strangers combing through and around their home made her uneasy, but what truly irked her was the five percent commission Kathleen had promised them.

"Five percent?" she scoffed when Kathleen broke the news. "That's a hell of a lot of money for people who haven't even stepped foot on the property yet."

Kathleen, expecting this reaction, remained calm. "Matilda, we don't have the equipment or the expertise to do this ourselves. If we want to find those diamonds, we need help. And five percent of something is a lot better than one hundred percent of nothing. Plus we have that much money now that we don't really know what to do with it"

Matilda folded her arms, unconvinced. "We don't quite have enough to throw away though sister. I just don't see why we have to foot the bill for the whole operation too. Travel, accommodation, meals, why should we be the ones financing this wild goose chase?"

Kathleen sighed. "Because no one works for free, Maddy. They're not going to take the risk unless we show them we're serious."

Matilda shook her head, still doubtful. The whole thing felt reckless, and deep down, a part of her wondered if they were chasing shadows. What if the diamonds weren't there? What if they'd been tricked by this story passed down too many times, warped by memory and wishful thinking?

She spent the afternoon pacing the veranda, mulling over the possibilities. Every argument against the plan seemed rational, yet the tiny flicker of hope, the what if, gnawed at her.

By dinnertime, something shifted. Maybe it was the warmth of the evening air, or perhaps it was the way Kathleen spoke about the search with quiet determination. But as they sat down to eat, Matilda found herself asking question after question.

"What kind of equipment do they use?" she asked, spearing a piece of roast pumpkin with her fork.

"Ground-penetrating radar, metal detectors, sonar, whatever it takes," Kathleen replied, her confidence unwavering.

"And how long will they be here?"

"A week, maybe more, depending on what they find. They are concentrating on looking under the house"

Matilda nodded slowly. The doubt hadn't completely faded, but now, curiosity had taken hold. By the time they cleared the table, she was leaning forward, completely engrossed.

"So,… when exactly do they arrive?"

Kathleen couldn't help but smile. "The day after tomorrow. There are three of them and I have already booked them into the Royal Hotel Motel."

The three men arrived at Girraween late in the afternoon, much too late to begin the search, but with plenty of time to meet with Matilda and Kathleen and lay out a plan. The sisters stood on the veranda as the dust from the approaching vehicle settled, watching as the visitors climbed out of the dual-cab ute.

Peter Manning was exactly as Kathleen remembered, tall, broad-shouldered, and slightly hunched with age, his sharp eyes scanning the property with the air of a man who had spent a lifetime searching for things buried beneath the earth. His grandson, Greg, was a wiry young man with a mop of sun-bleached hair, his easy grin revealing a youthful enthusiasm. Beside him stood Mark, a lanky teenager with an air of quiet curiosity, his baseball cap pulled low over his forehead.

Introductions were brief but warm. The sisters quickly gathered that Greg and Mark had only recently completed Year Twelve and were in the midst of a well-earned gap year.

"They're trying to figure out what to do with their lives," Peter said with a smirk. "In the meantime, they've decided to spend it digging up the past, sometimes literally."

Greg laughed. "Pop's got the best stories. Not just about bomb recovery and weapons searches, but real treasure hunts too. Mark and I thought, why not put his gear to good use?"

Matilda raised an eyebrow. "So this is more of an adventure for you boys?"

Greg shrugged. "Maybe. But if there's really something out here, we want to be the ones to help find it."

Peter gave a gruff chuckle. "Don't let their age fool you. They know how to handle the equipment, and they're willing to put in the hard work."

Kathleen nodded, exchanging a glance with Matilda. She could still sense her sister's skepticism, but at the very least, they had a team willing to give it their all.

With daylight fading, they decided to walk the property, discussing possible locations to start the search. As they made their way around the house and outbuildings, Peter listened intently to the sisters' accounts of the legend, the diamonds, the whispers of hidden wealth, the decades-old clues that had led them here.

By the time they returned to the house, the plan was clear. At first light, they would begin.

That night, before the men prepared to head to town to their hotel, Matilda had invited them inside the house for drinks. Peter was a fan of Dimple Haigh, it seemed, and the boys enjoyed a beer. As they left for their hotel in Dalby that night, Matilda found herself staring out over the darkened landscape, the weight of anticipation pressing on her. Part of her still doubted they would find anything. But as the wind stirred the dry grass, she couldn't help but wonder, what if they did?

The plan was straightforward. Matilda and Kathleen were reasonably confident that they had searched every conceivable hiding place inside the house, so much so that they had lost count of how many times they'd answered the inevitable questions:

"Did you check under the floorboards?"
"What about inside the walls?"
"Did you remove all the power outlets and look behind them?"

Yes, yes, and yes. Every crevice, every nook, every improbable hiding spot had been examined, pried open, and scrutinised. If the diamonds were inside the house, they would have found them by now.

So, they turned their attention elsewhere.

The primary focus would be beneath the house, around the footings where the timber stumps met the earth. If something had been buried decades ago, that would be a logical place to start. From there, they would extend the search to the outbuildings, the old sheds, the workshop, even the disused chicken coop. Each structure had its own foundations, its own corners where secrets could have been long forgotten.

And then there was the bore.

It had been there for as long as either sister could remember, a deep, narrow shaft drilled into the earth to draw water. Matilda had never thought much of it before, but now, the idea of something hidden at the bottom, a place no one would think to look, sent a shiver down her spine.

"That's a long shot," Greg admitted when they brought it up. "But I suppose if you were trying to hide something permanently…"

"Exactly," Kathleen said. "It might be a dead end, but we have to check everything."

Peter, ever the pragmatist, nodded. "We'll scan the ground first, see if we get any hits. If nothing turns up, then we can think about more extreme measures."

With the plan in place, the team turned in for the night, their minds racing with the possibilities.

Tomorrow, they would begin. And with any luck, they'd finally uncover something.

After nearly six gruelling days of searching, the team was forced to concede defeat, at least as far as the diamonds were concerned. Despite their best efforts, there was no sign of the elusive treasure.

The most promising lead had come on the sixth day. While crawling under the house, roughly beneath the end of the hallway, Greg had paused, eyes fixed on the screen of the ground-penetrating radar. The device had detected a disturbance in the soil, an area about two meters long and eight hundred millimetres wide. It was large enough, intriguing enough, to warrant immediate excavation.

Excitement surged as they dug, the dry earth giving way beneath their hands. Then, after what felt like hours, Mark's trowel struck something solid. He reached down, brushing away the dirt, and pulled out an old wristwatch.

"A Junghans," Peter said, inspecting it closely. "German-made. From the 1930s, I'd reckon."

The watch's face was clouded with age, its hands frozen in time. The leather band had long since deteriorated, leaving only a few brittle fragments clinging to the lugs. It was an interesting find, but hardly the treasure they were hoping for.

Hoping for more, they brought the metal detector over and swept it across the disturbed earth. Almost immediately, it gave off a sharp, insistent beep.

"There's something else here," Greg said, eyes bright with anticipation.

They dug deeper, carefully sifting through the soil. Then, Greg's fingers closed around something cold, something unmistakably metallic. He lifted it into the light, and the group fell silent.

A handgun.Closer inspection revealed it was a Sauer model 1913. A German military issue handgun.

The weapon was rusted, its grip worn, but there was no mistaking what it was. A chill settled over the group as they examined it.

"Encouraged by the discovery, they pressed on, unearthing more artefacts, a set of metal buttons, a set of three car keys on a very rusty key ring, a tarnished belt buckle and a polythene wallet which was yellowed and brittle and appeared to contain a passport. Then, as Mark sifted through a handful of dirt, something pale caught his eye. He bent down, brushing away the soil, then froze.

"Bones," he whispered.

Peter, who had been watching quietly, stepped forward. He knelt, studying the fragments in Mark's hand, his face unreadable. Then, after a long pause, he exhaled heavily and shook his head.

"We're on the wrong track," he said firmly. "There are no diamonds here."

The weight of his words settled over them like a thick fog. They didn't ask what he meant, didn't press him for an explanation. Some things were better left buried.

Peter took a deep breath before addressing Matilda and Kathleen, his voice calm but firm. "What we've found here," he said, gesturing toward the unearthed remains, "are, in my opinion, human bones. And based on the other artefacts, the passport, the watch, the belt buckle, the buttons, I'd say they've been here a long time."

He crouched down and carefully picked up the weathered passport, its edges frayed and its cover nearly disintegrated from time. "This passport," he continued, flipping it open, "was issued in Brazil to an Otto Kleinwohz in 1949. It shows a single entry into Australia in 1952." He paused, his brow furrowing as he carefully unfolded a fragile piece of paper tucked inside. "And this… appears to be a receipt from a Brisbane motor dealer. The dealer's name is too faded to read, but the details are still clear, purchase of a 1951 model Ford Pilot in 1953 for the sum of £549."

Peter let out a slow breath, looking from one woman to the other. The weight of his discovery settled over them like a heavy fog.

Kathleen swallowed hard. "So whoever this Otto Kleinwohz was… he came to Australia, bought a car, and then what? Just disappeared?"

Matilda frowned, glancing down at the shallow grave. "Or was made to disappear."

Peter hesitated before standing. He dusted his hands on his jeans and looked them both in the eye. "Which means you have a decision to make. If we report this, the authorities will come in. They'll excavate, investigate, and piece together who this man was and how he ended up buried here." He let his words sink in before adding, "It won't be a quiet matter."

The air between them grew thick with unspoken thoughts. The past had clawed its way back to the surface, demanding to be acknowledged. Now, it was up to them to decide what came next.

Matilda and Kathleen exchanged uneasy glances, the weight of Peter's words sinking in. The unearthed remains, the aged passport, and the relics of a past life hidden beneath their home painted a story they were not sure they wanted to unravel further.

Matilda reached for the passport, her fingers trembling slightly as she examined the faded pages. "Otto Kleinwohz," she murmured. "Arrived in Australia in 1952. Bought a car in '53. And somehow, ended up here." Her eyes flickered toward the shallow grave.

Kathleen exhaled, folding her arms. "Which begs the question, who buried him? And why?"

Peter cleared his throat, choosing his words carefully. "That's where your decision comes in. If we report this, the authorities will investigate, and given how long these remains have been here, it could be a lengthy process. Excavations, forensic analysis, inquiries into the property's history, it won't be a quiet matter."

Matilda pursed her lips, weighing the implications. The house had been in their family only for one generation, but its past had always held whispers of secrets. But this was no longer just a whisper. This was a truth clawing its way back to the surface.

Kathleen shook her head slowly. "What if we don't say anything?"

Peter hesitated. "Then you live with the knowledge that someone was buried here, deliberately. You live with the unanswered questions. You will also have to be very careful not to tell anyone, and I mean anyone. "

Silence stretched between them, thick and heavy. Outside, the wind rustled through the trees, as if the past itself was waiting for their next move.

"If you want my advice, forget about the diamonds. Some things are better left alone."

The weight of his words hung heavily in the air. The search for the diamonds, their grand adventure, was over.

That evening, as the sun dipped below the horizon, the sisters bid farewell to Peter and the two young men, Greg and Mark. The searchers packed up their equipment, their once-bright enthusiasm dampened by the eerie turn of events.

Before Peter climbed into the ute, Matilda pulled him aside and discreetly pressed a tightly rolled bundle of fifty-dollar notes into his hand.

"Thank you," she said simply.

Peter smirked, shaking his head. "I appreciate it, but this was more interesting than most jobs I've done."

They exchanged a knowing glance, and he pocketed the cash with a nod of gratitude before driving off into the fading light.

A few days later, as the sisters sat on the veranda sipping a Dimple Haig whisky and ice, Matilda chuckled to herself.

"What's so funny?" Kathleen asked.

Matilda smirked. "I slipped Peter a five hundred dollar tip!"

Kathleen nearly choked on her drink before laughing. "So did I!"

They burst into laughter, picturing Peter receiving both cash bundles and shaking his head in amusement.

But their laughter slowly faded as their thoughts drifted back to the unsettling mystery they had uncovered. The conclusion of the search hadn't brought answers, only more questions.

Who had been buried beneath their house? Was it someone from the Reimer family's turbulent past? Another would-be assassin who had met his fate before carrying out his task? The only people who could answer that question were dead.

They would never know how a single act of battlefield survival had changed the course of one man's fate.

In the bitter winter of 1944, amid the chaos of retreating German forces in Poland, a young German Feldwebel, Otto Klein, found himself deployed under General Maximilian Freiherr Which's 2nd Panzer Division. The front lines had become a desperate and brutal landscape, where survival depended as much on instinct as it did on training.

During a ferocious skirmish near Tomaszów, Klein's unit found itself in disarray, caught between advancing Soviet forces and the crumbling German defensive lines. It was in that moment of confusion and carnage that Klein spotted SS Oberst Martin Von Ghetch, pinned down and wounded, surrounded by enemy fire. Though he had no great love for the SS, Klein acted without hesitation. Risking his own life, he fought his way through the enemy assault, dragging the wounded officer to safety amid the deafening roar of gunfire and artillery.

For Von Ghetch, a high-ranking officer with deep connections within the Nazi hierarchy, such a debt could not go unpaid. In the days that followed, as the German forces struggled to reorganise, Von Ghetch took decisive action. He had Klein transferred out of the Wehrmacht and into the SS, promoting him to SS-Oberleutnant, a move that elevated his status and, more importantly, placed him under the direct protection of the Reich's elite forces.

But Von Ghetch's reward did not end there. Recognising that the war was lost and knowing that men like himself would soon face retribution, he arranged for Klein to secure something far more valuable than rank, a passage to Brazil. It was a carefully orchestrated escape, a lifeline that would ensure Klein's survival long after the Third Reich crumbled into history.

And so, while the world burned and the Reich fell, Otto Klein vanished into the shadows, leaving behind the smouldering ruins of war-torn Europe for the distant promise of a new life on foreign soil.

In 1953, Otto Klein's fluency in English, honed through years of survival and adaptation, earned him a mission of grave importance. He was selected for an operation that would take him halfway around the world, to a remote town in Queensland, Australia, named Dalby. His objective was clear: locate and eliminate Carl Reimer and his wife, Peta, individuals who had betrayed powerful men and vanished with something of immense value. The stolen diamonds, priceless remnants of the Reich's hidden wealth, were believed to be in their possession, and Klein's orders were to recover them at all costs.

Arriving in Brisbane under the guise of an immigrant seeking work, Klein took careful measures to conceal his true identity. Aware that Germans were still deeply unpopular in Australia following the war, he adopted the alias Otto Kleinwohz, claiming Polish heritage to avoid suspicion. It was a calculated deception, one that would allow him to move undetected among the wary population.

With efficiency and precision, he secured a reliable means of transport, a Ford Pilot motor car, sturdy and unassuming, perfect for the long journey inland. His destination: the Commercial Hotel in Dalby, where he had booked a room under his assumed name. From there, he would begin his search, blending into the dusty streets of the small Queensland town, watching and waiting for any sign of Reimer.

Though far from the battlefields of Europe, Klein understood that this mission was no less dangerous. The hunt for Reimer would be a game of patience and cunning. And in the quiet expanse of the Australian outback, where secrets could be buried as easily as bodies, failure was not an option.

Locating Polish migrants in the district had proven relatively easy that year, as their numbers were few and their presence did not go unnoticed. For two weeks, Otto Klein maintained his cover at the Commercial Hotel, posing as a migrant labourer seeking work. He frequented the local pub, struck up casual conversations, and listened carefully for any mention of Polish families in the area. His patience was soon rewarded.

Through whispered exchanges over pints of beer and idle chatter with townsfolk, he learned of a Polish couple named Petryczek. The description given of Anton Petryczek bore a striking resemblance to Carl Reimer, the same age, the same quiet demeanour, the same foreign reserve that set him apart from the locals. Klein's instincts sharpened. Could it really be that easy? Had Reimer and his wife successfully buried themselves in the Australian outback under new names?

Pushing further, Klein made inquiries about possible employment, careful not to appear too eager. It was suggested that the Petryczek's might be looking for an extra hand at their property, a stroke of luck that could not have played more perfectly into his plan. With practiced ease, he expressed interest, mentioning that he too was Polish and eager for honest work. It was all the encouragement his informant needed. Within minutes, Klein had the address of the Petryczek property in his hands.

Slipping the scrap of paper into his pocket, he suppressed a satisfied smile. The hunt was nearly over. Now, all that remained was to confirm their identities, and finish what he had come to do.

Otto drove slowly down the dirt road, the fading light casting long shadows across the dry landscape. As he neared the entrance to the property, he cut the engine and coasted the last few yards to a silent stop. The heavy stillness of the approaching night settled around him. With practiced precision, he exited the vehicle, locking it carefully before beginning the short walk toward the house.

The Petryczek residence stood ahead, bathed in the dim glow of interior lights. Through the curtained windows, shifting silhouettes hinted at movement inside. Klein's pulse quickened, though his face remained impassive. He reached into his coat pocket and wrapped his fingers around the cool grip of his Sauer & Sohn 7.65 pistol, drawing it slowly.

Approaching the glass-panelled front door, he kept to its left side, pressing himself into the shadows. The house was silent, save for the muffled sounds of radio music inside. Crouching low, he steadied his breathing, every nerve alert, every muscle taut with anticipation.

Then, in an instant, everything went black.

The last thing Otto Klein saw was the glint of light reflecting off the glass-panelled door.

Carl Reimer had just secured the tractor for the night, wiping his hands on a rag as he made his way back toward the house. The evening air was still, the land stretching out in hushed silence under a sky just beginning to darken. His thoughts were already on supper, Peta would have something warm waiting, but as he neared the house, something caught his eye.

A shadow moved near the front door. Someone was crouching, pressed against the wall just beyond the glass-panelled entrance. The figure was deliberate, purposeful. This wasn't a neighbour dropping by or a passing traveler looking for help. A cold realisation gripped Carl's chest.

They had been expecting this. The past was never truly buried, and despite the years that had passed, he and Peta knew the day might come when someone from the old world would come looking. They had been watchful, cautious. But lately, they had let their guard slip, lulled by time and the quiet rhythms of life on the land.

Carl's heart pounded. His gun was in the laundry, inside the house. There was no way to reach it without being seen. He hesitated only a moment before turning back toward the shed, moving with the careful steps of a man who knew his life depended on silence.

Inside the darkened shed, his hands closed around the worn wooden handle of a mattock. It was heavy, solid, an old tool, but one that could be just as deadly as any firearm in the right hands.

Gripping it tightly, Carl stepped back into the night, his body tense, his mind clear. He was no longer just a farmer on a quiet Queensland homestead. He was a man fighting for his survival.

As Carl exited the shed, he took a different approach, veering around to the far side where the shadows were deeper, offering him better cover. His pulse drummed in his ears, but his grip on the mattock remained steady. Every step was deliberate, his bare soles moving soundlessly over the packed earth.

The intruder remained fixated on the house, crouched low, peering through the glass panels of the front door. The dim glow from within illuminated his features in ghostly flickers, but Carl wasn't interested in studying the man, only in stopping him.

Holding his breath, Carl closed the distance in a few swift strides, lifting the mattock high. The heavy tool arced downward with brutal precision, the pick-end slicing through the night air before sinking deep into the crown of the stranger's skull.

A dull, sickening crunch.

The man's body stiffened, then collapsed in a heap against the verandah, his limbs twitching before falling still. Blood, dark and glistening, pooled quickly beneath him, seeping into the cracks of the verandah's timber floorboards.

Carl remained motionless, his breath coming in ragged gasps as he waited for any sign of movement. None came.

He exhaled, shoulders sagging, but the relief was fleeting. He had known this day would come, had spent years dreading it, and now that it had arrived, the reality of what he had done was settling in.

He wiped a trembling hand across his face, then turned toward the house.

"Peta," he called softly, his voice hoarse. "I need you to come here."

Carl caught Peta just in time, pressing a firm hand over her mouth before she could let out a scream. Her eyes were wide with terror, darting from his face to the darkened figure sprawled on the verandah.

"Shhh," he whispered urgently. "There may be more. Go and bring my gun, quietly."

Peta swallowed hard, nodding, and disappeared soundlessly into the house. Carl remained still, ears straining for any sound beyond the soft rustling of the wind through the trees. His heartbeat thundered in his chest as he crouched beside the lifeless man, his breath shallow and controlled.

A few tense minutes passed before Peta returned, her steps nearly inaudible against the timber floor. In her trembling hands, she held Carl's prized Vis pistol, the Polish-made firearm he had kept hidden for years, a relic of a past neither of them could forget.

"I turned off the lights and the radio," she whispered, handing it to him.

Carl nodded, gripping the pistol tightly. The weight of it was familiar, reassuring, though his hands were slick with sweat.

"I'll check the paddock," he murmured. "Lock the door behind me. Don't open it unless it's me."

Peta hesitated, her lips pressing into a thin line, but she obeyed. The door clicked shut softly behind him as he slipped into the darkness.

The moon, though veiled by drifting clouds, provided just enough light to navigate the yard. Moving carefully, Carl kept low, scanning the open space, ears attuned to every rustle and distant night sound. The scent of dry grass and earth filled his nostrils as he made his way toward the driveway.

At the gate, he halted.

A car.

It was parked just beyond the entrance, its dark shape barely distinguishable against the night. Carl froze, every muscle tensed, watching, waiting.

Had the man come alone? Was someone else inside, lying in wait?

He gripped the pistol tighter, levelling it instinctively, his finger hovering just above the trigger. His breathing slowed as he let his eyes adjust, scanning the contours of the vehicle.

Nothing. No movement. No sound.

Minutes stretched painfully long. He remained still, heart pounding in his ears, but the car remained lifeless. No shadow emerged from within. No second intruder followed.

Finally, after what felt like an eternity, Carl decided. If anyone else had been here, they were either long gone or waiting for dawn. He took one last glance at the silent car, then turned, making his way back toward the house, moving just as slowly, just as carefully.

It was going to be a long night, for both of them.

They had made a contingency plan years ago, a grim necessity born from the fear that one day, an unwanted visitor would come looking for them. It was a plan that accounted for everything, even the disposal of a body. Or more.

The house, unlike many in the area, was not fully high-set but rested on wooden stumps of varying heights to accommodate the natural slope of the land. At the front entrance, the verandah was only three steps above the ground, barely two feet. But at the rear of the house, where the land fell away more steeply, the back verandah stood almost five feet high. Beneath it, the cool darkness stretched deep under the house, a place of shadows and dust, where few ever ventured.

It was there, beneath the house, that Carl now dragged the body. His breath came in short, sharp bursts as he pulled the dead weight across the dirt, the limp limbs catching against the uneven ground. He worked quickly, heart hammering in his chest, driven by instinct and terror. The grave had already been prepared years before, hidden between the stumps, just high enough that he had to crawl on all fours to reach it. He had dug it no deeper than four feet, just enough to suppress any scent, to ensure nature would do the rest.

Carl didn't search the man's pockets. He didn't want to know his name, didn't want to see any identification that might tell him who had sent him. The less he knew, the less he could ever be forced to reveal. Instead, he rolled the body into the grave unceremoniously, dust and loose soil spilling over the stranger's still form. He pulled the pistol from where it had fallen on the verandah and tossed it in after him. One less problem. One less risk.

He worked swiftly to cover the body, pressing the dirt down firmly with his hands, patting it into place as if smoothing out an old wound. His fingers trembled, but he forced himself to move methodically, as though following a rehearsed routine.

By the time Carl crawled out from beneath the house, his arms and shirt smeared with soil, Peta had already scrubbed the verandah clean of blood. The boards, damp from washing, bore no trace of the violence that had unfolded there.

They stood in silence for a long moment, staring at each other in the dim moonlight. Neither spoke of what had just happened. They didn't need to.

The next morning, Carl made his way to the front gate to retrieve the car. His pulse was steady, his mind clear, but his body carried the weight of the night before. As he approached, he took a moment to properly examine the vehicle. It was a current-model Ford Pilot, a sleek, powerful V8. He had to admit, he was impressed. It was a fine machine, and under any other circumstances, he might have admired it a little longer.

But admiration was the last thing on his mind. The car was a problem, one that needed to disappear quickly.

He tried the door handle. Locked.

Carl exhaled sharply, realising almost instantly what that meant. The keys were likely still in the visitor's pockets. His stomach twisted at the thought, but he shoved it aside. He was not, under any circumstances, digging up that grave. That was a line he would not cross.

Instead, he turned to a different solution. He knew how to get into the car without a key. A bit of fencing wire and a steady hand would do the trick. He retrieved a length from the shed and worked the wire carefully between the glass and the door frame, feeling for the mechanism. It took a few tries, but soon enough, he heard the satisfying click of the lock releasing.

He pulled open the door and climbed inside. The next step was bypassing the ignition. He leaned over, looked beneath the dashboard before opening the bonnet, and removed the ignition switch from under the bonnet. Years of working with machinery had given him the skill to make quick work of it. With a few deliberate movements, he crossed the wires, sending power to the ignition. Then, with a firm pull on the starter button, the engine roared to life.

Carl allowed himself a small breath of relief. Now, he just needed to move the car, get it out of sight before anyone started asking questions about an abandoned vehicle at the gate.

Just as he was about to close the bonnet, a voice called out from behind him.

"Anton!"

Carl's entire body tensed. For a split second, his mind struggled to process the name. Anton? Who the hell was Anton?

Then it hit him. The neighbour.

He turned his head slowly, his face carefully neutral as he stepped out of the car. His pulse pounded in his ears. He had been so consumed with his own thoughts that he hadn't heard anyone approach.

The neighbour stood a short distance away, looking toward the house, clearly expecting to see someone else. Carl forced himself to relax, shifting his stance casually.

"Morning," he said, keeping his voice even as his neighbour admired his new car.

Matilda sighed, swirling the amber liquid in her glass. "It seems that Otto Kleinwohz was the owner of our old Ford Pilot. Such a mystery."

     Max Barrington

"Just one more to add to the growing list, sister…" Kathleen mused, tapping her fingers on the table. "So that now makes… what? Three deaths in this house?"

"That we know of so far!" Matilda corrected, raising an eyebrow. She took a slow sip of her drink before adding, "I'll bet Kleinwohz drove out here to kill the Reimer's, and somehow, they turned the tables on him."

Kathleen shuddered at the thought. "It must have been a job and a half burying him under the house, though."

"But," Matilda said, leaning forward, "how clever. Who would think to go looking under a house for a missing man? And if he came all the way from Brazil, who was even missing him? Other than the people who sent him here to do his ghastly deed, of course."

"At least the Reimer's, got a new car out of it all" Kathleen could at least find some amusement to help keep things from becoming too morbid.

Kathleen poured them each another drink, the golden liquid glistening in the dim light. "And then there's Axel Emmerich…" she mused. "He was the second operative, wasn't he? Sent from Brazil, probably after Kleinwohz never returned. Very strange."

Matilda nodded thoughtfully. "Perhaps… perhaps it wasn't just about getting the Reimer's, but about getting the diamonds."

A heavy silence settled between them as they contemplated the dark possibilities. They both knew the house wasn't done revealing its secrets, not yet.

Kathleen sighed, raising her glass. "One last Dimple Haig for the night, then."

Matilda clinked her glass against her sister's. "To unsolved mysteries," she murmured.

The house, with all its ghosts and hidden past, seemed to watch and listen. And for now, at least, it would keep its secrets, besides, Matilda and Kathleen were in no hurry, they took the days as they came.

Max Barrington

Fed up with the incessantly jarring sound of the telephone ringing, Kathleen had finally had enough. The shrill, persistent tone that sharp, metallic trill produced by two brass bells being struck by a small hammer inside the phone echoed through the house every time it rang and the vibration of the metal bells continuing to tremble for a fraction of a second after each strike. It had been slowly sending her mad and had begun to feel like an unwelcome intruder, a constant reminder of things past.

In an attempt to bring a sense of peace, Kathleen had bought Matilda a mobile phone, hoping it would offer a more modern, quieter alternative. She had even suggested, with a certain level of exasperation, that perhaps it was time to cut off the landline altogether.

"Why not just get rid of that awful thing?" Kathleen had asked, her tone pleading for a sense of relief.

But Matilda had objected immediately, her voice firm and resolute. "No!" she had said, shaking her head with a quiet determination. "Too many memories lie in that telephone, both good and bad. That telephone has been a part of this house for as long as I can remember. It's seen our joys, our sorrows, our family's ups and downs. It carries echoes of the past in a way no other thing in this house does. That telephone shall remain in the hallway of this house forever!"

Kathleen had tried to argue, but she quickly realised that Matilda's attachment to the telephone ran deeper than just the sound it made, it was in a way connected to her lost family. It wasn't about the modern conveniences of a mobile phone, or the quiet that Kathleen longed for. For Matilda, the old telephone was a tangible connection to a lifetime of memories, a symbol of the people and moments that had shaped her. It was a relic, yes, but one that held a place in her heart, a place that could never be replaced or erased by the hum of a modern device.

So, despite the annoyance of its relentless and, nauseating, ring, the telephone remained, firmly stationed in the hallway, just as it always had been, an unyielding link to the past that Matilda was unwilling to sever.

At 74 and 75 years of age, the Collins sisters were, to put it mildly, very active. Despite their years, Matilda and Kathleen were far from slowing down. Their energy and determination still fuelled them, and they continued to keep their hands in the operation of Girraween, albeit in a more supervisory role. The property, once their family's heart and soul, had evolved over the years. Now, Girraween was no longer just a farm, it was a fully operational, thriving business.

The day-to-day running of Girraween had long since been handed over to Rob, the dedicated manager who had been with the property for over three decades. Under his guidance, the operations had expanded significantly, and now, he was supported by a team of five full-time staff members. The business was becoming increasingly professionalized, and to accommodate this growth, Girraween had recently employed a full-time accountant and an assistant. They worked out of a small but highly efficient office in Dalby, which had been rented specifically for this purpose. The office, though compact, was a hub of organisation and productivity, a far cry from the farmhouse that had once served as the headquarters of the entire operation.

Girraween was no longer just a family farm or a small-scale business. It had transformed into a thriving company, Girraween Holdings Proprietary Limited. The shift from a small family-run operation to a fully fledged business was a testament to the hard work and vision Matilda and Kathleen had put into the property over the years. But while the company had expanded, the Collins sisters had retained full ownership. They were the sole directors and shareholders, their names still proudly attached to the company that had once been their family's lifeblood.

Though Girraween Holdings was a far more sophisticated operation than it had ever been, it still held the same place in Matilda and Kathleen's hearts. They may have handed over much of the day-to-day management, but they were very much involved in the decision-making, their influence still strong. Girraween was their legacy, and they intended to ensure its continued success for as long as they could.

By 2020, the progression of Kathleen's Alzheimer's disease had become undeniable. What had once been subtle memory lapses and moments of confusion had escalated into more severe cognitive decline, affecting her ability to perform even the most basic daily tasks. Her once sharp mind, full of wit and clarity, was now clouded by a disease that relentlessly eroded her memory, leaving her vulnerable and increasingly disoriented.

Kathleen's diagnosis in 2015 had been a blow to Matilda, but at the time, they still clung to the hope that she might be able to maintain her independence for many years. The early signs of Alzheimer's had been manageable, and for a while, she could continue living at home with her sister supporting her as best she could. But as the disease progressed, it became clear that Kathleen needed more than Matilda could provide.

By 2020, Kathleen's memory lapses had become more frequent and more troubling. She would forget where she had placed things, or even forget what she had been doing moments before. The moments of clarity became fewer and further between. There were occasions when she became confused about where she was, or who people were, and even struggled to recognise familiar faces. She had become increasingly unable to manage her own personal care, and simple tasks like preparing meals or maintaining a routine were beyond her. Their once orderly home was now cluttered, and she was unable to care for herself in the way she had done for so long.

The decision to move Kathleen into an aged care facility was one of the hardest decisions Matilda had ever faced. It was a decision borne out of necessity, but it was still heartbreaking. Matilda had watched her sister slowly fade away, and the thought of her no longer living independently, of no longer being the strong and capable woman she once was, was difficult to accept. But as much as Matilda wanted to care for her sister at home, she knew it was no longer possible. Kathleen's safety was at risk, and Matilda's ability to provide the level of care needed was no longer enough.

Matilda researched local options in Dalby, searching for a facility that could offer the level of care and attention Kathleen needed, while also providing her with the comfort and dignity she deserved. After much consideration, they decided on a small, well-regarded aged care home in Dalby that had a strong reputation for its caring staff and comfortable environment. It was a place where Kathleen would have access to medical care and support around the clock, as well as the companionship of other residents who were also living with dementia.

Matilda had generously set up and annual donation of one hundred thousand dollars per year for the nursing home and had also made a generous provision in her will.

When the day came for Kathleen to move into the aged care home, it was a deeply emotional moment for both sisters. Matilda, her heart heavy with sadness, helped Kathleen pack her belongings. Kathleen, though confused and uncertain about what was happening, trusted her sister completely. She didn't understand why she was being moved, but she clung to Matilda, as she always had, and allowed herself to be guided through the transition.

The facility was warm and welcoming, with soft lighting, cozy lounges, and a well-maintained garden where residents could sit and enjoy the fresh air. Kathleen's room was small but comfortable, with familiar photographs and personal items placed around her to create a sense of home. Still, it wasn't the same. It wasn't the home she had known, where she had lived independently for so many years. It wasn't the place where she had made so many memories with her only family, her sister. Yet, in this new environment, Kathleen would have the care and supervision she needed to keep her safe and supported as her condition continued to decline.

Matilda visited Kathleen regularly, as often as she could, bringing her favourite books and stories, and sometimes simply sitting with her, holding her hand in quiet moments. There were times when Kathleen seemed lost, confused about where she was or who Matilda was, but there were also moments of clarity, when she would smile and say something that reminded Matilda of the vibrant, witty sister she had always known. Those moments were bittersweet, fragments of the person she once was, fleeting but precious.

The decision to move Kathleen into the aged care facility was one that Matilda never stopped grappling with. It was a painful reminder of how much her sister had changed, how much the disease had stolen from her. But it was also a step toward ensuring that Kathleen was cared for in the way she deserved, with dignity and love, in an environment where she could be surrounded by those who understood her condition and could provide the best possible care.

As time passed, Kathleen's condition continued to decline, but Matilda never stopped visiting, never stopped caring. The bond between the sisters remained unbreakable, even as the shadows of Alzheimer's deepened. Matilda held onto those fleeting moments of recognition and clarity, cherishing them as the most precious gifts in a world that had been irrevocably altered by the disease.

Matilda, ever devoted, visited her sister every single day. Rain or shine, she would make the drive to Dalby, refusing to let distance, or time, diminish her presence in Kathleen's life. But in 2021, her routine was threatened when the Queensland Department of Transport refused to renew her driver's license. Matilda was outraged but undeterred. If she could no longer drive herself, she would find another way.

Her accountant, understanding both her stubbornness and her need, hired a young woman named Alaina to serve as Matilda's driver. Alaina was twenty-two, the same age Alison had been when she had left for Thailand, when she had left and never returned. Perhaps that was why Matilda felt an immediate, almost unspoken connection to the girl.

Alaina, like Matilda and Kathleen in their youth, was an orphan. She had travelled from Melbourne to Dalby in the hopes of finding farm work, but her lack of experience had proven to be a barrier. She had resilience, though, and an eagerness to work. Seeing something of herself in the young woman, Matilda made a proposal.

Instead of merely acting as a driver, why not expand the role? Alaina could be her companion, her housekeeper, her assistant, whatever was needed. She would live at Girraween, and her salary would be adjusted accordingly. The arrangement suited them both, and Alaina accepted without hesitation.

In the sprawling quiet of Girraween, Matilda had once again found someone to share her days, to help stave off the loneliness that had, for too long, threatened to consume her.

And now, as if in the blink of an eye, it was 2025. Matilda was 92 years old and no longer made the daily trips into Dalby. There was no longer a reason to, Kathleen had passed away the previous year, also at the age of 92. The house at Girraween felt emptier than ever, despite Alaina's presence.

Matilda could still recall with absolute clarity the last time she visited Kathleen. It had been the day before she died. The memory played in her mind like a scene from a film, every detail etched in sharp relief. She remembered the nurse who had escorted her to Kathleen's room, a young woman, confident and sharp-tongued, too sure of herself for Matilda's liking. There was something about her that grated, an air of superiority that suggested she believed she knew more than she did.

As they walked down the hallway, the nurse had made a remark that still burned in Matilda's mind.

"I don't know why you go to so much trouble to visit her," the young woman had said, her tone dismissive, almost indifferent. "She doesn't even know who you are."

Matilda had stopped mid-step, her spine straightening as she turned to face the girl. Her eyes, steely and unyielding, locked onto the younger woman with a gaze so sharp it could have cut glass.

"That may be so," Matilda replied, her voice calm but laced with quiet intensity, "but I know who she is." She let the words hang in the air for a moment, allowing their weight to settle. Then, with a tilt of her head and a piercing stare, she added, "But tell me… who are you to make such suggestions?"

The young woman faltered, shifting uncomfortably under Matilda's scrutiny, her confidence wavering in the face of something far greater than mere words, an unshakable bond that time, nor illness, could ever erase.

She had left it at that, but the moment stayed with her. And on her way out of the nursing home, she had stopped at the reception desk.

"Who was that nurse?" Matilda asked, her tone clipped and controlled. "The super-smart one, the one with all the answers."

The receptionist hesitated, her fingers hovering over the desk as if weighing the consequences of her response. Finally, she sighed and provided the name. "Barbara Holden."

Matilda simply nodded, her expression unreadable. But in that moment, her decision was made.

"Please advise the Director," she said, her voice cool and deliberate, "that I will be contacting my solicitor later this morning to have this nursing home removed as a beneficiary from my will. I will then contact my bank to ensure that the annual donation I have been making ceases immediately."

The receptionist's eyes widened, but Matilda was far from finished.

"If this facility sees fit to employ individuals like Barbara, people with no passion for their work, no sense of duty, and not even the faintest desire to be here, then it is clear to me that this place has neither the understanding of value nor the common sense required to manage money responsibly."

She adjusted her handbag on her arm and cast one final glance around the room, a place she had once believed in, supported, and trusted.

Without another word, Matilda turned on her heel and strode toward the exit, never once looking back.

Now, a year later, she still felt no regret over that decision. Kathleen had deserved better. And in the quiet solitude of Girraween, Matilda carried on, holding onto the memories of those she had loved, and lost. She also had made Alaina the sole beneficiary in her will.

It was Saturday night, and as always, Matilda followed her nightly routine. After savouring a generous Dimple Haig over ice, she made her way to bed at her usual time. The warmth of the whisky had become a quiet comfort in her evenings, a small indulgence she allowed herself without apology.

Tonight, the house was particularly still. Alaina was away, as she often was on Saturday nights, spending time in town. Matilda suspected she had a boyfriend, though Alaina hadn't mentioned one outright.

"Young love," Matilda mused to herself as she climbed into bed. She made a mental note to tell Alaina to bring the young man out to Girraween one day. If he was someone important in her life, she ought to meet him. After all, she thought with a sly grin, he might have some say in what happens here one day.

The thought amused her, and she chuckled softly in the dark, the sound barely above a whisper. Settling into the pillows, she allowed the comforting stillness of the house to wash over her. Within moments, she was asleep, her mind drifting effortlessly into slumber.

BRRRRINNNGG! BRRRRINNNGG!……………….

BRRRRINNNGG! BRRRRINNNGG!

Matilda stirred.

BRRRRINNNGG! BRRRRINNNGG!……………….

BRRRRINNNGG! BRRRRINNNGG!

Matilda was starting to get from her bed.

BRRRRINNNGG! BRRRRINNNGG!……………….

BRRRRINNNGG! BRRRRINNNGG!

"Who on earth could this be?….and at this time of the night?"

The telephone had stopped ringing almost as soon as Matilda had reached the little desk that the telephone sat on. As Matilda looked at the phone she could see that the hand piece wasn't sitting on its cradle on top of the telephone, rather it was lying beside the telephone, as one would place it when waiting for someone to take a call that had already been answered.

"Strange" she thought and then remembered that the telephone was disconnected. This was seeming to be a repeat of what had happened last weekend, She had since convinced herself, that she had been dreaming last week when a similar thing had happened….so..was she again dreaming?

She carefully picked up the telephone receiver and gently placed it to her ear…….feeling a little stupid..she said into the mouthpiece…."Hello!"

All of a sudden!…realising how stupid she was being and that her sister had been right.."Get rid of the fucking old prick of a phone!" Kathleen had screamed at her, "It has nothing but bad news!"

Matilda gently placed the receiver back onto the cradle, her movements slow and deliberate. For a moment, she sat in silence at the small desk, her fingers resting lightly on the smooth surface of the telephone. Then, with a deep breath, she rose to her feet, her expression unreadable.

Max Barrington

With a firm grip, she lifted the telephone by the recessed handle behind the cradle, feeling the weight of it in her hands. Standing at her full height, she raised it high above her head, her arms trembling slightly, not from weakness, but from the quiet rage simmering beneath her composed exterior.

Without hesitation, she hurled the telephone down onto the polished timber floor of the hallway. The sharp crack of impact echoed through the house as the handset separated from the base, skidding across the floorboards. Matilda didn't pause to assess the damage, nor did she look back. With unwavering resolve, she turned away, her steps measured as she made her way to her bedroom.

Slipping beneath the covers, she exhaled softly, her body relaxing into the familiar embrace of her bed, she grinned to herself as she remembered her sister's words. "That Fucking Telephone!" Within moments, sleep took her, deep, undisturbed, and final.

She would never wake again and the smile on her lips would be forever.

Alaina returned to Girraween on Sunday afternoon, stepping through the front door with an air of familiarity. She set her bag down, already forming a mental list of the tasks awaiting her. But as she took her first steps into the long hallway, she froze.

Tiny, glistening fragments littered the polished floorboards, catching the afternoon light in dazzling, scattered brilliance. Diamonds.

Her breath hitched as she instinctively crouched down, fingertips hovering over the sparkling chaos. She reached out, picking up one of the stones, turning it between her fingers. Alaina, like most, knew nothing about diamonds, but these, the weight, the clarity, there was little doubt in her mind, these may be real. But how? Why?

It was only then, as her gaze followed the erratic trail of scattered gems, that she noticed the second anomaly. Near the small desk in the hallway, the Bakelite telephone lay shattered, its black casing fractured, the receiver detached and resting a few inches away.

A creeping unease settled over her as she slowly straightened, her mind racing. The telephone hadn't merely fallen, it had been thrown and thrown hard, by the looks.

And the diamonds… they hadn't simply been misplaced. Something had happened here.

Something she wasn't ready to understand.

End….

Max Barrington

Did you enjoy this book?...

If so please tell your friends and I would appreciate it greatly if you could rate it.

Thanks! ... Max

Max Barrington

Max Barrington

Other Books By Max Barrington

Woolgar River Park

Task

Dying To Find Gold

Harry Croft

The New March

Bad Company

The First Ten Years in Australia

Fifty Five More Years

You Couldn't Make This Stuff Up

The Writer & The Written

What's Mine is Yours

The Darkie's Gold

The Intrusion

The Premonition

Revelation at Narern

King to Spare

Max Barrington